DEADLY
Fantasies

KELLY MILLER

© **2016 by Kelly Miller**
contactkelly@kellymillerauthor.com
www.kellymillerauthor.com

Also by Kelly Miller

Dead Like Me (Book 1 in the Detective Kate Springer Series)
Splintered (Book 1 in the Detective Emma Parker Series)
My Blue Nightmare (Novelette 1 in the My Nightmare Series)

ACKNOWLEDGEMENTS

After the first book poured out of me with such amazing speed, I worried whether I could do it again. *Deadly Fantasies* is the proof I needed to know that this passion is here to stay. Hopefully, you'll enjoy this story as much as the first Detective Kate Springer novel. But before I can share it with you, I'd like to thank all the people who helped me along the way. I couldn't have pulled it off without their help. As always, any mistakes are mine.

Thank you God for this wonderful life you've blessed me with. Getting to write every day is simply icing on the cake.

My amazing husband who loves me beyond measure, indulging this crazy passion of mine. And to my children Emily, Andrew, and Daniel who don't mind hunting me down when I've gone into hiding, looking for a quiet space to write down my latest idea.

My mom, Cindy Bass, for being my biggest supporter and promoter.

My best salesperson, Janene Miller-Thiele, for always having a copy of my book on hand, ready to tell a friend about a great new writer she knows.

Danny and Tracy DeGrace for always having the answers for me. They're my go-to team for police procedure and medical questions.

Alina Font for answering my questions about Cuban culture and Lorelei Vitulli for providing just the right flavor for my character Ana Lopez.

Lisa Vogt for her skilled hand at shaping up my marketing copy.

My critique group: Jessica Ruth, Chris Coad Taylor, and Lisa Vogt. Your suggestions and opinions make me a better writer.

My beta readers: Laura Caruso, Craig Roberts, Jenny Roney, Lorelei Vitulli, Lisa Vogt, and Denise Westlake. Thank you for giving so freely of your time and offering invaluable insight to make my story a better read.

Jana Bayne for her suggestion of the character name Maggie Eaton. Congratulations on winning the first annual Name a Character Contest.

To all of the book club members who chose my first novel as a reading selection. I hope you're ready to discuss this second book.

This book is dedicated to my husband.
A man who loves me without strings, a man
who supports me in every way.
His love has changed me for the better,
shaping me into the person I am today.
I thank God for allowing me another day to
stand by Winston's side,
braving all that life has to throw at us.
Together. Always.

FRIDAY

CHAPTER 1

The evening flooded back like snapshots in a memory book. Hotel. Celebration. Drinks. Skin. Lots of skin. I grabbed my ringing phone with one hand and moved the bedside alarm clock closer with the other. The numbers burned 1:17 am, mocking my now awakened state.

After three years as a homicide detective, a call this late, or early depending on your point of view, could only mean one thing—a dead body. It was just a matter of time. Tampa hadn't had a murder victim laid at its doorstep in four days.

A voice next to me grumbled, begging me to make the ringing noise stop.

"Detective Springer," I croaked into the phone.

Nothing but dead air.

Great, crank call. I twisted sideways, getting ready to switch on the nearby lamp, but stopped midair when a whimper, childlike yet aged with the sound of regret, broke free from the phone's speaker. "Kate? Kate?"

I knew that voice. But from where? The cobwebs from too much partying cluttered my mind. The crackling of bad reception filled the airways.

"Kate, I think I killed my husband."

Dr. Nina Grace. Finally attaching a name to the confessor, I asked, "What? What do you mean—" I stopped midsentence, knowing any more words would be wasted. Our call had been disconnected.

I grabbed my clothing scattered around the room and began dressing. "Last night was wonderful," I said, leaning over Jeffrey, "but I gotta go. Keep sleeping, I'll call later." He was so out of it, I doubted he'd even remember me leaving. Hell, we'd been asleep for less than two hours.

Jeffrey turned away from me, rolling over onto his side. He pulled the covers up tight underneath his chin and mumbled, "That's okay. My wife's not expecting me home tonight."

What! Bastard told me he'd separated from his wife six months earlier. Said he'd filed for divorce three weeks ago. I should have known better than to trust a lawyer. Should've stopped by the courthouse and looked up the records myself. Unfortunately, the sort of justice he deserved called for more time than I had at the moment. And the right power tools. I had to get to Dr. Grace. She saved my life last year. Now it was time to return the favor.

CHAPTER 2

It's true Dr. Nina Grace had saved my life, though in more of a metaphorical sense. Last fall, I underwent psychiatric counseling with her after I shot a suspect in a kidnapping case. Only spent three weeks on her couch, but she had a way about her. One that made me want to unload my darkest secrets. And did I ever. Nina was unlike any shrink I'd ever been to before. I opened up, let her in, and most importantly, let her help me. So I owed her. That's why I hadn't called this into dispatch. Not yet. First, I needed to get out to Nina's house to assess the situation for myself.

On the drive over, I kept redialing the number Dr. Grace had called from only to be frustrated with a busy signal. Maybe she was on the line with a 911 operator. Reaching the Davis Islands Bridge, I flipped on the car's interior light and checked the directions on my map one last time. The address was on the southwest side of Davis Islands, a land mass created by dredging mud up from the bottom of Tampa Bay. The area had a curious mix of residents. Mainly the middle class living next door to the uber rich. The wealthy folks had invaded the island, knocking down many of the small homes that faced the water to build in excess. But you still had quite a few of the hundred-year-old block houses saddled up next to the McMansions.

I picked up my cell phone to call Dr. Grace again, but it started ringing before I could dial the number. Hopefully, it was her calling back. Instead, I got a notice about a signal seven—a dead body—at the very address I was headed to now. Lady luck was finally on my side. Since I was the on-call detective, it saved me the hassle of finagling an assignment to the case.

I pulled into the Graces' sprawling circle driveway, passing two unattended squad cars. Sirens off but lights on, the strobes maniacally turned, lighting up the palm trees. My haggard reflection flashed blue and red in the car window. Looking down at my outfit, I remembered I was dressed for clubbing, not an investigation. In my pocket, I came across a band to tie my dark blonde hair back. I clipped my badge to my waistline and threw on a blazer I'd found in the trunk. The boots I exchanged for a pair of running shoes. Not exactly fashionable, but better than the ribbing I'd take walking into a crime scene in my previous attire.

Dr. Grace's house was built in a Spanish Mediterranean style, a trend popular on the island. Lights shone from every window of the massive house, illuminating the darkness like a beacon in the night. Even though the front door stood ajar, most likely due to the responding officers, the doorframe looked intact. No pry marks suggesting forced entry, at least from this location.

I rested my hand on my sidearm and shouted, "Police entering the premises." I didn't want shot by some rookie thinking I was the perp.

To my right, a decorative iron-rail staircase wound upwards from the open foyer to the second floor. The luxurious downstairs had wood flooring that spread across the entire length of the house back to a wall made entirely of glass. The Graces' home faced the Bay side. I bet their view was incredible during the day.

To the left of me lay a large oriental vase in pieces on the floor. The small antique table it had been sitting on had also toppled to the ground.

Bloody footprints seemed to originate from the room to my left. Red pathways shot out into the foyer crisscrossing the open expanse of the first floor. In the air, a coppery scent mixed with a stench of loosened bowels. The unmistakable smell of death. I pushed open the cracked door and rapidly sucked in my breath, holding it. A veritable blood bath. Something very wrong had happened in this room.

"—won't leave her husband," a voice said.

"Wh . . . what did you say?" I stammered, still in shock from the visual of such violence.

"The woman hasn't left his side since we got here. When I tried to coax her from the body, she flipped out. I thought it best to let her stay so she didn't destroy any evidence. The other officers are clearing the house and outside perimeter."

As if on cue, a deep baritone voice boomed out of a radio mic attached to the officer's lapel. "The house is clear."

A few moments later, another voice broadcast, "Perimeter's clear."

I crouched down, covering my shoes with the paper booties I'd brought in from my trunk. Then I pulled on a pair of latex gloves. My eyes stared ahead the entire time, transfixed to the blood-soaked body strapped to a chair in the center of the den. Presumably Nina's husband, Mr. Grace. Though I'd previously seen a picture of the couple on her office desk, the person sitting in front of me was so unrecognizable, I couldn't tell if this was the same man. What looked like duct tape crudely bound each wrist, firmly securing them to the chair's armrests. The blood-drenched tape had also been wrapped around his midsection, ensuring he would endure the torture without his body slumping forward.

In my fourteen years on the force, I'd never come across such a grisly scene. Blood sure, but a body bruised, cut, and beaten this badly—no. The man's right eye had disappeared into a lump of swollen flesh. What appeared to be his left ear lay on the floor almost lost in a puddle of blood. So much blood, it looked like a perverse wading pool. I had to rub the hair down on my arms. The room felt galvanized by the rage that had exploded in here.

Sitting on the floor, clinging to her husband's leg was Dr. Nina Grace. She seemed oblivious to the sights or smells of the room. My heart ached watching her vacant expression. I hoped wherever her mind had taken her, she'd be able to stay there a little while longer. When she finally snapped back, she'd be forced to face a new ugly reality.

Nina's once white nightgown clung to her body now heavy with drying blood. The front of the gown was saturated, but as I walked around the couple, leaving plenty of space so as not to add my own prints, I could see the back of the nightgown from the waist up was still in pristine condition. Nina's long, chocolate brown hair fell forward over her shoulders. The ends were caked with dried blood.

With great effort, I pulled my eyes away from the carnage and looked around the masculine room. An enormous entertainment center stood against one wall, a large couch sat against the other. The couch was trendy yet comfortable looking. It bared a few worn spots, making me wonder if Mr. Grace often fell asleep while watching the game.

I stood beside a large, tidy desk. Tidy except for the blood covering the phone receiver and a red handprint stamped in the center of the desk. Custom-made bookshelves lined the entire wall next to the door. The spines held a variety of titles. I questioned if Nina's husband had actually read all the books or just filled the shelves to portray a scholarly air.

I could only focus on the details of the room momentarily. The blood kept pulling my gaze back toward the grisly scene. Because the blood was everywhere, my eyes didn't know where to land. Streaks of dark red, now turning brown in color, covered the walls. It was as if an artist had been turned loose in the room, deciding to create a splatter painting using all the possible shades of red. Just standing in this room made me nervous. A normal reaction but one ill afforded a detective. I focused on calming my fingers which had been tapping out a concerto against my legs since the moment I'd arrived.

As I made my way closer to the door, I heard familiar voices. Crime scene technicians appeared at the doorway and abruptly halted. It felt as if all the air was being sucked out of the room by the simultaneous intake of breaths. I glanced down at Nina. Not even a flinch. She was completely unaware of the people around her.

"How'd you get here so quickly?" Lucy James, the lead crime scene tech, asked me. Her eyes never left the bloodshed before her.

I mumbled that I was in the area when the call came in. Hoping to shift the conversation, I waved my hand at the room before us. "This is going to be a nightmare of a scene to process."

Lucy sighed, pushing her glasses up higher on the bridge of her nose. "Why is there a woman still sitting in the middle of my crime scene?"

"An officer tried to move her, but she wigged out. Thought we should find out how you wanted to handle it before we forcibly removed her." Now wasn't the time to tell Lucy the woman surrounded by a puddle of blood was Dr. Nina Grace, my ex-shrink, not to mention the shrink of plenty of other decorated Tampa police officers.

"Good idea. I don't want her destroying evidence. Especially if she's the doer. We'll take some photos first."

When the light from the first flash exploded, Nina furiously blinked as if trying to exorcise the spots from her vision. Forced into the present moment, she looked around as if seeing the scene for the first time. Then Nina let out a shriek I knew would haunt my dreams for weeks to come. Eyes wide with terror, she kept wailing. Emotion rolled off her in waves, spasms wracking her body with brutal force. Two EMTs rushed in with a backboard. Nina began to flail her arms. She clutched a cell phone tightly in her hand. Just as the phone was about to make contact with the temple of an EMT, I jumped forward breaking it from Nina's grip. I placed the phone in an evidence bag that Lucy had opened for me and watched Nina being strapped onto the backboard. When the last buckle clicked into place, her sobs died and struggles ended. Maybe she had finally clawed her way back into oblivion.

All the commotion had drawn the responding officers' attention. They were milling around the foyer, waiting for their next assignment. I grabbed Hank Barrett, a six-year veteran on the force. Someone I knew I could count on. "I want you in the back of that ambulance with Dr. Grace. If she has a flash of lucidity and ends up making a declaration, I want it noted. Also make sure the ER staff doesn't hack up her clothes trying to examine her. Do you understand?"

Barrett nodded and jogged to catch up.

Sometimes we'd get stuck with a newbie ER nurse who would slit the patient's clothes right up the middle. Especially if the patient was combative. Experienced nurses knew to cut around bullet holes, stab wounds, all in an effort to maintain trace evidence. But stationing a police officer in the exam room would ensure proper handling of the evidence.

I motioned for another officer to come over. "You're in charge of the crime scene log. Stand outside the front door, and get the names of everyone in and out of this house. You got me?" The officer nodded and told me he'd get additional help to cover the other exits.

"I guess money *can't* solve all your problems," said a voice from the doorway of the den. My partner, Detective Patrick Jessup. I had to stamp down a stab of bitterness at his impeccably dressed person. How he could look so together at two in the morning was beyond me. Not a blond hair out of place, not a wrinkle in his highly favored khakis. Though, I shouldn't be surprised. After three years as partners, I knew his hot buttons. Buttons I often pushed for a mid-day mood boost. And there was nothing like a rumpled look to sour his normally easy going attitude.

"How did you get here so quickly?" Patrick asked me.

Really? Again with that damn question. Just because I wasn't the most prompt person, didn't mean I was always last to a crime scene.

"We need to talk." I grabbed Patrick by the arm, carefully

maneuvering us around the various bloody footprints in the foyer. We moved deeper into the open living room area, stopping beside the back of a large tan sectional.

During a case last fall where I was less than forthcoming, I'd damaged my relationship with Patrick. It had taken months to repair the lost trust. In the interest of patching the leaky holes, I knew I had to be completely honest, filling him in as quickly as possible. Anyway, he was sure to find out Nina had called me once he looked at her cell phone history.

"The woman you saw wheeled away is Dr. Nina Grace."

Patrick's eyes grew large as awareness registered.

"She called me a little after one o'clock saying her husband was dead." Okay, maybe I wasn't willing to cough up the whole truth just yet. But I knew Nina couldn't have killed her husband. Why start off by admitting she thought she might be the one responsible for the murder? It would immediately set a tone for the whole investigation. Hell, might as well paint a red target on her back. After what that woman did for me, the least I could do was make sure everyone involved kept an open mind.

"Why'd she call you? Why not 911?"

"I haven't spoken with Dr. Grace since last September. Before I left our last counseling session, I gave her my card and told her if she needed anything to call me. Dr. Grace only got a few words out before her call dropped. She must have also dialed 911. Either before or after, I'm not sure, but two cruisers were parked outside when I arrived."

Patrick nodded slowly, digesting the information. "O . . . kay." He looked around the living room. "Have you had a chance to check this place out yet?"

"Only the den." I pointed at the drying footprints on the floor. "The highest concentration of blood is in the prints coming out of the den. They look smaller than my feet. Guessing a size six, six and a half. Probably Dr. Grace's. She was barefoot when they took her away."

"The footprints lead to the kitchen," Patrick said, following the darkened marks. "Luckily, it's not wall to wall carpeting in here."

Blood was smeared on the kitchen countertop next to an empty cell phone charger. "Dr. Grace had her cell phone in her hand. She almost clocked one of the EMTs with it."

"She must have used it to call 911."

"But there's blood on the phone in the den? Why didn't she call 911 from her home phone?"

Patrick picked up the receiver from the wall unit at the far end of the kitchen. "No dial tone. We need to find out if the line was tampered with."

"I saw an alarm keypad on the wall. Since the system works through the phone land lines, wouldn't the monitoring company have been alerted if the house phone had been disabled?"

"You'd think. We'll check into it later today."

We followed the blood trail out of the kitchen into the living room near the windows facing the Bay water. The footprints and blood drops were faint but still led us to an oversized purse. It'd been discarded next to a brown suede chair. The purse's contents were strewn all over the floor.

Patrick pointed at the blood on the zipper and strap. "Somebody was looking for something."

"Do you think the perp searched it?"

"Maybe, or it could have been Dr. Grace. The lab will tell us if the bloody prints belong to her."

I nodded, thinking through the scenario out loud. "So Dr. Grace discovers the home phone didn't work, comes over here to get the cell from her purse. Could account for the multiple paths of blood." I pointed at the different trails circling around the living room and foyer. There seemed to be no rhyme or reason to them, unless you considered the person leaving the marks could have been searching for something. "In her panic, maybe Dr. Grace forgot where she left her purse."

"I only see one set of footprints," Patrick said.

"The killer may have worn protective footwear."

Patrick nodded but remained quiet until he asked, "By the way, what are you wearing?"

Leave it to me to be partnered with the only guy who actually noticed my mismatched clothing. I punched him in the shoulder. "Come on. We need to get back in the den before the clown with the balloon animals shows up."

CHAPTER 3

The crime scene had definitely turned into a three-ring circus. Anymore people in this room, and we'd have to start charging a cover. I walked around Patrick, trying to ignore his reaction as he fully absorbed the savageness of the crime. Lucy James stood in the corner, adjusting her camera lens. My best friend always seemed a little uncomfortable in her own skin. Small framed, her clothes seemed to wear her instead of the other way around. When she glanced up and saw me, a crooked grin escaped. Then she seemed to remember her surroundings, and the smile quickly disappeared.

"You better hope that one picture turned out," I said after I'd made my way over to her. Red shoe prints marked the floor surrounding the victim.

"You're telling me. The EMTs completely obliterated my crime scene." Lucy let out a sigh of resignation.

"How can this not completely piss you off?"

"What's done is done. I can't change the fact the floor got trampled. All I can do is work with what's left."

Not me. I fumed at the idea of having to reconstruct the scene. A key piece of evidence could have hitched a ride on the bottom of an EMTs shoe never to be seen again. But the evening was still young. Maybe I'd catch some dumb rookie screwing up. A good ass chewing would help ease a little frustration.

"Where do you want to begin?" Lucy asked, handing me the Vicks VapoRub. Normally, I didn't like to deaden my sense of smell. I might miss a telling scent skirting the air. But this time the only odor was the rancid stench of death.

"Let's start at the desk." I rubbed the cool menthol salve under my nose, coughing at the overpowering vapor smell.

Stacks of papers sat beside the Graces' computer screen. I picked them up, leafing through them. Jonathan, according to his signature. The victim's name was Jonathan Grace.

"Photograph everything, print it, and pack it," I told a tech standing beside Lucy.

Patrick stood with another crime scene technician in front of the bookshelves. The killer was likely trying to extract information from Jonathan Grace. A clue could still be hidden in one of the novels. A bit old school, but it wouldn't be the first time. During my first year as a homicide detective, a tech found a receipt for some diamond jewels, ironically enough, in the book *The Maltese Falcon.* Cracked the case wide open.

While Lucy shot pictures of the body, I decided to walk the scene in the killer's shoes. Bloody finger and hand smudges marked various spots around the room, but there were no prints outlined in the blood. The killer must have worn gloves. Indicated premeditation. Also no torture instruments were left behind. It's probable they were brought here. Even so, I'd keep an eye out for empty spots in the garage and kitchen drawers indicating missing tools and other sharp instruments.

I jotted down a reminder in my notebook to check with the alarm monitoring company. I needed to know if and when the system was armed. Also, if the passcode was entered last evening to allow entry into the house. I wondered when the killer arrived. If the alarm wasn't on, he could have waltzed through the front door. Or did he break in through another entry point and disable the alarm? Maybe he knew the passcode and simply punched in the four digit number. Another thought occurred to me, but I didn't want to linger too long thinking about the easy access Nina had to her husband.

"Patrick, come check these out." I pointed at the unusual marks on the floor. They were situated behind the body where the EMTs had left the blood pool untouched. "You know what those look like, don't you?"

Patrick hunched down, examining the marks more closely.

"Bootie smudges," I said, answering my own question. I lifted my foot slightly, indicating the same protective footwear on our own shoes. For us, it helped cut down on cross contamination.

"Could be," Patrick said. "Or it could be from something else. We'll have to see if the lab can confirm your hunch."

Wearing booties reinforced the idea of premeditation, and it said the perp knew enough about forensic science to cover his tracks. The smudges in the blood pool looked similar to the size of Patrick's feet. If they were bootie marks, we were looking at about a size eleven foot impression.

"Do you know who's probably familiar with crime scene collection techniques?" Patrick asked. "Dr. Grace. Think about how many cops have spilled their guts on her couch."

"You think she tortured her husband?" I asked, continuing to look around the room at the different smudge marks.

"I don't know about motive yet, but she had ample opportunity. And the stats back me up on this. You know as well as I do, three-fourths of homicides are committed by someone known to the victim."

"Sure, but that doesn't mean Dr. Grace is the perp."

"Kate, I know you have a connection with her, but you need to stay objective. Are you going to be able to handle it if we find out she's responsible for . . . for all of this?"

"Yes, of course." Though I didn't sound as sure as I'd hoped.

Walking out of the den, I pointed at the fallen table in the foyer. "When I arrived on the scene, there were bloody smudges coming from the den. They stopped at the table. The perp might have realized he was tracking blood into the foyer, stopped to take off his booties, and inadvertently knocked the table over, causing the vase to shatter."

"Thanks to the EMTs that will be difficult to prove now." Patrick pointed at the dizzying array of bloody shoe prints marking the space between the den door and the front entrance.

I exhaled in frustration. "We'll have to ask Dr. Grace if she heard a crash."

"Or see if forensics can find a sliver of the vase in her clothing."

"Do you really think Dr. Grace, wearing gloves and booties, subdued her husband, who outweighed her by more than a hundred pounds, tortured him, then changed clothes, dumped them, as well as all the torture devices, and sat at his feet pretending to be catatonic when the cops arrived?"

"Maybe."

I threw my hands up and started back toward the den. Patrick grabbed my shoulder. "Kate, I don't know for sure. That's the point. I simply want you to keep an open mind. We'll finish gathering the evidence then look to see where it leads us. I'm not solely focusing on Dr. Grace, but I refuse to discount her as a suspect either. It's too soon."

"You're right," I conceded. "I shouldn't allow our previous relationship to cloud my judgment." It was as close to an apology as I could get.

"Well you better watch what you say around Sergeant Kray. You know when we update him, your previous relationship will be the first topic we discuss. Even if Dr. Grace didn't kill her husband, she could still be guilty. Wives have been known to hire the job out. Wouldn't be the first time." Patrick walked past me, stopping short right inside the doorway.

"Murder sure," I said, "but . . . this? It would take some serious rage for Dr. Grace to pay someone to torture her husband like this."

"Have you noticed Jonathan Grace's mouth wasn't duct taped?"

"The killer wanted answers. Can't hear 'em if his mouth is shut."

"Right but you saw his body—hole in his knee, fingers shattered, ear lying on the floor. He wouldn't have been quiet. How could Dr. Grace have slept through that kind of screaming? This place is big but not that big."

"Why don't we test your theory out?" I suggested, patting him on the back. "We'll have one of the officers scream his head off while we sit in Dr. Grace's bedroom. Find out for ourselves what's possible."

CHAPTER 4

I motioned an officer over, explaining to him and the others in the room how we were going to test a theory. Patrick grabbed a radio and said he'd call when we were ready. Assuming Nina slept on the second floor, we headed upstairs.

On the way there, one of the responding officers explained about the condition of the house when he arrived. The front door was ajar. The only light came from the den and foyer. All the upstairs doors were closed except for two.

The officer led us to a room tucked into the opposite end of the house. The door to a women's sitting room stood open. He explained that this door and another, leading to a bedroom, were found opened.

When I looked around the bedroom, I noticed Nina's glasses resting on a small stack of books on a nightstand. This had to be hers. The room's design, as with the entire house, had a cold feel. It was impeccably furnished and beautifully decorated, but it didn't have the touches that made the place feel like a real home. Felt more like a designer showroom. I was a pretty good judge of character and though I'd only known Nina professionally, it didn't seem like much of her personality made an appearance. Jonathan had probably hired a decorator and more of his tastes had shown through than Nina's. Made me wonder how firmly Jonathan had grasped the reigns of control in their relationship.

I radioed downstairs, telling the officer he should begin screaming like a madman had a switchblade to his balls. We could hear the screams with both doors open, but they sounded more like muffled groans when they were shut. I radioed back to the officer, telling him to cut the death act and send up the first available crime scene tech to help catalog our search.

During the experiment, I'd noticed a bottle of pills sitting on the bedside table near Nina's glasses. I pointed it out to Patrick then bent down to read the label.

"What is it?" Patrick asked. "Valium, oxycodone?"

"No. Something called Relpax."

"Relpax? That's used for migraine relief. My wife has it in her medicine cabinet."

"What are the side effects? Does it make her sleepy?"

Patrick nodded. "Puts her right out. That's why it's effective in relieving her pain."

"So can you concede that with Jonathan screaming for his life downstairs at the opposite end of the house with all the doors closed, and Nina possibly medicated in her room, she probably wouldn't have heard a peep."

"If all those conditions were true, then yes, I'd say she slept through the whole damn thing."

But I still had to wonder, did the killer know Nina was home? Would he have killed Jonathan's wife if she'd stumbled down the stairs investigating a noise in the night? Maybe her deep slumber had actually saved her life.

I headed toward the Graces' walk-in closet, a room large enough to have Thanksgiving dinner in. With both sets of in-laws. "This doesn't look good."

Patrick peered around the corner. I pointed to the empty side of the closet. If there were two sides—a his and hers—then his side of the closet stood barren. Only a couple of padded hangers dangled on the left side of the room. If Jonathan had moved out of the bedroom, it looks like Nina had stayed on her side. Maybe she'd hoped it would only be temporary. Hell, if it would have been me, I would've said good riddance. More room for my shoes.

"I wonder where the husband slept," Patrick said.

"Let's go see if we can find where his clothes ended up."

Before we reached the hallway, Lucy walked into the room. "Did your theory pan out? Was it possible for Dr. Grace to hear her husband being tortured downstairs?"

"Unlikely," Patrick answered, a look of defeat on his face.

Unfortunately it didn't seem like this would be an open and shut case.

"Too bad Dr. Grace didn't have a dolphin's hearing," Lucy said, cupping her ear.

Patrick frowned. "Excuse me?"

"A dolphin's hearing is so acute it can pick up an underwater sound from fifteen miles away."

Last year, Lucy was on an Albert Jack kick. She was constantly giving us the origins of everyday sayings. Now it seemed she had moved on to weird animal facts.

"O . . . kay then."

Rescuing Patrick, I piped in, "This place is ridiculous. It's going to take forever to search it all."

Though I loathed the idea, I knew we needed to call Sergeant Kray and get a couple more detectives out here. It was always a crap shoot on who would be assigned. Most of the detectives were top notch, but a couple of them were real assholes. Five guys worked homicide, plus me, the only woman. We were still waiting for a new assignment to get our count back up to seven. A twenty-year veteran had just retired from our squad, leaving an open space. With the combination of the Tampa homicide rate decreasing and crappy economy increasing, the brass wasn't in too big of a hurry to fill the empty slot. A winning move of rock-paper-scissors ensured I wouldn't be the one waking up Sergeant Kray.

Patrick shot me a dirty look. "Fine. I'll call Kray then figure out where Jonathan Grace bunked." Patrick stormed off, punching numbers into his cell phone.

"I don't know why he's pissed," I told Lucy. "I'm the one missing my beach plans this weekend."

"He does seem a little snippy."

Patrick's body language definitely read edgy. My partner was the even keeled one, the one guy who knew how to defuse *my* explosive temper. There must be something more going on, but I'd have to get it out of him later. Still too much to do and too many listening ears nearby.

"Nice to get a short reprieve from the carnage downstairs?" I asked Lucy. "The other techs must have drawn the short straws."

"Being senior tech does have its advantages."

While Lucy went about photographing the items I requested, I trailed behind her searching Nina's bedroom. I looked under the handfuls of decorative pillows, the mattress, and in each drawer mostly in an effort to find a journal. Nina was a big fan of writing toxic thoughts down on paper. At least for her patients. When I didn't find anything, I figured not so much for herself. Though she could have kept a journal locked away in her office.

I did find something interesting at the bottom of Nina's drawers. Something obviously very important to her. There was a blue onesie wrapped in white tissue paper. A newborn outfit with the words *Mama's Little Angel* written on the front. I wondered if it was a keepsake from one of her children. I hadn't even realized Nina had kids. There were no pictures of them proudly displayed on her office desk at work, and I hadn't noticed any in her house.

Searching through all the clothing in Nina's room made me smile. I'd already noticed green was her favorite color when each time I'd been in her office she'd worn a different shade. With her bronze skin and vibrant green eyes, the color suited her. Looking around, I realized pops of green embellished the space, everything from emerald green knick knacks on her dresser to sea green accent pillows on top of her bed.

When Jonathan moved out of their bedroom, maybe Nina felt comfortable enough to add some personal touches. The more I thought about Jonathan, the more I looked forward to sifting through his life. Must be the voyeur in me. Everyone's dirty little secrets were revealed during a homicide investigation. If the victim had a stash of old nail clippings, we'd find it. Dominatrix fetish—it wouldn't stay secret long.

I would research Jonathan's past and everyone involved in his life. Once I knew all the cast of characters, I'd be able to wear his persona like a second skin. It's a technique that would help me figure out Jonathan's mindset leading up to the murder, thus bringing me closer to the killer.

"Kate," Lucy said, getting my attention. "Please don't jump down my throat at what I'm about to say because I'm only asking as one best friend to another. But . . . are you going to be able to handle working Dr. Grace's case?"

Again with that damn question?

"Don't give me that look," Lucy said. "I'm serious. I know what she means to you."

"You're right." I sighed. "I'm torn. Part of me wants to shield Dr. Grace from this investigation to repay her for helping me become whole again. I couldn't have gotten over my past if she hadn't been the one gluing the pieces back together. The other part of me, the detective part, reminds me that I have to follow the letter of the law. I can't cover up a crime for her. If I find evidence, implicating Dr. Grace in a murder, I have to bring it to light. But until then, I want to make sure the department doesn't get tunnel vision and focus solely on her."

"If you need anything, even a moral sounding board, you know you can always talk to me."

"Thanks, Lucy. I really appreciate it."

We finished searching Nina's sitting room and began the hunt for Patrick.

"By the way, how's it going with Chuck the vet?" I asked.

"You mean Charles?"

I did, but after all the pictures I'd seen of Mr. Wonderful, not to mention the numerous gushing stories I'd heard about him, I couldn't help but call him Chuck. Helped knock him down a peg or two, at least in my mind.

"Umm . . . he's fine." Lucy pushed her glasses farther up the bridge of her nose.

"Yeah, right. Now you *have* to spill it."

After a moment's hesitation, Lucy answered. "You know how I was over the moon when Charles asked me out a few months ago. I'd had a crush on him ever since I first brought Felix into his office."

"You mean after the dumb cat got his head stuck in a vase?"

Lucy blushed and nodded. "Anyway, Charles is a really great guy. Charming, intelligent, witty . . ."

"Yes?"

"But I've yet to see where he lives. He keeps making the excuse that he's too embarrassed to show me his bachelor pad. I'm sure that's it, but I want to get to know him better. What better way than to see his living environment?"

"Just remember his house isn't a crime scene you need to investigate. Most guys would be offended if they caught their girlfriend collecting hair samples from the shower drain."

I made light of the situation hoping to get Lucy's mind diverted but made a mental note to check into Chuck's background. If my best friend were in love with an ass, that would be one thing, but refusing to show her his place? That was a major red flag in my book. Chuck could be married with seven kids at home. I knew how easily men lied about their marital status. In fact, I still felt the burn from Jeffrey's betrayal.

CHAPTER 5

On the opposite end of the second floor, we found Patrick and crime scene tech Frankie Russo kneeling in front of an assortment of sex toys.

"Find anything you like?" I asked, bumping Patrick on the shoulder. A flash of color raced across his cheeks. Lucy let out a squeal of laughter. That signature sound of a pig getting stepped on with a six-inch stiletto heel.

The tech coughed, admirably controlling his reaction. "We found a duffle bag containing two sets of metal handcuffs, a leather neck collar with the word 'bitch' stamped on it, a cat o'nine tails, a blindfold, a half empty box of condoms, and one bottle of lubricant."

I squatted down to get a closer look at the spread. "A bit tame compared to some of the treasures we've uncovered in bedroom searches. Where did you find the bag?"

"Right out in the open, sitting in the bottom of this closet," Patrick said. "It looks like Jonathan slept in this room."

"Do you think his wife was into kink, too?" Lucy asked.

"Who knows?" I said. "They were obviously sleeping in separate bedrooms. Doubt they were participating in extracurricular nighttime activities. Anyway, if they were using these items together, they'd be stored in a container closer to their bed."

"Is that experience talking?" Patrick fired back.

I ignored his uncharacteristically harsh tone. "You said these items were found in a duffle bag. Very portable. Jonathan could have a jealous mistress."

"Doesn't seem like he tried to hide the bag," Patrick said. "Maybe Dr. Grace knows her husband's having an affair."

Mexican standoff.

"Did you find anything else?"

Patrick let out a long breath. "No but Russo lifted various prints. If Jonathan had a mistress, he may have brought her back here. We'll see what turns up. But other than clothes, the room's pretty bare. Doesn't feel like Jonathan spent much time here."

After searching the second floor, all of us headed back to the den. My mouth tasted like something had died in it. I looked at my watch, 5:17 am. I was in desperate need of a toothbrush. And while I was wishing, I might as well add a shot of caffeine and a shower to the list. Breakfast too.

Black dusting powder marred the den walls and furniture. Yellow numbered placards, indicating evidence locations, dotted the room. A crime scene tech was bent over the pool of blood at Jonathan Grace's feet. He held an eyedropper in the blood, suctioning out 5cc to put into a tube for later analysis. Lucy and Frankie left our group, heading over to the desk.

"We may have gotten lucky, detectives." Harry Ellis, the medical examiner, held a gauze pad over the corpse's right cheekbone. "May have found saliva on the victim's cheek. If we can't find a blood sample from the killer in all this mess, we can at least get a blood type from the saliva if the killer's a secretor."

"The killer must have spit on the body when he was in a rage, torturing our vic," Patrick said.

"Odd how the killer's careful wearing booties and gloves," I said, "but leaves physical evidence like this behind. We thought the killer might have a working knowledge of forensics, but if that turns out to be saliva, it seems a bit sloppy. Maybe our perp's just a fan of *Law and Order*. Doubt he has a degree in criminal justice."

I stopped talking, expecting Patrick to look at me. When he didn't, I couldn't help but poke a little harder. "Like you said, Patrick, Dr. Grace would know the intimate details of forensics. I can't imagine her being this careless."

He ignored me, instead asking Ellis, "What's the cause of death?"

I jumped in. "You mean besides the hole in the knee, the missing ear, and massive blood loss?" The dig wouldn't help Patrick's mood, but I couldn't resist pushing his buttons. Especially when he made it so easy.

"I'll have to examine the body back at the morgue," Ellis said. "I'll tell you after the autopsy."

"Detectives? We found a ring underneath the couch." Frankie Russo held up an evidence bag containing a plain gold band. "There's an inscription that reads, 'I love you Snookums.' That means the wearer of the ring has the pet name Snookums."

I turned to Patrick, confusion etched into my face. "It's a thick band, the type a man would wear. Do you think it belongs to the killer? If so, why would the killer take off his gloves, allowing his ring to fly under the couch?"

"The bloody smudges in the den suggest the perp wore gloves. I can't understand how he didn't notice it missing? Mine feels like an extension of my finger." Patrick held up his left hand. "When it's off, I'm constantly touching the empty space with my thumb."

"Wait a minute, Ellis." I placed my hand on the ME's arm. "Is Jonathan Grace wearing his wedding band?"

Ellis moved away from the body. We could all see the victim's ring missing even though blood caked his hands.

"It could be his," I said.

"Or Grace could have stopped wearing it when he moved out of his bedroom," Patrick countered.

"If it's not Grace's, whose would it be?" Just another question to add to the mounting list.

"We'll measure the ring and see if it's a match to the victim," Ellis responded.

A booming laugh echoed outside the den. I cringed. That thunderous sound could only belong to one person—Detective Donald Wozniack. Also known as *the* department asshole. Could I really have that much bad karma banked that Wozniack got assigned to my murder case? I walked toward the doorway hoping to block his entrance before—

"What the hell happened in here? No wonder you need my help, Springer. Looks like you've got a real cluster fuck on your hands."

Heat rushed up the back of my neck. I could feel years of taunting and insults coming to a head. I was ready to pop when Patrick moved around me, motioning for the two detectives to follow him into the foyer.

Wozniack was accompanied by Detective Yeo Jung. I didn't mind Jung, except for the fact that he tended to defer to the senior Wozniack. Not the best career move, considering Wozniack was only five years shy of retirement and not real motivated to bust his ass in any way.

"Thanks for coming out guys," Patrick said once we'd all congregated near the stairs. "Considering the neighborhood, we thought it best to get a couple more hands on this thing."

"I can see why. Look at this place." Wozniack let out a sharp whistle. "Mayor's probably a regular at their dinner parties."

I pointed at Wozniack, telling him Patrick and I were lead on the case. "Don't think for one second you're gonna bulldoze your way in here calling the shots."

"Don't go getting your panties all in a bunch, Springer. I don't want this nightmare. Who the hell needs the headache? Ain't that right, Jung?"

"We're working on the Masterson case anyway," Detective Jung said.

"So what can we do for your highness?" Wozniack sneered, mocking me with a bow.

I ignored him, deciding not to rise to the bait. I started with the den, walking them through the crime scene, outlining the evidence we'd found so far. Once everyone was up to speed, I explained which rooms still needed searched and asked Wozniack and Jung to interview the Graces' neighbors at daybreak.

Wozniack looked down at his watch. "We sure would hate to wake the good folks of Davis Islands before sunrise. The chief might get all sorts of nasty complaints if we started asking questions before the neighbors had their morning cappuccinos."

I brushed off Wozniack's sarcasm. "Later today, I need you two to look into anyone who's had access to the Graces' house in the last three months. Gardeners, electricians, pool boy. Anyone. I don't care if it's a homicidal Mary Kay lady."

A row of questioning eyebrows shot up. "You obviously haven't attended one of their pink cult meetings." A couple of months ago, I was lured to one with the promise of a free skin care system. Almost left with my own sales kit. Car salesmen could take pointers from those sharks.

"Should we get a list of the hired help from the Mrs.?" Wozniack asked.

"No," Patrick and I answered in unison. I didn't want Wozniack anywhere near my main witness—or suspect depending on which detective you asked.

"Get the names from the housekeeper," I said. "Earlier, I found a note on the kitchen counter from an Ana. Maybe we'll get lucky, and she'll be in later this morning."

"Anything else?" Wozniack asked in a bored tone.

"Yeah, on second thought, Jung, you should let Wozniack finish up here. I need you to get the ball rolling on the paperwork for the warrants. The wife couldn't give her consent to search the house, so we'll need one for this place. Don't forget to include the cars, any outlying buildings, and a boat if they have one. Patrick will probably head over to Jonathan Grace's office later. He'll need a search warrant on that location and a subpoena for all their bank records."

At first glance, Wozniack didn't give the impression of a competent detective. He had a protruding belly and a bald head that had a dusting of white hair on the sides, circling around the back of his head. But I had to admit, it was in my best interest to assign him the task of interviewing neighbors. Wozniack had mad skills with eyewitnesses. I swear that man could talk a nun out of her habit.

***

Patrick and I stood outside near a palm tree after we'd completed the search of the Graces' house. Sunlight began to seep over the horizon. I wiped away the sweat collecting on my neck. Even early July mornings topped the upper 70's.

"Just got a call from Hank Barrett," I said. "He told me Dr. Grace remained unresponsive the entire ride to the hospital. EMTs explained she was in shock, her pulse weak and rapid. Pupils were dilated. They didn't administer any medication, only evaluated her vital signs."

"Any spontaneous declarations of murder?"

"No. Once they got to the hospital, Barrett stood in the corner observing. Said the ER staff ran a battery of tests on her. Still waiting on the results. Barrett bagged her clothes and is in route to the crime lab. Dr. Grace's body didn't show any signs of physical trauma. All the blood must have come from her husband. You saw her catatonic state in the den, Patrick. There's no way she killed her husband."

"Stop it, Kate. You know Dr. Grace is a psychologist. If she's the killer, we can't let her play us. She knows the signs of shock. It wouldn't be that difficult for her to fake. Or what if she hired someone to kill her husband? Maybe the guy went overboard, and the sight of the murder pushed Dr. Grace over the edge. Add that to a huge helping of guilt and it could have sent her into shock."

"We just started the investigation, and you've already convicted her."

"No ... I ... haven't. Unlike you, I simply haven't found her innocent yet."

Unwilling to jump on that merry-go-round again, I threw out a trivia question, trying to diffuse Patrick's uncharacteristic anger. "Eight presidents were born in one state. Which state was it?" Questions like these were our little way of passing the time, taking our mind off a particularly craptastic event, or just showing each other our dumb side.

When Patrick didn't answer, I poked him in the ribs. "Come on, this is an easy one."

Patrick practically exhaled my name. "Kate, I'm not in the mood."

"What's going on with you?"

"Nothing!"

I stopped talking, deciding to wait him out. Patrick had seen me in an interrogation room. He knew I could outlast him.

"My wife's pregnant. Again."

Patrick's angry outburst shocked me. I didn't know what to say. "So you don't know which state was home to eight presidents?"

Patrick glared at me.

I threw my hands up in submission. "Sorry. Didn't sound like you wanted to hear congratulations."

Patrick let out a deep sigh and rubbed his hands against the back of his neck. "You're right, I should be happy. My three little girls are gifts from God. I just don't know how I can afford one more gift."

"What does Alina have to say about it?"

"She's excited. She's always wanted a big family, but on a cop's salary, that's not very realistic."

"Money's your objection?"

"Coming from the single lady. Do you have any idea what it costs to keep three girls clothed? And the shoes! Does a four-year-old really need a closet full of shoes?"

"Oh, come on. Most of those are probably hand-me-downs."

Another dirty look told me I should shut up and let Patrick vent.

"I'm not ready for another baby in the house. It wasn't that long ago we got Raina potty trained, and now we have to start all over. It's not just the money thing bugging me. It's no sleep, spit-up on my shirts, no sex. *Lots* of no sex."

"Think on the bright side, you might finally get a Patrick Jr."

"Great. Then we'd have to buy all new boy clothes. You're not helping, Kate."

I clapped Patrick on the back. "Come on, Daddy. Let's get out of here. I'll spring for breakfast. You need to start saving up for diapers."

CHAPTER 6

Patrick and I watched the sunrise as we formed the day's game plan over a couple of breakfast skillets. The scrambled eggs wiggled too freely for my taste, but the hash browns had a nice crunch to them.

"You should handle the search of Jonathan Grace's office," Patrick said. "I'm really not in the right frame of mind to interview his office staff."

That surprised me. Quite the role reversal, considering he usually angled for the interviews. He hated being cooped up in the office all day.

Patrick swallowed a last piece of toast. "I'll start researching Nina and Jonathan Grace," he said. "We need to arm ourselves with as much background information as we can get. Especially before our interview with Dr. Grace."

"Don't trust me to come clean with the dirt I dig up on the good doctor?" I picked up the check and headed toward the register. I ignored the raspberry I heard behind me.

Back in my car, I headed north to Jonathan Grace's office in the Channelside District. Tampa was such a diverse city, little pockets of unique neighborhoods sprinkled throughout the city. Channelside was home to the Port Authority, Florida Aquarium, and St. Pete Times Forum. Within a few short miles, visitors could touch stingrays, head for Mexico on a cruise, check out a Lightning hockey game, or watch a concert with 20,000 new friends. The prime location wasn't only a tourist destination but also a popular hangout for the locals.

Sitting at a red light, waiting for the trolley to pass, I brooded over the possibility that Nina Grace killed her husband. Nina's a petite woman, measuring about 5'3" and 100 pounds. I doubted she had the physical prowess to carry out a murder, the magnitude of which was handed out to Jonathan Grace. But was her heart callous enough to hire an executioner? Unhappiness could morph into bitterness, which left long enough to fester, turned black and rock hard.

No one knew more than I the evil that could lurk, simmering right beneath the skin. With some people, the malice leaked out of their pores, an evil so foul, you could almost smell it. Others were better at hiding their heart's desires. Was Nina one of those people? In front of Patrick, I had to portray unfailing allegiance toward Nina. At least until the evidence told me otherwise. But in the emptiness of my car, I couldn't help but wonder about her innocence.

Nina and I had met last fall. A rough time for me both personally and professionally. The Tampa PD was still recovering from having lost two officers, shot after a routine traffic stop. It happened in June, but the entire force was on edge for months afterwards. Later that fall, I caught a case where the victim resembled me at the age of thirteen. It brought up a lot of issues with my past and the childhood sexual abuse I'd suffered. If it weren't for Nina, I wouldn't have been able to conquer my demons once and for all.

Not to say I was completely cured. I still had some lingering effects. Mostly trust issues. But how could I not when all of the people I'd loved most had let me down. I trusted a man more than seven times my age to take care of me. He took advantage of that trust and used it against me. I trusted a mother who, instead of protecting me, handed me over to the pedophile. Unknowingly, I'll admit, but still a violation of trust in a child's eyes. Dr. Grace had helped me work through most of my issues, but I still struggled with allowing myself to fully open up to others.

Maybe I simply trusted the wrong people. Take Jeffrey, the supposed ex-husband I'd been dating for the last three months. In the end, a horse's ass, but at least he had served a purpose. He'd taken my mind off Carlos Diaz. Just the thought of Carlos turned my insides gooey. A fact, which in and of itself made me cringe. The man was six feet of pure Latin hunk. Dreamy brown eyes a girl could get lost in. And I almost did.

We met last fall after he'd written an embarrassing article about me in the *Tampa Tribune*. At first, I hated the man. Carlos had practically stalked me while I worked a murder case, hoping a lead would further his career. Eventually, I had to pay him back for his help in the investigation, giving him an exclusive. After that, things got too steamy, too quickly. I panicked and shut him out. It may have slowed him down a little, but he hadn't given up his pursuit. His persistence had always driven me nuts, but a small part of me, that often times hidden part of me, thought it was endearing. But it didn't matter how much Carlos wanted a relationship. He was a reporter. How could I trust him not to use our bedroom talk against me?

I pulled into Jonathan Grace's office parking lot next to a CSU van. Lucy James sat in the driver's seat talking on her cell phone. When I walked up to the window, she gave me an exasperated look. She held up a finger indicating she needed a moment longer.

She finally lowered the glass, an apologetic look on her face. "It was Charles."

"Trouble in paradise?" I asked a little too hopeful.

"Oh, no. Nothing like that." Lucy looked down at the steering wheel and started pulling at the duct tape. Her straight, reddish-brown hair fanned around her. "Charles called asking if we could reschedule our date for later in the week. When I asked him what was more important than spending time with his best girl, he got a little cranky. I don't know, maybe he thought I was being too nosey."

Lucy looked up and saw my scowl. "It's no big deal, Kate. I'm going to be busy with this case anyway."

I silently berated myself again for not running a background check on Chuck. I filed a note in my memory box to stop procrastinating and do it once I got back to the station later today. For now, it was best to change the subject. "I'm surprised you're here. With all the evidence from this morning's crime scene, I figured I wouldn't see you for a couple of days."

"I left instructions for the boys. They're quite competent. Anyway, I needed some fresh air. That was one rough scene. Thought I'd take advantage of searching a room without a dead body."

"Let's hope so."

Lucy took off her glasses and started to clean them with the end of her shirt. "How do you want to handle this?"

"Give me a few minutes to check out the place, interview the employees." Experience told me if I went in waving a warrant, they'd clam up. Right before breakfast, Detective Jung had delivered the search warrant granting us permission to search Jonathan's office, but it would stay in my pocket until I'd exhausted my list of questions.

"No problem." Lucy pointed across the street at the corner diner. "Truth be told, I came a little early to get some food. Most of my guys won't eat after processing a scene like the one we had, but for me, a full belly is a happy belly."

I smiled as Lucy and I parted ways, thinking how lucky I was to have her as a best friend. She'd always been there for me, holding my hand when I needed to talk, providing a shoulder to cry on during one of my many breakups. I don't know what I'd do without her support.

I stopped outside the elevator doors that would take me up to Jonathan Grace's second story office. According to the directory, Grace Developers Group shared this building with a lawyer, CPA, brokerage firm, and a not-for-profit.

I stepped off the elevator and turned left. Smoky glass doors opened up to a small but upscale waiting area. I smiled at the thought of Grace's rich clients barely containing their impatience as they cooled their heels with a copy of *Architectural Digest* in their laps.

"Excuse me," I announced. "Is anyone here?" I looked down at my watch. 8:17 am. If they had banker's hours, it was still early, but the door had been unlocked.

I heard a phone drop onto its base and a sultry female voice answered from a room to my right. "You're early this morning."

I heard the clicking of heels as a tall bombshell turned the corner. She stopped when she saw me. The woman was in her early twenties and had a 40s pinup girl vibe. Her look was complete with the formfitting, vintage dress and black, rolled-up hairdo. I wondered if Nina knew her husband spent his days in the company of this eye candy and what the good doctor had to say about it.

"You're not Jamie."

"Not the last time I checked." I chuckled, hoping to create a light mood, putting her at ease.

Her hands rose to her hips, immediately on guard, like a Star Wars force field had risen up from the floor separating me from her. Maybe nonchalance wasn't my strong suit.

"I'm Detective Kate Springer with the Tampa Police Department. Do you have somewhere we can talk?"

The woman pointed to the left and led me to a large conference room. Her steps were quick and measured. I could tell this lady was used to being in charge and getting what she wanted.

"Is there anyone else in the office today?" I asked, taking a seat.

"No. Only two of us work here." The woman sat across the table from me. "Mr. Grace isn't in yet. May I ask why you're here, Detective?"

"I'm sorry, ma'am. What was your name?"

"Ms. Tyler. Lauren Tyler."

I remained silent, hoping she'd fill the awkward, empty space. Most people did. They were intimidated when confronted with a police officer. Instead, she sat silent on the edge of her chair with her back ramrod straight and green eyes boring into me. Lauren Tyler wasn't the type of woman to offer up information freely. She probably had two ways of dealing with people, both based on gender. If I were a man, she'd use her sex appeal to play the situation to her advantage. Instead, I received the cold, corporate Lauren.

"Ms. Tyler, I'm afraid I have bad news. Someone murdered Jonathan Grace in his home late last night."

Lauren let out a yelp and covered her mouth with her hands. Tears welled up in her eyes, though she allowed none to escape. Her reaction communicated shock, but I didn't know if it was sincere. This kind of woman, the accomplished actress type, was probably used to playing a variety of parts. Who knew if the rapid appearance of tears indicated she truly cared for her boss or if it was only an act.

Lauren stood and had me follow her into the office she'd exited earlier. The pictures on the desk told me it was her personal office. Grabbing a tissue from a decorative box, Lauren dabbed her eyes, ensuring her makeup remained flawless. She sat in her rolling chair, and I took the seat next to her desk. Having entered her inner sanctum, I hoped she would finally let her guard down.

"Obviously, you cared for Mr. Grace. I'd like to ask you a few questions. Anything you can give me might help us find who killed him."

"You're sure he was murdered?"

Flashing back to the crime scene, I shuddered. I could guarantee that grisly scene wasn't an accident. I nodded and once again, Lauren dabbed her eyes as fresh tears moistened the pink tissue.

"What's your function in this office?"

"I'm Mr. Grace's Executive Assistant. I do anything and everything from booking meetings and arranging flights to creating marketing materials."

"And you mentioned earlier only you and Mr. Grace work here. Then who makes up the 'group' in 'Grace Developers Group'?"

"Excuse me?"

"Does Jonathan Grace have any partners?"

"Not anymore. Mr. Grace bought out his partner, Sean O'Brien, after the bubble burst." When I raised my eyebrows, she clarified. "When the real estate market crashed in '08."

I wrote down the ex-partner's contact information. "What exactly did Jonathan Grace do at Grace Developers Group?"

"In layman's terms, Mr. Grace bought property, building luxury condominiums on them."

"How did he weather the downturn in the economy?"

"He was one of the few real estate investment groups that remained solvent. Many condo developers declared bankruptcy. No buyers means a big empty building with no way to pay for it."

"Do you know of anyone who might have wanted to hurt Mr. Grace?"

Lauren, about to shake her head, stopped short. "Actually, Mr. Grace did get quite a bit of hate mail earlier this year. He told me to throw out the letters, but I thought it would be wise if I hung onto them for a while." Lauren wheeled her chair backwards to a tall filing cabinet. From the bottom drawer, she pulled out a file folder labeled *Crazies*.

Mighty convenient to have a list so readily available. I quickly scanned the first few letters in the pile. The most recent ones were from an environmental group angry over Grace's plans to build a new condominium.

"What's the real story behind the hippies' anger at your boss?"

Lauren sat rigidly with her mouth pursed and arms folded across her chest.

"Come on, Lauren. You know I can easily find out what's going on. Save me the trouble and tell me Mr. Grace's side of the story."

She began chewing on her bottom lip. Probably figuring out the best way to spin the story. Company girl to the end.

After another moment's hesitation, Lauren let out a sigh. "Mr. Grace bought property on the outskirts of Orlando with the intention of building on it. Two months ago, he was indicted by a grand jury for alleged felony violations of the federal wetlands protection law. Attorneys for the US Environmental Protection Agency sought an indictment citing allegations Mr. Grace improperly bulldozed and filled in wetlands. It's ridiculous. Some invasive plants are uprooted on a small patch of undeveloped pasture land and all the tree huggers descend like it's a two for one sale on Birkenstocks."

I couldn't hide my smirk. It's a shame Lauren and I hadn't met under different circumstances. I respected her tough attitude. Probably cultivated from working in a predominately male-dominated field. I could relate. "What kind of sentence went along with a guilty verdict?"

"If convicted, which was highly unlikely, Mr. Grace could face six years in prison and fines up to $500,000."

Definitely not a little slap on the wrist. Being out of circulation for six years, Jonathan's finances would have taken a big hit, but I'm guessing the jail time wouldn't have been too tough. Most likely, he would have been thrown into one of those cushy Club Med types of federal penitentiaries.

I'd run down this new list of environmental loving suspects later to find out if any of them had a record of violence. I leafed through the rest of the hate letters but nothing major jumped out. Lauren copied the mail, allowing me to keep the originals. I would finish reading them back at the station.

"What about enemies?" I asked. "You can't build a company like this without stepping on a few people along the way."

"I'll write down the names of Mr. Grace's biggest competitors." Lauren grabbed a tablet of paper off her desk. "At the top of the list is Goro Yamamoto."

"Goro, who?"

"Yamamoto. Ever since he lost out on a bid to build in the Channelside District, he's hated Mr. Grace."

"Must happen a lot in this business. Losing a bid is one thing; being angry enough to kill someone over it is another. Was Yamamoto pissed because Grace got the contract in some back-door deal?"

For a moment, Lauren forgot herself and a sly smile escaped. "Just because Mr. Grace knows the right people doesn't make him a cheat."

"And who are the right people?"

Lauren dropped the smile and grew quiet again.

"Okay," I said moving on. "I need to retrace Mr. Grace's last steps on the day he died. Do you have that information?"

"I can pull up his calendar on my computer." After a few keystrokes, an electronic schedule popped up on the screen. "Looks like he got into the office right before a 9 am conference call with Adhil Gupta. Mr. Grace considered working with him on a future land deal. This was their first meeting. It lasted a couple of hours. Mr. Grace worked in his office from 11 am to 12:30 pm. Then he went to Jackson's Bistro for a lunch meeting with his lawyer, Curtis Cavanaugh. I assume they discussed the pending wetlands case."

After I got the lawyer's contact information, Lauren went back to Jonathan's calendar. "Mr. Grace drove to Orlando after lunch. He wanted to get another project in the pipeline, so he met with Jamar Washington to scout out possible locations. I remember Mr. Grace called me around 6:30 that evening . . . yesterday, was that only yesterday?"

Lauren fell silent.

"You said Mr. Grace called?" I prompted.

"Right." Lauren shook her head slightly as if to clear her mind. "I was working closely with a print company on a project they seemed hell bent on screwing up. When Mr. Grace called, I dropped everything to email him a file. He told me he was getting ready to sit down to dinner with Mr. Washington. That's the last time I heard from him. I don't know where he went after dinner."

"Looks like Jamar Washington might have been the last person to see Jonathan Grace alive. Do you know anything about the guy?"

"Never met him. Sounded decent enough on the phone."

"Can you print a copy of your boss's schedule for the entire week prior to his death?"

"Sure."

I'd noticed Lauren had yet to ask about Nina's wellbeing. I decided to steer the boat in that direction, see what kind of murky waters we ended up in.

"Ms. Tyler, I want you to know, you don't have to worry about Mr. Grace's wife. She was home at the time of the murder, but she's unharmed."

Was that a shudder? Quickly stifled, but not fast enough. I wondered if Lauren only knew Nina through the photographs on Jonathan's desk, or if the assistant was a shoulder for Jonathan when he complained about the old battle ax. If Lauren and Jonathan had an office romance, there's nothing like a woman scorned to bring out the claws. Or in this case, the power tools.

"Were you close with Mr. Grace?" When Lauren tensed, I started to clarify my question. "I mean—"

"You mean, did Mr. Grace confide in me about his marriage?"

I nodded.

"No. He and I kept our relationship professional. I was his Executive Assistant, not a Personal Assistant."

Lauren's body language shouted the opposite, but I had no proof of this. I'd table the tough questions until I had something definitive.

"One last question. Where were you last night?"

"What do you mean?"

"Mr. Grace was murdered around midnight. What were you doing then?"

"Sleeping."

I arched my eyebrows.

"No, not alone. My . . . girlfriend stayed over." By her red cheeks, I could tell girlfriend meant partner not BFF. "Analise came over for a late dinner, around 7:30 pm. She stayed until 6 am when she had to head home to get ready for work."

That answered one question. But it was interesting Lauren never asked how her boss died. That's usually the first question family and friends asked. She may be on the bottom of the suspect list, but Lauren Tyler was still on it.

CHAPTER 7

I'd served Lauren Tyler with a warrant, and now Lucy and I were searching Jonathan Grace's office. Numerous sets of files had been packed up in boxes to be reviewed later. Lucy was removing the hard drive from Jonathan's computer.

"Lucy, there's something off about this picture." Before me a large photograph took up much of the wall across from Jonathan's desk. The evocative picture showed a silhouette of a naked female body. There was no overt nudity, it simply celebrated the natural curves most women had today.

Lucy stopped turning her screwdriver and looked up. "The frame's slightly askew."

I moved over to her vantage point and realized she was right. I walked back over to the picture, grabbed the bottom of the frame, and pulled it up away from the wall. "Lookie here. There's a safe behind this photograph. Come help me with this, will ya?"

Lucy and I each grabbed hold of a side, gently lifting it from the hook and slid it down the wall to the floor.

"Give me a sec," I told her and left to check with Lauren to see if she knew the combination.

When I returned, I told Lucy, "Apparently this is Jonathan's personal safe. Lauren said she didn't have access to it, but I don't believe her. When she answered, her voice raised about an octave. Dust it and let's see what we find."

Only two sets of prints were viable. The rest were too smudged to get a good sample. Lucy visually confirmed they were from two different people.

"The ME will give you Jonathan's prints for a comparison," I said. "How much you want to bet the other set is Lauren's?"

"Don't think she'd willingly volunteer to let us check, do you?"

"I seriously doubt it. Let's not put her on the defensive yet. We might need more information from her later." At this point in the investigation, it was best to keep Lauren as an ally. I waved the file folder holding Jonathan's hate mail. "How about we pull her prints off this?"

It wouldn't be admissible in court, if it actually came to that, but it would be helpful to know if Lauren's prints matched a set found on Jonathan's safe. Depending on how the investigation shook out, I could always get a warrant for her fingerprints at a later date.

Lucy finished dusting the manila folder. "See how this loop pattern curves over the top ridge on both the print from the safe and the one from the file folder? Could definitely be a match to our Ms. Tyler. I'll have to confirm it back at the lab though."

Lucy looked over at the safe and then back at me with a mischievous smile playing on her face. "You know what time it is?"

"Big Beula time," we sang out in unison.

Lucy let out her piggy squeal of laughter. She grabbed her keys and bounded out of the office to grab the monstrous drill from the van.

A few minutes later, Lucy adjusted goggles over her glasses and tightly gripped the drill in both hands. She wore a silly grin as she started up the machine. The loud whir of metal on metal drowned out my laughter over Lucy's obvious glee. I had to admit it was exciting breaking into someone's personal space. Would I find a clue leading to Jonathan Grace's killer? What kind of secrets did he want to hide away from home in the safety of his private office?

My ears were still ringing when Lucy opened the safe. I peered over her shoulder as she photographed its contents.

"All that trouble for a small stack of cash and a key?" Lucy held up the long, silver key about the size of a credit card. "The number 3154 is etched into it."

"Looks like a safe deposit key. Wonder what made Jonathan feel like he needed an extra layer of security? Whatever he's hiding, he obviously didn't feel comfortable stashing it in his office. Are there any other distinguishable marks?"

Lucy turned the key over inspecting it. "No, nothing." She photographed, printed, and bagged it.

"Wait a minute." I hunched down and looked up into the safe. When I didn't see anything, I ran my gloved hand along the inside walls. Near the top ledge of the door's opening, my fingers touched a small raised surface. "Bingo!" Clear tape secured something tiny and square. I removed the tape and pulled out an SD card. This type of digital storage, about the size of a quarter, was commonly found in digital cameras.

"Should we wait and have our computer guys run this?"

"Are you kidding me?" I was like a kid at Christmas, unable to wait one more second to unwrap my present.

"Jonathan Grace's computer is already dismantled," Lucy reminded me.

"I'm sure Lauren wouldn't mind if we borrowed hers."

After Lucy photographed and printed the storage card, we walked to Lauren's office and found it empty.

"Maybe she went to the bathroom." I sat down at her computer and inserted the SD card into the slot, opening the computer's directory. When I clicked on the card's icon, thumbnail pictures started uploading.

"Oh, my." Hunched over my shoulder, Lucy squeezed my shoulder, digging her nails into my blazer.

What seemed like hundreds of photographs recorded a sexual encounter. The digital camera must have had an automatic timer clicking off a shot every thirty seconds or so. The first few pictures caught Jonathan Grace fiddling with the camera's buttons. Once he got the proper angle, the photos recorded his movement toward a bed. The shapes of two people were silhouetted under a sheet. The only thing peeking out was their feet.

The room wasn't at the Graces' house or even a garden variety hotel room. It looked like a jungle-themed sex room. The walls were painted in an array of dark greens, creating a nighttime rain forest. An imposing tiger crouched in the corner, spying on the threesome.

In the next photograph, Jonathan pulled the sheet off the twosome in the bed. By the eighth shot, I could tell both were women. All the photos had a date stamp of earlier in the year, 03/17/11. As I enlarged the next shot, I heard a gasp behind us. Lauren Tyler had returned just in time to see her face and other exposed body parts fill the computer screen.

"What are you doing?" Lauren frantically tried to grab the mouse away from me. I put one hand up to her chest, stopping her futile advances. She finally gave up, dropping down into the extra chair beside her desk.

Lauren seemed intelligent. The type of woman to easily navigate the shark infested waters of the corporate world. But when you added her beauty into the equation, she could've had any job she wanted. Yet, she settled for an Executive Assistant job in a small two-person office.

When I asked her about this, she reluctantly explained. "I'd recently graduated from college and couldn't find a job."

I shot her a disbelieving look.

"No really," she said. "The economy had tanked. The commercial real estate market was in the toilet. Nobody was hiring, especially someone so green. Plus a few of my grades were less than stellar." She shrugged her shoulders. "I felt lucky when Mr. Grace gave me a shot. Only an Executive Assistant position, but I knew I could learn the ropes of Tampa real estate then move on to something bigger. That was my plan anyway."

"What happened?"

"I enjoyed the lifestyle a little too much. Jonathan paid real well, and I'd often find presents on my desk—diamond bracelets, emerald earrings. Bonuses, that's what Jonathan called them. We'd go out for late working dinners at the most expensive restaurants in town. Growing up, I didn't have a pot to piss in. It was nice to finally have anything I wanted. It didn't take long before an affair began."

"What about your girlfriend?" I asked.

"It was before I met Analise."

"Then who's the other person in the pictures?" I pointed to a thumbnail photograph of Lauren and a redhead kissing.

"Some girl at the club." She gave a flippant wave of her hand. "The beginning of the relationship with Jonathan was perfect. The nights we spent together were wonderful. But he changed. I mean, I'm no prude, but Jonathan was very . . . experimental. He knew I was bisexual, so he asked if we could have a threesome. I don't know why I agreed to be photographed."

"Would you even consider a ménage à trois experimental these days?" Lucy asked absently. "Seems kind of tame if you ask me."

I gave her a stern look for interrupting the interview, but you better believe I filed that little nugget away for later.

"What club?" I asked Lauren.

"The Sext Club."

When I didn't respond, this time Lauren filled the silence. "It's a club in Ybor City. Members only, very exclusive. You have to be invited by a member in order to get in." Lauren blushed when she said, "I'm a member. I introduced Jonathan to the club."

"This sex club—"

"No *Sext* Club. You know sexting. It's all the rage these days."

It took a second to digest what she meant. People texted messages all the time using their cell phones. "Sexting" is like phone sex where people text sexual notes back and forth. Since a written record of this flirtatious chat is created, sexting had been known to get quite a few married politicians in hot water.

"Anyway," Lauren said, "the Sext Club has an ingenious hook. You're assigned an avatar that is completely customizable. So when you're at the club, you're totally anonymous. You're given a handheld device you can use to sext other avatars. It's fun to try to figure out which avatar belongs to which patron. You can hang out at the club and talk dirty, or if you take an interest in someone, you can hook up in one of the rooms."

Now the jungle room made more sense. "You said Jonathan Grace changed?"

Lauren glanced at Lucy. "You're right, threesomes aren't that risqué, but after I said yes to the first suggestion, Jonathan pushed me to do more. Even when it made me feel . . . uncomfortable. I finally put a stop to the relationship after he crossed the line. I *do not* enjoy being bound and gagged. And wearing a school girl uniform is just creepy."

"How'd he take it?"

"Surprisingly well. Jonathan had met someone else at the club and was quickly losing interest anyway. After we split though, things got uncomfortable at the office. Awkward doesn't even begin to scratch the surface. When I gave him my two weeks' notice, I found a copy of these pictures on my desk with my resignation letter lying beside it ripped in half. It didn't take a genius to figure out I was staying."

"Why would Jonathan want you around if things were tense between the two of you?"

"Jonathan did not like to lose the things he considered his." Lauren nodded her head, a sad knowing smile on her face. "Though he didn't want me in his bed any longer, Jonathan still thought of me as his. He thought he owned me."

"When did all of this take place?"

Lauren searched her memory for the dates. A realization hit her, easily readable from her frown and forehead crease. The timing of the affair and breakup probably scared her, made her think she'd climbed higher up the ranking of my suspect list. Lauren crossed her arms, visibly closing down.

I stood up, moving closer inside her personal space. "Let me guess, Jonathan blackmailed you. Wanted you to stay with the company. You didn't want those pictures getting around town. It would ruin the reputation you'd worked so hard to create. Not only would it obliterate your chances to move to a larger company with a better title, you'd be lucky if you weren't working at the dollar store by the end of the week.

"Tell me Lauren, when Jonathan was out of the office, did you slip in and try various combinations on his safe? I mean, the pictures had to be there, right? Where else would he keep them? Definitely not at home with his wife. But you couldn't figure out the combination, could you? The winning numbers weren't the date of his anniversary, his lucky numbers, or even his dead dog's birthday.

"What'd you do, Lauren? Hire some low-life from the club. Did you promise him ten minutes in paradise if he got Jonathan to talk? I have to give it to you. Good choice. The guy did a number on your boss. Cut off his ear. Even drilled a hole in his knee. All for three little numbers." Lauren's already pale skin grew a shade lighter after hearing the description of Jonathan's death.

I put my hands on the armrests of Lauren's chair, moving in closer. "We found two sets of prints on the wall safe. Did your hired killer give you a bogus combination?"

Lauren's mouth dropped open. I didn't know if it was from surprise I'd figured it out or my assumption that she could possibly have something to do with Jonathan's death. Things were definitely starting to look up for Nina.

Lauren turned her head to look at Lucy and then glared at me. "I am done talking."

"Oh, don't worry. We'll be in touch."

CHAPTER 8

I dropped a fast food bag on Patrick's desk. "What does SPAM stand for?" I asked him.

"Is that what's in the sack?" He hesitantly opened it, peering inside.

"With your behavior lately, it should be. Now answer the question."

Patrick picked up his cheeseburger and took an enormous bite. He started talking through the food.

I sighed and answered for him. "SPAM stands for Shoulder Pork And Ham."

"Gross."

Patrick swiveled his chair around facing my desk. He brought his bag with him, dumping the fries on top of a napkin. I swear the man had more lunches at my desk than I did.

"Interesting morning you had," he said after thanking me for the meal.

I'd called Patrick on the way back to the precinct, relaying everything I'd discovered at Jonathan Grace's office. "Definitely one for the record books. At least we have a couple more suspects to add to our list."

"You'll be sad to hear you missed Wozniack. He and Jung stopped by when they got back from the crime scene."

"Did they finish their to-do list?" I swiped a fry from Patrick's mountain. I was already busting at the seams from my own lunch, but couldn't help pushing his buttons. The baby of the family, Patrick grew up fighting off his six older sisters. Food was no exception.

Patrick sighed. "Almost. Wozniack said all of the neighbors were shocked, but morbid curiosity struck a few of them, and they started asking for details. One old guy who lives in the house directly across from the Graces saw the two of them arguing four days earlier. The neighbor was pushing his trashcan to the curb when he witnessed Dr. Grace yelling at her husband through an open car window."

"Did the neighbor hear their conversation?"

"No. Said he didn't have his hearing aids in. Guess his wife drives him crazy. He keeps them out for as long as he can get away with it."

"Then how did he know Dr. Grace was yelling?"

"Wozniack asked the same thing. Guy said he was seventy-six, that he knew when a woman was yelling at a man even without his hearing aids."

"Did Wozniack actually learn anything useful canvasing the neighborhood?"

Patrick held up a finger until he finished chewing. "Lots of folks weren't home, but we got lucky. When Wozniack and Jung were pulling out of the Graces' driveway, a truck from Janz Security showed up. Dr. Grace had called them Wednesday, requesting they come out to beef up the security system. They planned on installing outdoor motion detector lights and security cameras at the front and back entrances."

"Why now? What explanation did Dr. Grace give them?"

"Said she caught someone watching her house. Some guy sitting in a car across the street staring. It gave her the willies. Janz Security said the husband urged her to call."

"It could have been the killer staking out the place, learning the Graces' schedule." I made a note to remind myself to ask Nina for a description of the vehicle. "We need to have Wozniack check back with the neighbors, especially the old guy. See if anyone noticed any strangers in the area."

"It's taken care of. Wozniack said he already had plans for tomorrow to follow up with the neighbors who weren't home this morning. Said he would add this new information to his list. In true Wozniack fashion, he bitched about us getting our shit together. Said he wouldn't recanvas a third time."

"Yeah, yeah. What did Janz say about the alarm system?"

"The technician did us a favor and checked the lines outside the Graces' house. There's a phone box out by the street. It's responsible for routing calls to their place as well as five other houses. The killer didn't tamper with it. Instead, the line was cut near the house. The tech checked with the security office and found they hadn't received a notification that the phone line had been tampered with. The tech blamed inferior equipment. Newer systems send out an alert if the line's been tampered with whether the system's armed or not. Janz hasn't made the necessary investment needed to upgrade its hardware."

"Let me guess, there's no record of whether or not the Graces' set their alarm last night."

Patrick shook his head. "It's unbelievable that someone would spend so much money on a house and then scrimp on its security system."

"I'm confused." I rubbed my temples. "Did the perp stake out the house, waiting for an opportunity? Watching for the day someone forgot to turn on the alarm?"

"Seems like a long shot. If the Graces were sticklers for arming their system, might be a long wait."

"True enough. If Dr. Grace saw someone watching her house, you'd think she'd be conscientious about arming their system. Although Jonathan was most likely the last one in the house last night. Not much crime in their neighborhood. Maybe he didn't take his wife's warning seriously."

Patrick shrugged, wiping his hands on a napkin. Greasy fingerprints stained the white paper. "Something to check on with the housekeeper. She'd know how diligent they were. She'd be the one to turn off the alarm—if it was set—when she arrived each morning."

Inwardly, I smiled. For the moment, Patrick had jumped on my bandwagon. He'd stopped offering a competing story on how Nina could have killed Jonathan.

Patrick looked down at Wozniack's report on the search of the crime scene. "By the way, there were no signs of forced entry at any of the windows or doors. We know one person in the house at the time of the murder that didn't have to worry about the alarm passcode."

Short-lived moment. Patrick was back to pointing the finger at Nina.

"When you think about it, someone staking out the house wouldn't know if the alarm was armed or not," I said. "Where the keypad's located on the wall isn't visible from the outside. What about the large bush to the left of the garage? It's conceivable the killer hid behind it, slipping into the garage as the door lowered."

"When? After Dr. Grace came home or later when Jonathan arrived?"

"Either."

"I think you're grasping at straws, Kate. How would the killer know the Graces' schedules?"

"Not hard to find office hours on a company website."

"Still seems like a lot of supposition. We could go round and round like this all day. How about we table it until after we've talked to Dr. Grace? There's still a lot we don't know. We need all the puzzle pieces to get a clear picture of what happened. Or at least more pieces than we have right now."

I raised my hands in defeat. "Speaking of which, what background information did you dig up on the Graces?"

"Lots." Patrick balled up his cheeseburger wrapper and shot it at the waste basket. "Damn."

"Graces? Background info?"

"Right. I'll give you the highlights. A Tampa native, Jonathan Grace was born April 18, 1965. That made him forty-six. I printed off an article about him in *The Maddux Business Report*—"

In response to my questioning eyebrow, Patrick handed me the article, continuing his summary. "It was a Tampa magazine that covered the commercial real estate market. Anyway, Grace grew up poor but became a self-made millionaire by thirty. Got rich buying and selling Florida real estate."

"Yeah, I see here he formed Grace Developers Group in 1992, when he was in his late 20's."

Patrick nodded. "His company built office high-rises, downtown Tampa condominiums, and a variety of luxury living projects on Bayshore Blvd, Clearwater Beach, and in the heart of St. Petersburg."

A picture of Grace ran with the article. He was ruggedly handsome. Dark brown hair cut short but with a mop of curls on the top, a dusting of gray in his sideburns. He looked more like a TV doctor than a real estate mogul. His tailored shirt and khakis emphasized his well-defined body. Not a weightlifter, a runner maybe.

I stared at Jonathan's picture, wondering what he did to incur the wrath of a killer. Was it a business deal gone bad? Did he sleep with the wrong man's wife? Or did he piss off his own wife one too many times?

"Ran a search on Dr. Nina Grace," Patrick was saying. "She was born Nina Garcia on February 17, 1971. Looks like she got to keep her monogram. Anyway, she's from Miami. Attended the University of Miami for ten years where she eventually earned her doctorate in psychology. Nina moved to Tampa and began working at USF's Florida Mental Health Institute counseling people with mental, addictive, and developmental disorders. In 2003, Nina opened her own practice and five years later added Tampa PD shrink to her resume."

"Wonder how she got that gig? Have to know some important people to land a city contract," I mused.

"Definitely. Jonathan and Nina got married in September of '06. On their wedding day, they would have been forty-one and thirty-five, respectively."

"Two months from now they would have celebrated their fifth wedding anniversary."

"Thirty-five seems kind of late to get married," Patrick said.

"Speak for yourself." Almost four decades in, I was in no hurry to tie the knot.

"This was Nina's first marriage but Jonathan's second."

"What happened to the first Mrs.?"

Patrick shuffled through a couple of papers, scanning the printouts until he found what he wanted. "Tammy Hildabrand and Jonathan Grace were high school sweethearts. They split after nine years. They have one son, Bobby Hildabrand. He's twenty-three now."

"Bobby doesn't have his daddy's last name. Be good to find out the story behind that."

"I'll start digging into the kid's background tomorrow."

"Did Nina and Jonathan have any children together?"

"No."

It made me wonder what the story was behind the baby outfit stored in Nina's dresser. "What about Jonathan's family? Parents, siblings?"

"Parents deceased, but he has one older brother living out west. I left a message for him, requesting a call back." Patrick slurped up the last bit of liquid through his straw.

"I think you got it all. Now would you like to hear about my morning?"

"By all means."

I updated Patrick on everything I'd discovered at Jonathan Grace's office, beginning with the federal investigation into the land deal and ending with the photographs of Jonathan, Lauren, and the redhead.

Patrick let out a long, soft whistle. "If Lauren Tyler is as motivated as it sounds to get ahead in the real estate business, knocking Jonathan Grace out may have been the only way to do it."

That's one of the things I admired most about Patrick. The other male detectives would've asked to see the pictures. For purely investigative reasons, of course. Not Patrick. He respected women. If this new baby turned out to be a boy, Patrick would be great at teaching the little guy what it meant to be a real man.

"What in the hell is that?" I asked.

The sound of a chicken clucking, a very loud chicken, had broken through the noise of the squad room. The detectives looked around trying to find the source. I finally realized the sound came from my belt. My phone was clucking like a chicken.

"Lucy!" She always complained about the harsh ring I'd chosen for my cell phone. Earlier at Jonathan Grace's office, she'd feigned a dead battery, borrowing mine to make a call. She must have changed my ringtone. Guess it's only fair. Last month I downloaded the sound of hippos mating onto her cell.

I looked down at the caller ID. "One sec, Patrick. I need to take this." I pushed my chair away from the desk and headed toward the hallway.

Covering my mouth so only the caller could hear my words, I spoke through a clenched jaw. "You lying sack of shit. You told me you were separated from your wife, that you'd served her with divorce papers."

"Honey, don't be like that," Jeffrey said. "I planned on giving her the papers back in June, but then her mom died, and I couldn't bring myself to do it. I'm not a heartless bastard."

"Yes. Yes you are." I mentally kicked myself for caring enough to fight with him about it. "Dammit, Jeffrey, I don't play in another woman's sandbox. You should have been honest with me."

"Honesty. You want honesty? Don't play the martyr, Kate. You chose me for a reason. You like not having to be emotionally available. Sex, no problem, but to actually feel something, forget about it!"

"Bastard!" I yelled into the phone but silence was the only response as Jeffrey had already hung up.

Did his words sting because I would miss him or because the truth hurt? If I was honest with myself, I knew something was hokey when

Jeffrey came up with one excuse after another on why he couldn't spend the night. He's right. I liked the sex without being burdened with the commitment. That's probably why I pushed Carlos Diaz away before the relationship had a chance to grow roots. Opening myself up to a man, allowing for the possibility my heart could get trampled on, not gonna happen.

I ran my hands through my hair in frustration. They came away coated with an oily residue that I wiped on my pants. A long night of partying and an even longer night at a crime scene left my hair heavy with buildup. Afraid of what I'd see, I hadn't looked into a mirror for hours. Before my next interview, I would use the station's shower room and change into a fresh outfit hanging in my locker.

On the way back to my desk, I changed my phone's ringtone back. "We've got a lot of balls in the air," I told Patrick, emphasizing the point with a juggling motion. "Let's figure out our next steps."

"I can interview Lauren Tyler's girlfriend," he said. "See if her alibi for last night holds up."

"Can you also interview Curtis Cavanaugh? I think I should stay away from lawyers for a while. Might have some misdirected anger, especially if he pulls that attorney-client privilege crap."

Patrick started to say something but after honing in on my mood, stopped.

"Make sure you ask the shark what happened when the granola-eater interrupted his lunch with Jonathan Grace," I added.

"Hey, you may not be kind to your body, eating all the crap you do, but don't go lumping granola-eaters with environmental activists. I happen to like granola."

"Great. Next time I'll bring you some tree bark for lunch."

"Hardy, har, har. Now what do you plan on doing while I'm stuck trying to get a lawyer to give me a straight answer?"

"Eventually, I plan on checking out Jonathan Grace's business rivals, but first I need to track down the Graces' housekeeper."

"About the housekeeper, Wozniack said he called Ana Lopez when she hadn't shown up at the house this morning. Got the list of workers from her like you asked. He's planning on following up with them this afternoon. Wozniack also broke the news about Jonathan Grace and told her someone would be out to interview her this afternoon."

"Lopez is definitely my next stop. If you want to find out what's really going on in a household, ask the one invisible person who's privy to it all."

CHAPTER 9

As it turned out, Ana Lopez was not my next stop. Before leaving the squad room, I got a call from a friend at Tampa General who worked in admissions. I'd asked him to give me a heads up when Nina transferred out of the ER. No sense waiting around a hospital wasting precious time.

Yet, that's exactly what was happening. Patrick and I were waiting to talk to the attending physician who'd treated Nina. I told Patrick I could handle this on my own, but he said he wanted to hear what the doctor had to say. Maybe he didn't trust me to tell him if Nina could have been faking her symptoms.

After an interminable twenty-six minutes, a short and slightly overweight man ambled over to us. The picture on his name tag showed a face ten years younger. Maybe the daily tragedies of the emergency room had taken a physical toll on his appearance.

"I understand you treated a woman this morning," I said after introductions. "A Dr. Nina Grace? Can you give us an update on her status?"

The doctor blankly stared back at me. I choked off my mounting impatience, reminding myself Nina was only one of a hundred patients the doctor must have seen today. I forced a smile and provided him with a brief description of her. Finally the memory caught hold.

"Oh, right." The doctor rubbed the back of his neck. "When EMTs brought the woman into the ER, initially she was unresponsive. She'd gone into shock, which in essence is a circulatory collapse. Her blood pressure dipped too low to maintain an adequate supply of blood to her body's tissues. As a result, her skin was cold and sweaty. She had a weak yet rapid pulse. During the examination, I discovered no physical trauma to the patient's body. No cuts, not even a bruise. The officer explained she'd been found sitting at the foot of her husband who'd been tortured and murdered. Is that right?"

"Yes," I answered.

The doctor nodded. "Severe emotional trauma could definitely cause the shock she displayed."

"You said initially she was unresponsive?" Patrick asked.

"We assessed her vital signs when she arrived. Started an IV. As I stated earlier, we cleaned her up and checked for any visual signs of trauma. There were none. The blood covering her wasn't her own. We sent a urine sample to the lab for a tox screen. Her system was clean. No drugs or alcohol present. We also checked for an infection or an electrolyte imbalance. Wanted to make sure nothing else had caused her erratic behavior at the scene. All tests were normal. She remained unresponsive until the end of the CT scan."

"What happened," I asked.

"I wasn't there at the time, but the tech told me it was as if a switch had flipped. The patient started thrashing on the table. He worried about the possibility of a seizure, but when he went to check, her eyes were large. She looked scared and confused. You can imagine how disconcerting it would be to wake up in a strange location, unaware of how you got there. When I arrived at the CT room, I explained to the patient I would have to sedate her if she didn't calm down. You mentioned earlier she's a doctor?"

"Yes, a psychologist," Patrick said.

The man nodded again.

"What is it?" I asked.

"After threatening her with sedation, the patient's agitation suddenly diminished. It was amazing how quickly she pulled herself together. Maybe in her line of work, she's sedated patients before. Could be her training kicked in, allowing her to calm down quicker than normal."

"So you're implying in a situation such as this, most patients need medicated," Patrick said. "Could Dr. Grace have been faking the shock?"

The doctor rocked his head side to side seemingly pondering the possibility. "Her physical symptoms were all legitimate. You can't fake a weak and rapid pulse, but . . . could that have been induced after she stumbled upon the body of her dead husband? Could be. I have no way to know if she faked the severity of her symptoms. Psychology is not my area of expertise."

I heard Patrick mumble under his breath, "No, it's Dr. Grace's."

I ignored the comment, asking the doctor if we could talk to her. Before he could answer, I added, "Dr. Grace may be the only witness to her husband's murder. It's important we find out what she remembers as soon as possible."

"She's undergoing a psychiatric evaluation right now. Dr. Grace got lucky, a spot opened up last minute. Normally, it takes a couple days before a patient's seen."

"How long will she be in the hospital, Doc?"

"We've ruled out a physical cause for her shock. Depending on the outcome of the evaluation, one of two things will happen. If her emotional trauma is so severe she's deemed a threat to herself or others, the psychiatrist might Baker Act her for further evaluation. On the other hand, if all goes well, you should be able to speak to her soon."

"So if the shrink says Dr. Grace is incapable of making decisions for herself, she'll be committed to a psychiatric facility." I sighed. "That means we might not be able to get her side of the story for another seventy-two hours."

"At least." The doctor looked down at his watch. "Excuse me, will you? I have to get back to the ER."

Great. More waiting. I looked down at my own watch. Only 1:34 pm, but it felt more like 8 pm. The initial burst of energy that had kicked in after my shower back at the station was seriously waning.

∗∗∗

Patrick and I discovered Nina had been assigned a private room here at the hospital. I took it as a good sign. We were camped out in a row of hallway chairs with a clear view of her door. Her room was empty, so we settled in for what we thought would be a long wait. But I hadn't even cracked open the can of Coke I'd talked Patrick into buying me when Nina turned the corner escorted by a doctor.

As Nina shuffled along the hallway, her limp hair hung down around her face. She stumbled slightly, but the doctor took hold of her arm, correcting her balance. When Nina's door closed, I jumped up hurrying over to it, waiting for the doctor to leave. Patrick stood so closely behind me, I could feel the heat of his breath on my neck. When the doctor finally came out of the room, he was looking down at his phone and ran straight into me. I quickly shuffled backwards and ended up on Patrick's toes.

"Sorry about that," the doctor said.

Numerous Doogie Howser jokes ran through my mind, but then again, maybe I was just getting old and everyone seemed younger than they really were.

I made our apologies then introduced ourselves. Patrick asked if the doctor was the one who'd administered the psychiatric evaluation on Dr. Grace.

"Yes," Doogie answered, "but you know I can't go into the specifics of what she and I discussed."

"We understand. Can you at least give us the outcome?" Patrick said, pushing a little more. "Are you committing Dr. Grace?"

"No. Her evaluation is complete, and I've ruled she's not a danger to herself or others."

"Let me lay it out straight, Doc. Your patient was at home asleep when her husband was murdered," I said. "She is potentially the only eyewitness to the crime. But she's also a suspect. I need to know what to expect from her behavior when we interview her."

The shrink mulled it over. So long in fact, I thought he might be thinking of another excuse not to answer. I was surprised when he played it straight.

"Dr. Grace presented with prolonged shock. She experienced severe emotional trauma that will have lingering effects in the weeks to come. I've diagnosed her with Acute Distress Disorder. This is a psychological reaction to the trauma she endured. Her mind tried to cope by sealing off the event from conscious awareness."

"Dr. Grace told you she doesn't remember what happened to her husband?" Patrick asked.

"You know I can't answer that, Detective."

I shot Patrick a dirty look. I wanted the shrink to keep talking. Asking questions we knew he wouldn't answer would shut him up permanently. For Nina's sake, I asked the one question I needed to know above all else. "When we interview Dr. Grace, I don't want to mistake a symptom of this disorder for a false sign of guilt. How does Acute Distress Disorder manifest itself?"

"Symptoms include emotional detachment, temporary loss of memory, depersonalization, irritability, problems sleeping, inability to concentrate, easily startled, and physical restlessness."

"Do you—"

"I'm sorry, Detective, but I really can't discuss this any further. I have to go. Another patient is waiting."

"Is it okay if we go in and speak with Dr. Grace?" I asked.

"Sure, but don't expect much. She's exhausted. Not only from the events at home but everything that's happened here at the hospital."

"Super," Patrick said after the doctor had walked away. "It's going to be tough reading Dr. Grace's body language when we question her. If she's jumpy, we won't know if it's due to the trauma of witnessing her husband bound and bloodied, or the guilt from killing him."

I gave Patrick a dirty look and punched him in the shoulder.

When I cracked open Nina's door, I heard the sound of tormented sobbing. Nina's body shook so violently, the motion of the crisp white hospital sheets played their own sad song. Nina laid facing away from the door toward the closed window shades. My heart went out to her. I'd always known her to be strong and confident. She probably felt now, finally back in the privacy of her own room, she could let go. I wished we'd given her a few minutes before barging in.

Patrick cleared his throat, causing Nina to look over her shoulder. Tears still streamed down her face, but she used the sheet bunched around her chin to quickly dry them.

"Dr. Grace, it's me Detective Springer. I am so sorry about your husband. I know this is a difficult time, and I don't mean to intrude, but I really need to ask you a few questions."

Nina turned over to face us. Patrick introduced himself as I walked over to the corner of the room and picked up a chair, carrying it over to Nina's bedside. I had to stop myself from reaching out to grab her hand in a show of sympathy.

Remember your place, Springer. I was a detective investigating her husband's murder. If I showed any kind of bias, I'd get kicked off the case. The new team might make Nina their sole focus. Best to keep the interactions between the two of us formal.

"What do you need to know?" Nina spoke slowly and instead of looking at me, stared at the wall over my left shoulder.

I leaned forward, taking the lead. "Can you tell me what happened last night?"

"Last night?" Her eyes flickered toward me, then back at the wall.

"Yes. Do you know what happened to your husband?"

"Jonathan?"

"Yes. Your husband, Jonathan. We found you sitting at his feet. Do you know what happened to him?"

Tears started flowing from Nina's eyes, wetting her hands propped under her face in a praying gesture. "Someone hurt him," Nina answered in an empty voice.

"Did you see who hurt him?"

"There was a crash."

"What—"

"Downstairs . . . so much blood."

Nina's eyes grew large. A look of horror settled over her face. She looked as if she were back in her husband's den, reliving the moment she'd found him. Nina's breathing quickened into shallow breaths. She started to hyperventilate. I pushed the nurse's call button. A few seconds later, help arrived.

"You two. Out. Now." The nurse pushed the chair out of the way to get closer to Nina's bedside. The loud scrap of metal against the floor caused Nina to cry out. She looked like a frightened animal searching for an exit. The nurse called for help. As I hurried into the hallway, another woman pushed by Patrick to get into the room.

"Great. Now what?"

"Dammit, Patrick. Have a little compassion, would you? If Dr. Grace isn't the killer, you're going to feel like a real ass."

I turned toward the bank of elevators, but I couldn't escape Patrick's retort. "And if she is the killer, you're going to feel like the world's biggest fool."

CHAPTER 10

The aroma of Ana Lopez's house wrapped around me like a warm hug. After introductions, Nina's housekeeper ushered me down the hallway, wooden spoon still in hand.

"Sorry, Detective. I hope you don't mind us talking in the kitchen. When I'm upset I cook." The tiny woman didn't take up much physical space, topping out at just five feet, but she had a presence that filled the room.

"No problem." I took a seat at the small dinette near the window. The smell of spices and caramelized sugar enveloped me. Every flat surface held a plate or aluminum pan full of both savory and sweet dishes. A few I recognized—arroz con pollo, carne con papas, flan—others were new to me. I inhaled a deep, greedy whiff of the aromas, hoping I'd soon benefit from her day's distraction. "As I understand, a detective contacted you earlier about Jonathan Grace's murder?"

"Sí. God rest his soul." Ana made the sign of the cross. "When I'm done cooking, I'll take all this food over to the house. Put it in the freezer for Nina."

"I'm sorry Mrs. Lopez, but the Graces' house is still considered a crime scene. You're not allowed in."

"Qué? You mean I can't go in the house? How will I get it ready for when the Mrs. comes home from the hospital? If what the other detective said is true, she can't come home to . . . it's not right."

"I'm sorry, but it will be at least a week before the house is released. Can you tell me how long you've worked for the Graces?"

"Almost five years now. The Garcias, her family, are close friends of mine. I've known Nina since she was pequeñita. When my husband died, God rest his soul, I was lost. Mi bebé . . . Nina, had just married and was kind enough to give me this job, taking care of her home."

"Can you tell me your work schedule?"

"I'm at the house Monday through Thursday from 7 am to 6 pm. Makes for long days, but I like to have a three-day weekend to visit my grandbabies. Every once in a while, the Graces will have a weekend dinner party where I do all the cooking, but for the most part, my schedule fits theirs. Those two are always working, so when they're home on the weekend, it's nice they can be alone. They don't need some old woman lurking around."

Satisfied with the contents of her pots, Ana wiped her hands on the flowered apron tied around her waist. She walked over to the cupboard, climbed to the top of the step ladder, and grabbed a colorful dessert plate. After she spooned up food from the dishes cooling on her countertop, she sat down handing me the plate and a fork.

"This looks delicious, thank you." I scooped up a large piece of the rich custard but stopped the utensil in midair when I realized Ana had no food in front of her. "You're not eating?"

"No." She shook her head. "No appetite. But you go ahead. I love watching people enjoy my food. Buen provecho."

After a few bites, I forced myself to put the fork down. "Mrs. Lopez, can you tell me what time Dr. Grace got home on Thursday?"

"She usually gets there at evening time, around 6 pm, but yesterday she came home early. Nina called a little before three o'clock. Said I could take the rest of the day off. She had a migraine and wanted the house quiet. I asked if there was anything special I could do to help, but she only asked I be gone before she got home."

"Does Dr. Grace have a history of migraines?"

"Sí. Since high school. Though they were worse back then. She didn't have the wonderful medicine she has now."

I couldn't stand it anymore. I grabbed a piece of chicken and worked at pulling a piece of meat off the bone. "What about Mr. Grace? What was his schedule on Thursday?"

"He left at his usual time in the morning, 7 am. He was still gone when I left that afternoon."

"Did you set the home security alarm before you went out for the day?"

"Of course. I'm very good at my job."

"And the Graces?" I asked. "How diligent were they at remembering to set the alarm?"

"Not too good. Most of the time when I arrived, it wasn't armed."

"Then it was likely Dr. Grace didn't set the alarm when she arrived home yesterday."

Ana looked down at her lap and adjusted her apron. She glanced up at me, silent.

"Mrs. Lopez, you've been working for the Graces for quite some time. How would you describe their relationship?"

Ana nervously rubbed the cross hanging around her neck, avoiding my gaze. Factual questions obviously didn't bother her, but since I'd started posing personal ones, she'd lost her voice.

I stopped my fork in midair, placing it gently back on the plate. "I know you'd rather not answer any of my questions. You're probably afraid you'll get Nina into trouble by saying the wrong thing."

When Ana raised her head to meet my eyes, I knew that's exactly what she'd been thinking.

"I really need your help, Mrs. Lopez. I'm not going to bullshit you or bully you into answering any of my questions. You need to know that

I'm on Nina's side. Last fall, she counseled me after I shot a suspected killer. I had some serious things going on in my life, but Nina helped me like no one else ever has. And I owe her. For the moment, I'm still assigned to this case, but I don't know for how long. I really need to find out who killed Jonathan Grace because I know Nina isn't capable of murder. So please, help me out. Tell me what was going on in that house. The uncensored version. I have to hear all of it if I'm going to help her."

Ana held her cross tightly in her fist. After a few mumbled words of prayer, she opened her eyes. "They met through a mutual friend. Fireworks from day one. Neither was looking for love, too wrapped up in their own careers, but once they found it, they had the good sense to grab on tight. They were lucky those two. The honeymoon lasted for years longer than most. I think it was the business about the bebé that started the downslide."

"The baby?"

"That's why they have the big house, have me. Nina wanted to have little ones as soon as she got married. We used to joke, at thirty-five, she was no spring chicken. Turns out it was a cruel joke. She tried to conceive for a couple of years then moved on to inveo."

"You mean in vitro?"

"Sí, but it no work. Every time Nina got the bad news, she sank deeper and deeper into a depression."

Ana got quiet. I opened my mouth ready to ask another question when Ana interrupted. "But I'm so proud of Nina, she dug herself out of that hole. I think she finally accepted the idea she'd never give birth. Though by that time, the damage to her marriage had already been done. The two talked about adoption, but I don't think Nina wanted to bring a child into an unhappy home. It wouldn't be fair to the bebé."

"When did Mr. Grace move out of their bedroom?"

"Early last year? Sí. That winter seemed to be the peak of their arguments. One morning, I heard them fighting. Nina wanted Señor

Grace to go to couples counseling, you know to work on their marriage. I hear him say he got all the psychoanalysis he needed at home. He didn't need to pay a stranger to tell him what was wrong with the marriage."

"What *did* Mr. Grace say was wrong with their marriage?"

Ana looked down at her praying hands.

"Mrs. Lopez? Please."

"He said she a frigid bruja."

"Bitch?"

"Sí."

"Did Nina confide in you about the problems in her marriage?"

"She used to. She missed her mama terribly. Nina worked so much she didn't get to visit her often and Maria's not able to travel anymore. I guess I was the next best thing. Lately though, Nina made lots of excuses. She says everything was fine. I think her troubled marriage embarrassed her."

"Did Nina seem different these past few weeks? Maybe distracted or angrier than usual?"

"Not that I noticed. Though she was rarely home, probably wanted to avoid her husband. But it's not like he was at home either."

I needed to know if Ana knew about Jonathan's extramarital activities. Though considering her obvious Catholic sensibilities, it would be a sensitive subject. I picked up my fork, rearranging the food on my plate. "When you were cleaning the Graces' house, did you ever find anything suggesting Mr. Grace was unfaithful?"

Ana brushed at some crumbs littering the table, sweeping them into her cupped hand. She stood and walked over to the trashcan to throw them away. Eventually she made her way back to the table and sat.

"Mrs. Lopez?"

"I don't talk ill of the dead," she said, avoiding my eyes.

"I understand, but Nina needs our help. If her husband was involved with another woman, I need to know about it."

Ana looked up at me. Unshed tears brimmed in her eyes. They

expressed a quiet strength.

"I found a bag in Señor Grace's closet. It had these . . ."

When she didn't continue, I helped her out. "Sex toys?"

"Sí. I wasn't being nosey, only cleaning. Mr. Grace often leaves his exercise clothes in a bag, and if I don't wash them . . . well . . . it wasn't his gym bag I found." Ana adjusted the apron tie around her neck. "I thought it might be something new the Graces were trying. Experimenting to, you know, rekindle the fire. I never mention it to Nina. I didn't want to embarrass her or have her think I was snooping. But then . . ."

"Yes?"

"What I said before, last winter was the worst of the fighting. I try to make excuses to stay late, you know, to keep an eye on Nina. I was worried about mi bebé. When she couldn't get her husband to agree to counseling, things got quiet in the house. I think they had nothing left to say. They lived separate lives, slept in different bedrooms. That is, when Señor Grace bothered to sleep at home. Nina seemed so sad, but he acted like a young man again."

"Do you think Mr. Grace was having an affair?"

Ana's cheeks flashed a rose-colored glow, and it wasn't from the heat of the kitchen. "Sí. I know so. Like I said, I don't like snooping, but if something was going on behind Nina's back, she had a right to know about it."

"How did you find out?"

"One Friday morning, I came back to the house. I forgot gifts I bought on my lunch break the day before. I planned on giving them to my grandbabies later that day when they arrived for a weekend visit. Señor Grace's car was in the driveway instead of in the garage, like he came back because he also forgot something. After I finished collecting my packages, I stood at the front door ready to leave. A woman wrapped in a sheet ran across the upstairs landing. She was laughing. A beautiful woman, very young. I heard Señor Grace's voice, and I ducked into the den so I wouldn't be seen. I waited until it was quiet, then left."

"When was this?"

"I remember it was a Friday, April Fools' Day. My oldest grandson loves to pull pranks. It's one of his favorite holidays."

I asked Ana to describe the mystery lady. It sounded like it could have been Jonathan's assistant, Lauren Tyler. The timeframe fit.

I moved my empty plate aside. "Did you tell Nina what you saw?" Ana's lower lip quivered, sadness shrouded her eyes. "Sí. I cried for weeks thinking about it, but I finally decided I had to say something. I knew Nina was miserable in the marriage. I thought telling her would be the final push she needed to gain the strength to ask for a divorce."

Or the final push in making the decision to have her husband killed. Unknowingly, Ana had offered up one of the oldest motives in the book. Revenge.

CHAPTER 11

After I left Ana Lopez's house, I headed back to the station. It neared 4 pm and the deserted squad room gave me a quiet space to think.

I knew I had to watch myself with this case. If I wasn't careful, it would drive a wedge between me and Patrick. Normally, we got along like a pair of shoes, the right side balancing out the left. But this case seemed to bring out my stubborn side, even more than usual, because of my prior relationship with Nina.

I knew the stats as well as anyone. Three out of every four murders were committed by someone close to the victim. Sure, the evidence could read like Nina was the killer, but the words spelling out her guilt could easily be rearranged declaring her innocence. I was sworn to uphold the law, and I would, but until I unearthed the evidence to put the final nail in Nina's coffin, it wouldn't hurt to hold the hammer, so no one else could prematurely pound it in.

Patrick's mood seemed out of whack, too. His usual easygoing attitude flew out the window with the news of his wife's pregnancy. Combine our two unstable mindsets and a volcanic eruption loomed on the horizon.

Even though I had defended Nina vehemently today, doubt had

still wormed its way into my mind. There was no way she committed the murder herself, but hiring someone to kill Jonathan was a whole different story. Had rage caused by her husband's affair pushed her over the edge? Tomorrow, I'd check Nina's financials and see if she had the means to hire a professional. Just because she had a mansion, didn't mean she was solvent. In this economy, plenty of people were in debt up to their eyeballs. The Graces might have owned a houseful of luxury items but still paid the bank for the pleasure of their use.

Hiring a hit man was simpler, in that Nina could form a certain detachment to the crime. She wouldn't get her hands dirty, thus making it easier on her psyche. Did the hired killer go too far with the torture? Maybe he was only supposed to rough Jonathan up and instead got over zealous. Guilt upon seeing her husband bound to a chair could have sent Nina into a near comatose state. Her physical symptoms could have been real even if she'd been the one to set the ball into motion.

The theories were piling up, but I was still banking on Nina's innocence. Jonathan Grace was rich, influential in the community. Powerful men didn't become powerful without pissing off a few people along the way. Tomorrow I'd rip his life apart, hoping to find a psychopath or two in his closet.

I opened my email inbox to make sure nothing had popped up in any of my other open cases. Nothing a little juggling couldn't take care of. I was about to close out the program when a new email from the Communications Supervisor appeared. He'd sent a message, informing me that a copy of Nina Grace's 911 call had been delivered to my desk. I looked through the piles of paper but didn't see any interoffice envelopes. Then I glanced over at Patrick's desk and saw a beige envelope sitting on top of his inbox.

Little things like this annoyed the shit out of me. Instead of giving me the mail, which I had clearly requested, someone had dropped it off at my partner's desk. Inconsequential, maybe. A simple oversight, I doubt it. More like another chance to throw it in my face that I worked in a male-dominated workforce.

I tried unwinding the stubborn string holding the envelope closed. *Screw it. Faster to tear the damn thing open.* I pulled out the CD and popped it into my computer. I opened the lone audio file and clicked play.

"911, what's your emergency?"

"My husband ..."

"Excuse me ma'am, can you speak up?"

"There's so much blood."

"Ma'am, has something happened to your husband?"

"I can't wake him up. Why won't he wake up?"

"What's your address?"

" ... "

"Ma'am, can you tell me where you're calling from?"

"Davis Islands. 674 Riviera. Please send someone. He needs help."

"We have officers on the way. Ma'am, can you tell me what happened to your husband?"

" ... "

"Ma'am, are you there?"

" ... "

"Can you hear—"

Throughout the conversation, a soothing female voice tried to calm a sobbing Nina Grace. As the recording went on, Nina became more hysterical. Yet when she gave her address, she sounded almost robotic. Must have been right before she went into shock. After a few promptings by the operator to persuade Nina to speak, the phone went dead.

Nina had called 911 from her cell phone at 1:14 am, only three minutes after I'd talked to her. When we spoke, she'd sounded frightened but coherent. She told me she thought she'd killed her husband. No matter which way I looked at the case, that one statement was the most damning. But it begged the question, how did Nina not know if she killed her husband? The way Jonathan died was no accident. I grasped onto the hope that Nina's thinking was a little off at the time.

I tried fixing the envelope, wanting to repair some of the damage I'd unleashed, but it was no use. I deposited the CD inside and put it on Patrick's desk so he could listen to it tomorrow. A loud yawn escaped as I stretched my arms over my head. Fifteen hours straight. Man I was getting old. I remember a time when I could breeze through a round-the-clock shift. Thirty-nine was kicking my ass.

I stood up then remembered I had one more task before calling it a day. Still had to dig into Lucy's new love interest, Chuck the vet. I slumped back down into the chair, hoping I wouldn't uncover any damning information on the guy. Lucy was too trusting, almost childlike in her ability to open her heart up. I envied that quality. I wish I could open up, freely give myself over to another. For a brief moment, I thought I would be able to close my eyes and dive in head first with Carlos Diaz. But fear had gripped me.

At night when I'd been snuggled into his arms, listening to the soft sounds of his sleep, I should have embraced the moment. Enjoyed the euphoric feelings. Instead I stayed awake, fighting the rush of emotion swirling around inside me. Emotions were new to me, feeling them felt dangerous. I knew if I let Carlos hold onto my heart, as brittle as it was, one mishap could irrevocably cause it to shatter.

I shook my head, forcing my mind to focus on Lucy and her new beau. Charles Kent owned his own veterinarian clinic. I hadn't met him yet, but Lucy had shown me an exhausting parade of pictures of the two of them together. He was tall, thin, and had a sharp patrician nose. He looked like one of the birds he regularly treated in his office.

Bingo! In 2001, Chuck was arrested on suspicion of domestic abuse. The police charged him with battery, but the charges were later dropped. *Liked to hit his women, huh?* That sure as hell wouldn't happen to my best friend.

You never really know what lurks in the depths of a man's soul. To think I started getting all sappy thinking about Carlos Diaz. For what? So I could get myself into a situation where some man could take advantage of me. Again. Just one more reason not to open up my heart.

How do I tell Lucy about Chuck's past?

Last year, I made the mistake of admitting I'd run a background check on her boyfriend. He had a misdemeanor theft charge on his record back from when he was a teenager. Lucy was pissed I'd gone behind her back. She saw it as a loyalty issue. Me too, but for different reasons. It had almost destroyed our relationship.

Maybe this time I'd play it differently, confront Chuck with what I found. After I was done with him, he'd break off the relationship for me. Lucy would never have to know about my role in it. Problem solved.

CHAPTER 12

I pulled my car out of the parking garage, merging into the left lane when a woman driving with her head down decided she wanted the same spot on the road. I slammed on the breaks to avoid hitting her, shooting a quick look into my rearview mirror. I expected to get nailed from behind, but the street was clear. Apparently, she opted to focus on her cell phone instead of watching the road. Her car's bumper sticker read, HONK IF YOU LOVE JESUS. TEXT IF YOU WANT TO MEET HIM. *Hypocrite.*

Though enforcing moving violations wasn't my job, it didn't stop me from wishing I could pull alongside her car, honk my horn, and scare the shit out of her. The only thing stopping me was the vision of her accidently hitting the gas and hurting an innocent bystander. Hell, at this point I just wanted to get home. Didn't even want to take the time to pick up dinner. My bed beckoned to me like a siren enticing a sailor with her enchanting love song. Hopefully, I'd avoid the shipwreck and make it home in one piece.

Speaking of hypocrites, I inwardly cringed as I pulled out my cell phone. But it wasn't like I was texting; my call was official police business. I dialed Patrick to update him on my meeting with Ana

Lopez. I kept the most damning piece of information until last—the housekeeper catching Jonathan Grace cheating on Nina.

"Makes a pretty strong motive for murder," he said. "Wonder if they had a prenup?"

"I also wonder about the life insurance policy."

"What's this? Have you had a change of heart? Do you think Dr. Grace knocked off her husband?"

"Not at all. I simply realize the importance of staying on this case. That means an unbiased investigation. I don't want whispers getting back to Sergeant Kray. From now on I'll consider all theories, no matter how asinine."

"Great. I think."

I adjusted my rear view mirror. "Were you able to get some face time with Jonathan's lawyer?"

"Yes, but let's talk about Lauren Tyler's alibi first. It's a much quicker discussion. When I interviewed Analise Lofton, she confirmed staying over at Lauren's last night from 7 pm to 6 am."

"Analise wouldn't be the first girlfriend to lie for her lover."

"No," Patrick agreed, "but I confirmed a restaurant delivered takeout to Tyler's place a little before 8 pm. We can't mark Lauren off our suspect list yet, but at least we know she started the evening with her girlfriend."

"That's a good start. So what was Analise like?"

Patrick groaned. "I felt like I was sitting in an Astrology 101 class. She's into the whole astrological sign nonsense. She kept asking if she could do a chart for me, whatever that means."

"Sounds like Analise is the complete opposite of Lauren."

"I'm glad I interviewed Analise in person though. She's one of those nervous talkers. I don't think she would have opened up like she did, if she hadn't felt so uneasy sitting across from me."

I laughed. "She must have been intimidated by your fierce presence."

"Ha. Ha."

Though Patrick was thirty-six, with his boy-next-door good looks, he barely looked thirty. The blond hair, blue eyes, and dimples usually had an effect on women, but intimidation wasn't one of the effects.

"What did Analise say?"

"She knew everything about Lauren's past relationship with Jonathan Grace, and her misery at being stuck in her dead-end job."

"She talked about that?"

"What can I say, I have a way with women. But you have to understand, everything she said was in the context of how it related to Jonathan's astrological sign. I heard all about how Lauren shouldn't have gotten involved with Jonathan because he was an Aries, a sign represented by the ram. I guess the ram symbolizes male fertility and aggression. Analise told me how his sign indicated he was a very sexual being, obsessed with living out his fantasies, a thrill seeker who craved adventure. She also explained Jonathan lacked communication skills, that he had a sharp tongue. So sure, I got plenty of information from her, but I don't know how useful it all was."

I could hear pages rustling in the background.

"Crap!"

"What?" I asked.

A few seconds of silence, then Patrick started talking again. "Nothing. I dropped my notebook."

"Don't get into an accident by trying to read, drive, and talk at the same time."

"Don't worry. I'm pulling into my driveway now. Let me tell you about Jonathan Grace's lawyer. I did a little digging into his background before I met with him. Wanted to know what to expect, have a game plan on handling him. Curtis Cavanaugh is not well liked in the State Attorney's office."

"Why?"

"Seems he represents the likes of the Ivanov family," Patrick said.

"Were those the Russians indicted a few months back for running a sex trafficking ring in Tampa?"

"The one and the same."

"What does a commercial real estate developer need with a lawyer that represents hard-core crooks?" I mused.

"Only one answer for that. When I met with Cavanaugh at his office, I don't think he expected to talk about Jonathan Grace. In fact, it worked to my advantage. Cavanaugh hadn't heard about the murder yet. Shock must have loosened his lips. For a lawyer anyway."

"Meaning he didn't throw that privileged crap in your face and ask you to leave."

"Exactly."

"What is all the screaming in the background, Patrick?"

"My girls. Just got inside the house. Let me pass out kisses then I'll head back to the den."

With a baby on the way, Patrick's office would probably be converted into a nursery. And knowing Alina, she already had a new paint color picked out.

It sounded like Patrick was arguing with one of his daughters. I heard a huff of resignation then, "Auntie Kate?"

Patrick's youngest daughter had obviously worn daddy down enough to talk him into handing over the phone.

"Raina, how are you?"

"Jacob pushed me down at school today."

"That's horrible. Do you want me to put him in jail for you?"

Raina squealed then broke out in a fit of giggles.

"Can I talk to your daddy now?"

"Auntie Kate, did you know in Florida it's illegal for me to sing in public in my swimsuit?"

"Well next time you're at the pool, try humming."

"It's also illegal to fart in a public place after 6 pm."

I laughed. The phone filled with the noise of Patrick wrestling the phone away from his giggling five-year-old.

"Sorry," Patrick said. The sound of a door closed in the background. "Jessup family bedtime stories," he said.

"Sleepovers at your house must be fun."

"By the way, if you talk to the girls don't bring up the new baby. Alina and I have decided to keep this under wraps for now. Until we can figure everything out."

"No problem. So . . . Curtis Cavanaugh? Jackson's Bistro?"

"Right. Cavanaugh and Grace met for lunch to discuss the investigation into the wetlands violations case. The lawyer said Grace was innocent, that the charges were baseless."

"Of course."

"The two of them were wrapping up when a guy shows up at their table spouting off environmental rhetoric. Grace told Cavanaugh he'd already had a few run-ins with this Owen Mitchell guy. He's head of an Orlando-based wildlife conservation group called Defenders of the Earth."

"Sounds more like a comic book series than an environmental group," I said.

"Looking at the verbiage on their website, they definitely see themselves as superheroes, defending not only poor defenseless animals but their natural habitats as well."

"Great. Does that mean we have to haul our asses all the way over to Orlando to interview this guy?"

"They say it's home to the happiest place on earth."

"Not in the mood, Patrick. My head's splitting. Let's table this until tomorrow. Is there anything else?"

"I called Jamar Washington. He confirmed he met with Jonathan Grace the day of the murder. They checked out potential condominium sites then went to dinner together. Grace headed back to Tampa around 8 pm. Everything checks out with his alibi. His wife and another couple met Washington at the restaurant's bar after the meeting and stayed until midnight."

"We'll get it up on the board tomorrow, but Jonathan Grace's murder timeline goes like this. He arrived at his office by 9 am Thursday where he had an overseas phone conference. He worked until 12:30 pm when he had lunch with his lawyer."

"Right. After the environmental protester breaks up the meal, Grace heads for Orlando. He's there until 8 pm, probably arrives back in Tampa around 9:30 pm. By half past one Friday morning, he's dead."

"We still don't know if Grace came right home," I said.

"We should have the paperwork from his credit card companies tomorrow. If he made a pit stop before home, hopefully a purchase will help us track his whereabouts."

"If that's everything, Patrick, I'm going to sign off. I'm pulling onto my street now."

"Sure. We'll get back at it, first thing tomorrow."

Thankfully the traffic had moved at a fast pace tonight. The schools were out for summer vacation, lessening the road congestion at rush hour. It seemed every kid in Tampa went to a specialized school and every parent drove them there. I could understand specializing in high school, but elementary school? Patrick's eight-year-old loved animals so much she studied them at a Montessori school. How could someone that young know what she wanted to do with the rest of her life? No wonder Patrick was stressed over the idea of a fourth child. I threw out a silent thanks that I didn't have kids. I couldn't deal with some needy person waiting for me at home.

CHAPTER 13

I wore my headache like a swim cap. Only two hours of sleep in the last thirty-six could do that. I forced myself to put on a pair of pajamas even though exhaustion weighed me down. The doorbell rang as I finished pulling up my pants.

"You've got to be kidding me!" Maybe they'll go away if I don't answer.

The bell rang again. Nope, faster to just shoot them.

I swung the front door open wide, practically growling. "What do you want?"

Carlos Diaz stood on my front step, Chinese cartons in hand, a lopsided grin on his face. Good thing I'd opted for the mint green pj's instead of the ones with the big yellow ducks on them.

"Thought you might be hungry." Carlos hastily set the take-out boxes down on the stoop and scooped up the cat before she escaped outside. He carried her past me into the house, laying her down on the window seat.

Come on in.

I sighed, trying to add as much indignation as one sound could hold. I grabbed the cartons of food and brought them to the table. My stomach growled at the smell. "Don't worry, the cat wouldn't have gone far. She hasn't eaten dinner yet."

"Have you?"

"No," I mumbled. My brain yelled at my stomach for being a traitor, but my heart melted at the compassion in Carlos's eyes. I tried to ignore them all.

"Wonderful." Carlos moved around my kitchen like he cooked there every day.

"How did you even know I was home?" I asked.

We both danced around the two-ton elephant in the room.

"I have spies everywhere."

Maybe that was his new tactic. Pretend I hadn't thrown him out of my house the last time we were together. Pretend I didn't tell him we were through. Impressive though. Seven months later, Carlos was still interested enough to track my whereabouts. The detective in me had to give him props. The girl in me thought it was romantic. The bitch in me was incensed.

"Are you stalking me now? What gives you the right—"

"Hold up. Truce. Will you please sit down, give me a minute?"

When I didn't move, Carlos held out a plate full of lo mein like an offering to the gods.

"Fine."

Carlos put the plate on the table and walked behind my chair. He pulled it out and didn't speak again until he took a seat across from me. "I thought about what you said last time we were together . . . after the initial sting wore off. You were right, we were moving too fast. We should have waited. The more I thought about it, the more I realized you were too vulnerable after the kidnapping. I took advantage of your lowered defenses."

"But—"

"But we were good together, Kate. There's no denying the passion between us. And more than the heat, we connected. You understood me in a way no one else ever has."

That's what scared me. What sent me running. Sure the sex was great, but that was the easy part. Carlos had such a tender way about him. The lightest touch of a finger stroking my cheek caused my heart to soar. Only a few short weeks and he had scaled my walls. What would happen if I let the relationship continue and it ended? Which I fully expected given my abrasive nature and enormous baggage. So I organized a preemptive strike. I left him before he could leave me. No matter what Carlos said tonight, I couldn't waiver.

"Holy hell, woman. I told you I that loved you." He pushed his chair away from the table and faced the far wall. Silent. I could read the tension in his shoulders. After a few moments, he exhaled and ran his fingers through his hair. He walked over to me and placed a gentle hand on my shoulder. "I still do."

"You wanted to hear me say those three little words back to you. I tried, Carlos, but you know I can't."

"I know, and I understand why. That monster forced you to say you loved him. Just a small child made to repeat those words over and over. They mean nothing to you now. They're an empty sentiment."

"Not only empty. Painful."

"I don't need to hear you say 'I love you.' I only ask that you don't run away when you feel the emotion."

My resolve crumbled. I brushed my check against his hand.

"Please. Sit." I handed Carlos a fortune cookie even though neither of us had touched our food.

He opened the wrapper and snapped the cookie in half. He took out the white rectangular piece of paper and read, "Someone you love will soon be returning to your life."

"It does not say that."

He smiled, folded up the paper, and shoved it in his pocket.

"How's work going? I see your byline in the Tribune all the time."

"Oh, now we're going to talk about work? Safer ground, right?"

I spun the noodles around my fork and shoved them in my mouth. Playing dumb, I blamed the silence on my mouthful of food.

Carlos nodded, smiling. "Fine. We can play this game. But you know as well as I do, the only thing people want to read about is the Casey Anthony acquittal. Even though the jury handed down a not guilty verdict on the murder charge of her daughter three days ago, the media spotlight hasn't dimmed a bit."

"Don't get me started on that woman. Four years with time served for providing false information? Whatever."

"I hear you're on the Davis Islands case," Carlos said. "How's that going?"

I dropped my fork. The clinking sound as it hit my plate was the only noise in the room. "What? Is that the real reason you're here tonight?" My heart screamed, pleading for my mouth to stop. "Angling for some quote to add to tomorrow's newspaper article?"

"Wait a minute, Kate."

"Don't you dare!" I stood up so fast, my chair tipped over. "I must have been out of my mind thinking you were still interested after all these months. The only thing you're interested in is reestablishing your link to the Tampa PD."

"For the record, you brought up work, not me."

I marched over to the front door and opened it. Carlos let out a soft sigh, walking toward me. Once he reached my line of sight, he stopped, forcing me to meet his gaze. "Kate, I know you still care for me. So much so, it scares the living shit out of you. Don't misinterpret a simple question for malicious intent. I know you're looking for an easy out, but don't accuse me of saying I love you just to get the inside scoop. That's not fair."

I opened my mouth to throw out a biting retort, something about not being able to trust a man. He stopped me before the breath could even pass my lips, laying a gentle finger over my mouth. "One day I will break through that hard exterior. I will love your pain away. And when you tell me you love me, you'll mean it."

SATURDAY

CHAPTER 14

This morning when I woke up, I realized I'd forgotten to pack up the Chinese food. The cat had finished off both meals. The good news, I didn't have to think up an excuse to confront Chuck the vet.

"If you could tell Dr. Kent that Lucy James's best friend is here to see him. It's an emergency. My cat ate the boat-load of food I accidentally left on the table last night . . . it's coming out both ends."

The receptionist at the vet's office wrinkled her nose and asked me to take a seat. Frank hissed from behind the wire door of her carrier when a Labrador came to say hello. I rubbed the dog's head and came away with a handful of black hair.

Eleven minutes later, Charles Kent walked toward me with his hand extended. "Ms. Springer, nice to finally meet you."

"*Detective* Springer," I corrected, tightening my grip. Chuck the vet was older than Lucy, pushing a little past forty. Handsome if you like that old money look.

"Right, right. Sorry about that. I feel badly we haven't had a chance to get together before now. I've been meaning to set up a time when we could all go out for dinner, but work's been crazy. I'm sure you know how it is."

"I don't have an appointment. Can you fit me in?"

"Not a problem. Any friend of Lucy's."

We walked back to an exam room. I took my cat out of her pet carrier, setting her on the table.

"Now what seems to be the problem with . . .?"

"Frank. She finished off the Chinese food I left out last night. Must have been some spice not agreeing with her."

"Right." Chuck laughed. "Lucy told me the story. You found the cat at a crime scene where her owner had been murdered. When Lucy asked what a good name would be, you said—"

"Frankly, I couldn't care less."

"Right. Funny stuff." Chuck ran his hand underneath the cat's belly and stopped when she made a purr of discomfort. "Did you know the ridged pattern on a cat's nose pad is as unique as human fingerprint?"

He and Lucy were two peas in a pod. The realization strummed my guilt strings making the tiniest of vibrations.

When I remained silent, he looked up at me expectantly. "Thought you might enjoy that one. You know, being a detective and all."

"Yeah, about that. Did a little checking on you Kent. Found out you were brought up on a domestic abuse charge in 2001."

Chuck's head shot up. "What?" Kent let go of the cat, and she jumped off the exam table.

"I think my best friend has the right to know who she's dating, don't you?"

"Yes, but you have it all wrong."

"You don't enjoy hitting women?"

"No, and if you'd give me a minute, I'd be happy to explain."

"I'd love to hear this."

Chuck exhaled, seemed to get his thoughts in order. "My wife and I were married for five years. It was a very . . . difficult marriage. Doctors diagnosed her with bipolar disorder. She was a very talented artist. At her highest highs, she'd paint the most beautiful portraits, but her lows barely left her with enough energy to crawl out of bed in the morning. I tried to get her to take her meds, but she hated them, said they stifled her creativity."

Chuck anxiously adjusted the stethoscope around his neck. "One night she became paranoid. There was a lot of screaming and furniture breaking. The neighbors must have called the cops. But before they arrived, my wife charged at me with a knife. In the process of trying to wrench it away, I must have used to much force pulling her arm back. In the struggle, it broke. The police showed up, found a knife in my hand, my wife writhing in pain, and understandably jumped to conclusions."

"Nice story, Kent."

"It's the truth."

"Really? Let me tell you how Lucy's going to see it. Husband can't take his wife's depression one more minute, snaps. They fight, her arm gets broken, the police break down the door right as her husband's about to stab his wife. Wife drops charges because . . . because that's what battered wives do. How many bloody crime scenes do you think Lucy's been to where the police haven't gotten there in time?"

"Why are you so hell bent on breaking us up?"

"Lucy deserves someone better. And you've got it all wrong, Doc. I'm not going to break you two up. You are."

"Excuse me?"

I picked up Frank and placed her back inside the pet carrier. A hiss expressed her displeasure at the rough handling. "You heard me. You're going to call Lucy and tell her you don't want to see her anymore. Make up some excuse. A good one. Now, before she falls too hard. You're not to see her again, do you hear me? If you do, I will make your life a living hell. Investigations into your business, detectives interviewing you in front of your friends and clients. By the time I get done with you, everyone will think you're a drugged out, thieving, animal sex freak."

Chuck stood silently. I expected an explosion, cursing, anything but the sad look on his face. He only nodded.

Am I wrong? Could Chuck be a great guy simply dealt a crappy hand? No. I couldn't think like that. If he were innocent, he wouldn't have given up so easily. He would have fought for his relationship with Lucy. I'm doing her a favor. I'm Lucy's best friend and that's what best friends do, they watch out for each other. I only have her best interest at heart.

I ignored the inner voice fighting to be heard. *When best friends fall in love, they leave.*

***

A text came in telling me Jonathan Grace's autopsy had started while I was in Kent's office. Arriving late was unavoidable. I still had to drop my cat off at her regular vet's office. They'd fix Frank up and board her until I could pick her up later tonight.

When I pushed open the morgue doors, it felt like I ran into a brick wall. The overpowering smell of bleach forcefully smacked me in the face. Though the scent of blood and feces hung thick in the air, the concentrated bleach mixture used to spray off the bodies after the external exam made my eyes water.

The medical examiner stood over a naked cadaver. I outfitted myself in the paper garb and plastic gloves, moving closer to the exam table. Harry Ellis's right hand had disappeared into Jonathan Grace's chest cavity.

"What took you so long? You missed all the good parts," Ellis said.

"Obviously not all the parts," I answered, nodding at the heart cradled in his hand. "My experiment of combining a cat with a large amount of Chinese food went horribly wrong."

Ellis stopped and stared at me.

I shook my head. "That came out wrong. What I meant to say was my cat ate all of last night's leftovers. She had it coming out both ends. Had to drop her off at the vet."

Ellis wrinkled his nose, a disgusted look on his face. How he could be grossed out by a cat's bodily functions yet unfazed by being wrist deep in human flesh was beyond me.

"You know it's Saturday, right?" I said. "What are you doing at work?"

"Filling in for Don. Right about now he's sitting on a beach in Puerto Vallarta with a margarita in his hand."

"In July. He's nuts."

"Cheaper this time of year. Anyway, one more week and it's my turn. Been saving up. This year's the big one, twenty-five years. I surprised my wife with tickets to the Galapagos Islands." Ellis removed Grace's stomach and weighed it. "She's crazy about wildlife. It was either that or a safari, and sleeping outside with hungry lions isn't my idea of a vacation."

Ellis's assistant photographed the stomach. Then Ellis cut a portion of the tissue for a sample. "I finished the external examination before you arrived. I'm almost done with the internal organs." Ellis cut into the stomach, opening it up, exploring its contents. "There's still some partially undigested rice, salmon, and what could be . . . avocado. Looks like your victim ate sushi before he died. It's mostly digested, would say he'd ingested it no more than an hour and a half before he died."

"What *is* time of death?"

"Patience, Detective. Grace's watch was pulverized at 11:42 pm." Ellis jerked his head toward the counter where the evidence bags containing Grace's possessions sat.

I walked over and picked up the plastic bag holding Jonathan's watch. Many of the links were crushed. Only a few shards of crystal still clung to the round face of the gold Rolex.

"The watch was hit with such force," Ellis said, "I had to extricate pieces of metal from the victim's left wrist. The markings on the duct tape binding his wrist indicated the killer used a hammer. A considerable amount of blood pooled at the wound site under the watch, telling me Grace was still alive when it was broken. So I can give you a pretty tight window on time of death. Because of the broken watch and stage of stomach digestion, Grace died between 11:42 pm and midnight Thursday evening."

"Interesting."

"What is?"

"The victim's wife didn't call 911 until 1:14 am. Looks like there could have been upwards of an hour and a half from the time Jonathan Grace died before his wife called for help. We found her at his feet nearly catatonic. I wonder if shock caused her slow response time." Patrick's voice echoed in my head telling me Nina may have used that time to dispose of the tools used to torture her husband.

"I'll leave that question for you to answer. The one thing I do know is your victim sustained serious head trauma." Ellis elaborated in detailed medical jargon the countless injuries Grace had endured. The highlights included multiple lacerated contusions, bruising to the brain, four teeth knocked out, neck sliced open, and left ear cut off. "When you get a copy of the photographs, you'll see the victim sustained blunt force trauma to the chest. The outline of the bruising suggests a beating from a lead pipe. Internally, five ribs were broken and the spleen and liver were lacerated. The killer unleashed some serious rage, drilling a hole into the victim's right knee using a three-inch bit. He also made hamburger meat of the genital area."

I shook my head. "What about hairs or fibers?"

"Just a minute. The body also showed signs of a previous beating, evidence of multiple rib fractures."

"Can you tell how long ago they were inflicted?"

"Not definitively but since there's no evidence of old bruising, I'd say it's been more than a couple of weeks. About your question on hair and fibers, multiples of both were found dried in the blood caking the body. Everything will be sent over to FDLE." The Florida Department of Law Enforcement analyzed all of our trace evidence.

Ellis turned his attention back to the body, working silently unless giving instructions to his assistant.

After the autopsy, he washed his hands announcing, "The official cause of death is asphyxiation."

"Excuse me, Doc?" I stuck a finger in my ear, hoping to clear out the cobwebs. "You sure he didn't bleed out from the big gaping slit across his neck?"

"The killer didn't slice deep enough to puncture the jugular or the carotid. Instead, he severed the trachea and nicked the inferior thyroid artery which bled down the victim's wind pipe into his lungs. The man choked to death on his own blood. See here?" Ellis pointed down at Jonathan Grace's neck. "The killer held a straight edge knife to the victim's throat. A struggle caused these grazing cuts. The killer pressed tighter, and I'd say accidentally pressed into the trachea."

"Accidentally my ass. This is a homicide."

"Well, you're right on that point. I'm simply saying I don't think the perpetrator meant to kill the man at the moment it actually happened."

"It fits with the scene," I said. "The killer binds Jonathan Grace, tortures him. No tape on the mouth because he wants information from him. The perp's done a number on the guy, beating the shit out of Grace, but he's still not talking. The killer holds a knife to Grace's neck trying to scare him into divulging his secrets, puts a little too much pressure on the knife. Game over."

Ellis grabbed a form off the counter and clicked his pen. "I wonder if the killer got the information he wanted before his victim expired?"

CHAPTER 15

Patrick looked up from his computer screen. "Where have you been?"

"Where do you think? It was my turn for morgue duty." I sunk into my chair and gave him a play by play of the autopsy, finishing with, "Eight fibers and four hairs were found on the body. The fingernails were clean, but it's not surprising considering Jonathan's hands were bound. The clothes, saliva sample, it's all been sent over to FDLE to check for trace evidence. Ellis said he'd send over his final report with a copy of the photographs later today."

I pulled out my desk drawer, rummaging through the junk until my fingers closed around a smooth wrapper tucked in the back. I pulled out a partly crushed protein bar, opened it, and popped a piece into my mouth. "How's your day going, dear?"

"Great. Thanks for asking, hon. You'll be happy to know Wozniack and Jung recanvased the Graces' neighborhood. They followed up at all the houses empty the first time around. The guys were batting zero until they interviewed a family living two doors down. Jung asked the parents questions, but they were clueless. Luckily, their teenage daughter remembered something. This past Tuesday, when the kid headed out to her summer job, she noticed a white SUV parked in front of their house. It stuck in her mind because the guy's vehicle faced the wrong way."

"A man sat behind the wheel?"

Patrick nodded. "The girl described a white guy with a baseball cap and sunglasses. He caught her staring at him and hightailed it out of there."

"Did she get the tags or remember what kind of SUV the guy drove?"

"According to Jung, she's like 'so not into cars'," Patrick exaggerated.

"Figures." I finished my last bite and threw the wrapper into the trash can. "Dr. Grace told the security company she'd caught someone watching her house. We'll have to see if her description of the vehicle matches. Maybe we'll get lucky with a nearby traffic cam or a house with a security camera directed at the street."

"That's already on my to-do list. Did I tell you Wozniack is on his way to Orlando to look into that environmentalist, Owen Mitchell?"

I shook my head.

"Jung had some leads to follow up on the Masterson case, but Wozniack was free. By the way, while you were off having fun at the morgue, I read through Jonathan Grace's hate mail. Looks like Owen Mitchell wrote eight letters on behalf of the group, Defenders of the Earth."

"What kind of letters? The kind asking 'please don't destroy our wetlands or we're gonna cause a public relations nightmare,' or something harsher like 'destroy one more plant, and I'm going to torture and kill you?'"

Patrick laughed. "Somewhere in between. The letters started back when Grace purchased a property on the outskirts of Orlando. At first, the notes had a friendly tone, informational about the types of plants and wildlife located on the property. The letters asked him not to 'obliterate the area with another concrete vacation getaway for spoiled rich families.' Obviously Grace ignored Mitchell because additional letters took on a nastier tone. Mitchell said his group would keep an eye on Grace's outfit. They knew Grace had been filling in the wetlands and planned on reporting the company's actions. The last letter dated one month ago said Grace should have 'heeded the warnings, now he was going to pay.'"

"It'd be good to find out if Mitchell's legit or just a blow hard."

Patrick nodded. "Most of the time, these guys who write hate mail are only letting off a little steam. Confront them about their ramblings and they morph into upstanding citizens, polite and respectful."

"True enough." It was easy to spew venom anonymously. Rarely did we encounter someone filled with enough hatred to show his or her true colors during an interview. "Since Wozniack's headed over to Orlando, we should've sprung for a Disney ticket. Like you said, it's the happiest place on earth. Even he couldn't keep up a scowl at Cinderella's castle."

"*They* say it's the happiest place on earth, not me. Try standing in line for an hour in the July heat, waiting with three girls under the age of eleven to go on a thirty-second ride. Happy my ass." Patrick continued on, grumbling under his breath about wet socks and sugar crashes, until his phone rang, breaking him from his little tirade.

"Mr. Grace, thank you for calling me back." Patrick pointed at the phone and mouthed the words, *Jonathan's brother. David.*

"Would you mind if I put you on speaker phone?" Patrick asked the caller. "My partner and I would like to talk to you . . . great, thanks."

"I don't understand why you're calling," a deep voice said. "You were very cryptic in your message, Detective Jessup."

"I apologize. Have you heard from your sister-in-law?"

"No, why would I?"

Patrick grimaced. "I'm sorry to have to inform you like this, over the phone, but your brother Jonathan died Thursday evening."

"What! How?"

"He was murdered."

A silence fell. It lasted so long I thought we might have been disconnected.

"Mr. Grace?" Patrick said.

"Yes, I'm here," David Grace answered, a hitch in his voice. "Jonathan and I have been estranged for almost . . . what, thirty years now, but I can't believe Tammy didn't call me."

"Tammy? No, Mr. Grace, Jonathan was married to a Dr. Nina Grace. Tammy and your brother divorced in 1989. How long has it been since you've spoken to him?"

"I cut off all ties at nineteen. Guess that would've made Jonathan eighteen."

"I hate to pry, especially at a time like this, but can you tell me why the two of you stopped talking?"

"I always figured I'd be getting this call. Only thought it would've come a little sooner." David's voice sounded flat now. He may not have had a relationship with his brother, but his tone indicated shock. Maybe he realized he'd never have the chance to reconnect with Jonathan, even if he wanted to.

After a moment's hesitation, he went on. "Jonathan and I had a falling out. But before I tell you the story, you have to understand my brother. Our dad was a real son of a bitch. Most of the time, he didn't have much to say. Usually let his belt do the talking for him. It motivated me to strive harder, to get out of the life I'd been born into. For Jonathan . . . it turned him cold and callous. Mom tried to make up for what Dad lacked in parenting skills but somehow the bastard always trumped her efforts. He brought out the worst in Jonathan."

David Grace croaked out a hard-edged laugh. "I remember one year my mom had saved a little extra from the monthly grocery money until she had enough to buy Jonathan a used bicycle. It was a real beat up piece of shit, but in Jonathan's eyes, it represented freedom. When Dad came home that night and found out about it, he took it away. Said it was bought with his money and the boy had no right to something he didn't earn. Jonathan cried all night, mumbling how no one would ever take anything from him again.

"I have a million stories like that, but you get the idea. I tried to step in, help guide him, but even after our folks died in a car accident, Jonathan wouldn't listen to me. The damage had already been done. Anyway, Jonathan started doing grunt work for the Carpelli family. It was innocent at first. I think he liked the attention Joe showered on him. A kind of substitute father type. Eventually Joe Carpelli brought my brother into the family business. Drugs, prostitution, you name it and they had a hand in it. I don't know the specifics of how it all went down, but Jonathan came to me one night begging for help out of a jam. He owed Joe ten grand. Asked me to loan it to him."

"Did you?" Patrick asked.

"When my parents died, my dad's employer paid out a life insurance policy. Dying was the only good thing that rat bastard ever did for his family. Of course, Jonathan had already blown his share. I'd saved mine for college. He knew how much I wanted to leave Tampa, to get away and start over somewhere fresh. He knew what asking me for that money meant. Sure I gave him the cash, but it ended our relationship."

Not wanting to interrupt the flow of the conversation, I held up a piece of paper toward Patrick that said, ASK HIM ABOUT BOBBY HILDABRAND.

Patrick nodded at me. "Did you ever meet Jonathan and Tammy's son, Bobby?"

"No," David answered, regret heavy in his voice. "I didn't even know Jonathan had a kid. Man, I've been a pig-headed fool. All these years wasted and now I can't ever get them back. Do you have Bobby's phone number? I'd like give him a call when I come back for the funeral. Has the service been scheduled yet?"

"I'm not sure. You'll have to check with the family."

Before Patrick hung up, he gave David Grace the contact information for Bobby as well as Ana Lopez's number. Since Nina's cell phone still sat in an evidence bag in lock up, I figured Ana would know how to reach her.

"It's amazing how two brothers, growing up in the same dysfunctional household, could have turned out so differently," I said. "It's like two sexual abuse survivors. One grows up helping victims, the other turns into a victimizer."

"You don't know how David Grace turned out. Not by one short, fifteen-minute phone call. The guy could be a drunk, beating his wife after every weekend bender. You know how people are, quick to point the finger at others' failings, slow to turn that finger on themselves."

"True enough." I grabbed the dry erase marker from the ledge of the white board. "Back to Jonathan Grace. What do we know so far?"

Patrick closed his eyes and took a deep breath. He let it out slowly. "Thanks to his brother we now have a glimpse into Jonathan's childhood but other than that, not much. He was definitely a powerful guy hated by many. A long list of people, including a wife who knew about his extramarital affair."

I made a few notes on the board. "Don't forget about Lauren Tyler. She could have had Grace killed because of the blackmail."

"We can tentatively add the environmentalist Owen Mitchell and Grace's son, Bobby Hildabrand, until we find out more."

"I also need to look into Grace's supposed arch nemesis, Goro Yamamoto." I wrote his name on the board.

"Yamamoto? Wasn't that the name of the corporation John McLane's wife worked for in the movie *Die Hard*?"

"Really?" I wrinkled my brow. "That was Nakatomi, not Yamamoto. This is why I never ask you movie trivia questions."

"Well, who has time to watch a movie? Unless of course, it stars Hillary Duff."

"Don't worry, in a few months you can go back to watching Winnie-the-Pooh."

Patrick shot me a dirty look.

"Come on, Patrick. We need to talk about this. Every conversation circles around to the impending birth of your newest child." I snapped the top of the marker back on and sat in my chair.

"For the record, you steered us there this time."

Whoops.

"I can't help it," he said, rubbing his temples. "Last night I get home, I'm dead on my feet. Alina wants to talk about baby names. I'd rather discuss the stats on women over forty giving birth. Not surprisingly, the conversation didn't go well."

"What do you want, Alina to have an abortion? That's not going to happen, she's a devout Catholic. I thought you were, too."

"No. I mean, I am. I mean . . ." Patrick took another deep breath. "I would never want Alina to terminate the pregnancy. And how could I give up my child for adoption, handing him over to complete strangers? I'm just pissed. I have no options, and I'm pissed about it."

"Sshhh."

"Don't shush me—"

"Hello, Sergeant Kray." I smiled up at our supervisor. "We were just coming to update you on the Jonathan Grace case."

Kray was an imposing African American man. Bald, sculpted out of granite, and steel eyes that could bore into your soul. His hard look had served him well on the streets before he worked his way up the food chain. Stories of his busts were legendary. Kray had always walked the fine line of obeying the law and skirting the rules, a character trait he could sniff out in his own underlings.

"I've heard rumblings about this case, Springer. I know Dr. Grace counseled you last year. Do I need to reassign you?"

"Hell, Sergeant, she's the department shrink. Who hasn't spent time on her couch?"

Kray stared at me with that deep intensity in his eyes. He knew I was being purposefully flippant.

"No sir," I said. "Our doctor-patient relationship will have no bearing on this case."

"Good. Now come in my office and give me an update."

"Do you want Jessup to come, too?"

"Nah. Looks like he's in the middle of something." Kray turned and headed back to his office, expecting me to follow him.

Patrick looked up from his stack of papers smiling. I stuck my tongue out at him and hurried to catch up with the Sergeant.

CHAPTER 16

After updating Kray, I'd spent a couple of hours poring over the Graces' financial records while Patrick sat at his desk reviewing the couple's phone logs.

"Hey, Patrick . . ." I looked up and saw his chair empty.

I grabbed my blazer and headed toward the elevator. Time to grab us a late lunch; we'd need food if we hoped to tackle the rest of the afternoon with clear heads. When the elevator door reached the eighth floor, I moved back to let the crowd of people off. Must be another tour. From the looks of it, Officer Rodrigo was stuck explaining the inner workings of the downtown precinct to half-a-dozen bored high school students. Standing behind the group, Patrick held up a couple of fast food bags.

"You read my mind," I told Patrick after he exited the elevator.

"Not much of a feat considering the time of day."

I grabbed a sack, thanking him. We walked the long way back to our desks, hoping to avoid being sucked into a Q& A with the kids.

Patrick and I took about ten whole minutes to savor our lunch before I couldn't stand it any longer. "I'm guessing you finished reviewing the Graces' phone logs. Since you picked up lunch and all."

"Thought the food might lessen the blow."

"What do you mean?"

"Nothing out of the ordinary showed up on the Graces' land line, mostly calls back and forth from Dr. Grace to her family. I'm still going through Jonathan's cell phone logs though and waiting on the fax transcripts for the Graces' text messages. It's been such a hassle—"

I sighed. "Patrick, you're killing me."

"Right. When I checked Dr. Grace's cell history, one number concerned me. She made three calls to an Emmitt Rutledge on April 23, May 18, and again on June 13—the day before Jonathan's murder."

"Emmitt Rutledge? Do I really want to know?"

"He's a divorce attorney."

"Are you kidding me? That's great news. It tells us Dr. Grace had decided to leave her cheating husband. Why would she kill Jonathan if she was making arrangements to divorce him?"

"Sure, that's one way to interpret the move. Here's another. A few weeks after Ana Lopez tells Dr. Grace about her husband's tryst in her own house, she calls a divorce attorney. Dr. Grace knew about the affair, Kate. That's motive. She could have contacted the attorney as a smoke screen. It's still early in the investigation. We might find out the Graces had a prenup. Divorce and the doctor gets nothing."

"Patrick, there was nothing *to* get. I did a credit check and also looked over the bank statements for the Graces' joint account, the ones packed up from the house. Then I went through the files I found at Jonathan's office. Their lavish lifestyle was all smoke and mirrors. They're in debt up to their eyeballs. The Graces still have twenty-five years left to pay on a four million dollar mortgage, and they're making monthly payments on a million dollar yacht, a country club membership, and two vehicles. Looks like they were used to living the high life and once the economy crashed, they didn't know how to rein in their spending. Not changing their lifestyle sent them into a downward spiral that would have eventually dumped them into bankruptcy court."

"O . . . kay." Patrick slowly leaned back in his chair. "Their financial life's in the crapper. We don't know how Dr. Grace would fair in a divorce settlement. What's Jonathan's life insurance policy look like?"

"I have no idea. Haven't come across it yet, but feel free to add it to *your* to-do list." I gave him a wink.

Patrick ignored me. "Maybe Nina decided it was easier to have her husband killed than to go through a long drawn out divorce. Remember what Lauren said about Jonathan? How he refused to let go of anything that was his. He doesn't sound like the type of guy to let his wife walk out on him."

"May I finish, please?" I flipped through a couple of papers until I found the page outlining the Graces' credit history. "They carried $230,000 worth of credit card debt. Most interesting is the fact that three-fourths of the debt was rung up on a Discover card issued in Jonathan's name only. All the charges were incurred this year and the mailing address for the statements lists his office address instead of his home."

"Was the card linked to his corporate account?"

"Jonathan has one corporate American Express card with a surprisingly low balance. I can't envision him taking out clients and paying with his Discover."

"Then what did Jonathan buy that he wanted to hide from his wife?"

"The first purchase was made in January of this year, $9,000 at Rowen Jewelers."

Patrick let out a soft whistle. "Nice hunk of bling. Wasn't that right around the time Jonathan started his affair with his assistant, Lauren Tyler?"

I nodded. "Lauren told me Jonathan would often surprise her with jewelry as bonuses."

"Too bad we couldn't get that kind of bonus policy instituted around here."

"Somehow I don't think you'd like working on your back to earn it."

Patrick conceded, shrugging his shoulders. "What else did he buy?"

"You ready for this? Besides multiple jewelry purchases, Jonathan took out six cash advances for $5,000 each. The withdrawals are spaced seven days apart starting May 21 through June 25."

Patrick flipped back through his desk calendar. "That's one withdrawal every Saturday."

"Thirty grand. No way in hell he made the same high price purchase every week."

"Blackmail," Patrick said.

"My thoughts exactly."

"The question is what did Jonathan do to make himself a target?"

"And who's his blackmailer?"

Patrick jotted down some notes.

I couldn't help but laugh. "I see you're still using those cute, pink notepads."

Patrick rolled his eyes but couldn't hide the hint of a smile. He'd received an entire box of little, pink steno pads from his three girls on his last birthday. His wife had steered them away from the tacky ties but couldn't help give in when they suggested the notebooks for daddy to use at work.

"Only two left, thank goodness."

"You didn't have to use them." The ribbing he'd taken from the other detectives had been ruthless.

"What? And waste perfectly good notepads? No way. But don't worry, I got my wife back. For Mother's Day, the girls got her a shiny, new yoga outfit, and I mean shiny."

Envy danced at the corners of my smile. Patrick and Alina made a great couple. They met in high school but had one of those on again, off again romances. Finally deciding they couldn't live without each other, they exchanged vows fifteen years ago.

"Focus, Jessup. Let's get back to the secret credit card account. Now the rest of the line items on the statements show up as charges from a

Whitington Enterprises."

Patrick turned away from my desk, pulling his chair closer to his computer. "Whitington? How do you spell that?"

I laughed.

"Hey, I may not have mad skills in spelling, but give me two minutes and I'll know everything there is to know about this company."

Patrick's fingers flew across the keyboard while I continued reviewing Jonathan's private credit card statement.

"There are charge amounts ranging from $100 to $2,500," I said. "Grace visited this place—"

"Got it. Whitington Enterprises is a holding company for a bunch of smaller businesses operating under it. The mailing address is a Tampa PO box, and a Rob Whitington is listed as the owner."

"What kind of businesses?"

"Let's see here. A dry cleaner, a print shop, two restaurants, dance club, online porn website, and something called the Sext Club. I figure the less reputable companies charge the credit cards with the name 'Whitington Enterprises' instead of the actual name of the business. That way if a wife gets ahold of a statement, she doesn't know what her husband's up to."

I snapped my fingers. "Wait a minute."

Patrick swiveled his chair facing me again.

"Did you say the Sext Club?" I asked.

Patrick nodded.

"Lauren Tyler told me she introduced Jonathan to this members-only club. He'd taken the pictures of Lauren and the redhead there, the same pictures he'd been blackmailing her with."

"I'm confused. Not only is Jonathan blackmailing Lauren Tyler, but he's also a victim of blackmail?"

"Are you thinking what I'm thinking?"

"That it can't be a coincidence?"

"No. I mean . . . yes to your question, it can't be a coincidence, but that's not what I'm thinking. It's Saturday. Tonight would be the perfect time to head down to Ybor City and check this place out for ourselves."

"Fine, but since it's your idea, you're the one telling my wife."

"Chill out, puss. It's for a case. She won't be that upset."

"You have met her, right?"

I sighed. "Why don't you check with Vice to see what we're up against? I'm sure this Whitington guy has flashed across their radar before. I'll give Lauren Tyler a call." A mischievous smile played across my face. "I'll persuade her that it would be in her best interest to get us on the club's invite list."

"Good idea. By the way, did you check with the banks the Graces do business with? See if Jonathan rented a safe deposit box at one of them?"

"Yes, but it was a dead end. Jonathan must have gone to a bank he didn't regularly use."

"Before I forget," Patrick said, tapping a finger on his desk, "we still need to find out what charges were made to Jonathan's credit cards the night of the murder. It might help us nail down his whereabouts during the missing time."

"Already done. When I stumbled onto the possible blackmail money trail, I got sidetracked and forgot to tell you. Jonathan rang up four charges on his credit cards Thursday. I checked with each business to get an accurate timeline. Jackson's Bistro was the first purchase of the day at 1:42 pm. That's where Jonathan and his lawyer met for lunch. At 7:54 pm, Jonathan paid for a dinner he shared with Jamar Washington. At 9:28 pm, Grace stopped for gas at a Tampa filling station."

"That proves Jonathan left Orlando after dinner."

"Right." I nodded. "The last credit card purchase was for $56 at The Blue Martini. When I called to find out what time Jonathan had been at the bar, I talked to the actual waitress who'd served him."

"It's been two days. They actually remembered him?"

"Yeah, surprising I know. The waitress said Thursdays are slow, and

I guess Jonathan's a regular. Since he's a big tipper, the waitress said she keeps an eye out for him in order to seat him in her section. Anyway, Jonathan paid for his bar tab at 10:12 pm. She said he usually has a woman on his arm, but Thursday night he came in alone."

"That's a pretty high bar tab for only one person," Patrick said.

"Jonathan must have been trashed when he left. Probably a good thing considering the brutality inflicted on him later that evening."

"We still don't know if he went right home or made another stop."

I sighed. "One more question to add to the ever growing list of what we don't know."

CHAPTER 17

"*Who's* waiting for me downstairs?" I snapped my fingers, trying to get Patrick's attention then continued my phone conversation. "Tell them to cool their heels until we're ready for them. I don't know, make something up. Say you're trying to find me."

I hung up the phone, stunned into silence.

"What?" Patrick gestured for me to hurry up with an explanation.

"You'll never guess who's in our lobby waiting to talk to me."

"You're right I won't. Skip the game of twenty questions and tell me."

"Nina Grace and her lawyer."

Patrick's mouth fell open. "What!"

"Yeah, I know. When's that ever happened? A suspect showing up on *our* doorstep."

"The woman's either a genius or certifiable."

What Patrick said was true enough. After a murder, we always made it a point to visit surviving spouses at their homes. It made them feel more comfortable in their own surroundings. If they were a suspect, there was no need to haul them into the station immediately putting them on the defensive.

"Patrick, go get Sergeant Kray and update him. See if he wants to watch the interview. I'll get Dr. Grace and meet you in room three." The biggest of our interrogation rooms, number three had more of an office feel instead of the two stuffy closets we used to sweat most of the perps.

During the elevator ride down to the lobby, I thought about the approach I wanted to take with Nina. I'd been caught off guard when she showed up here unannounced with her lawyer in tow. I looked at my watch, 3:14 pm. On Friday, the hospital said they were keeping Nina overnight, but I figured she would've stayed for a couple more days. Wonder how she got sprung so quickly?

I remember the last time Nina caught me off guard. A couple of months ago we ran into each other at a bakery near the precinct. We hadn't seen each other since my final appointment last fall. The first few moments were awkward, standing in such an informal setting next to the person who knew my deepest secrets, my darkest thoughts. Nina felt my tension and asked me to join her at a table near the window. We sat for a while, talking about all the new developments in my life.

That was the thing about Nina; she sincerely cared about my well-being. Her openness and nonjudgmental attitude had me opening up about Carlos Diaz and the relationship he wanted. At the time, I didn't even give it a second thought to ask how she was doing. Inquire about her marriage, her practice. Maybe if I hadn't been selfish, I could have helped her in some way. But this time would be different. Nina was in my house now.

I stepped off the elevator and turned right. Nina stood staring up blankly at the enormous tile mosaic beach scene covering the entire west wall. She wore an airy, sleeveless dress that mocked her rigid frame. Considering Nina's house was still a crime scene and no one was allowed on the premises, I wondered if her lawyer had given Nina the outfit.

Nina's hands were fisted at her sides while Bethany Dunbar

whispered into her ear. I'd had a few previous dealings with this attorney. Ms. Dunbar had a reputation for selling her services to the wealthiest criminals in the area, a definite don't ask, don't tell policy. She had a short, jet black bob and her features were as severe as her tongue.

"Dr. Grace?"

Nina slowly shifted her attention toward me. Her facial features remained flat, except for a momentary spark of recognition in her eyes. "Detective Springer."

"You didn't need to come all the way down here. Detective Jessup and I would have been happy to meet you somewhere else."

"Where? At the local motel?" Nina snapped. She raised a shaky hand and adjusted her glasses. "Sorry. This is . . . a lot to take in. I'm not even allowed back into my own house."

"If you need some clothes, some personal items, I'm sure I could get permission to remove what you need."

Nina ignored my offer. "My lawyer said I should get out in front of this thing. Come in before you had time to get your ducks in a row."

"Nina!" Dunbar hissed.

"I'm not interested in playing games, Detective Springer. Someone viciously . . . murdered my husband. I want to help you find the person responsible."

"Well, okay. Thank you for being honest with me, Dr. Grace. Let's go upstairs where it's more private."

On the ride back up to eight, Ms. Dunbar outlined the rules for the interview. Dr. Grace's visit today should be seen as an act of good faith and anytime they weren't comfortable with the line of questioning, they would leave. Nina stood motionless, staring at the numbers light up one after the other.

When I opened the door to the interrogation room, Patrick was already seated at the table. I made introductions and motioned for the two women to have a seat in the chairs facing the darkened mirror.

I'd hoped to get a few minutes beforehand to prep Patrick on Nina's mood and obvious fragile state, but since all the parties were ready, that wouldn't happen. For Nina's sake, I'd have to do my best to remain visibly impartial, yet steer the conversation away from any traps she might fall into.

"Dr. Grace, I want to tell you how sorry I am for your loss," Patrick said. "I know this must be a rough time for you. We appreciate you coming downtown to help us in the investigation into your husband's death."

Nina didn't acknowledge Patrick. She seemed lost in her own world, staring off at the wall behind him.

"When did you last speak to your husband, Dr. Grace?" he asked.

"Nina?" Bethany Dunbar placed her hand over Nina's.

The touch startled Nina, and she jerked her hands away. "What?"

"Detective Jessup asked when you last spoke to Jonathan," Dunbar repeated.

"Oh . . . two days ago. Thursday morning before work, we ran into each other in the kitchen. Literally." A hesitant smile played across her face. "Jonathan stroked my cheek and apologized for being such a klutz. It was the first time he'd touched me in months."

Nina remained silent, obviously lost in the memory. Eventually, the smile faded and pursed lips emerged. She finally looked at Patrick, telling him she'd grabbed her coffee and bagel and headed out the door. "That was the last time I saw him," she said.

"Did you drive straight to work?" Patrick asked.

"Yes, I had back-to-back patients all day. At lunch, I was fighting a migraine. Finally couldn't take it anymore. I cancelled my late afternoon appointments and went home. I hate rescheduling patients. They really depend on me, but I had no choice. By the time I got to my car, I could barely drive home."

"Do you remember what time you arrived at the house?"

"I have no idea," Nina answered flatly. "Probably thirty minutes after my last appointment finished."

"Was your housekeeper home when you arrived?"

Patrick knew Nina had called Ana Lopez around 3 pm, telling her to leave early for the day. He simply asked the question to see what answer she'd give. If Nina lied about the little details, she wouldn't hesitate to lie about the big ones.

"No, she wasn't home."

"Then no one can vouch for your migraine?"

"Detective Jessup?" Ms. Dunbar jumped in with a school teacher's scolding tone.

"I apologize. I meant nothing by it. So Dr. Grace, you finally get home, what next?"

"I headed straight for bed. Took some migraine medicine and I was out."

"Did you set the house alarm when you got home?"

Nina narrowed her eyes and tilted her head slightly. She was quiet, obviously struggling to replay the day's events back in her mind. "I . . . can't remember. I'm sure I did. I usually do . . . but I can't remember actually entering the code into the keypad."

"It's okay," Patrick said. "Can you tell me why you awoke in the middle of the night? You said you took your meds and headed straight to bed. What disturbed your sleep?"

"A noise. Something crashed downstairs. I was groggy and looked at the clock. It was a little after midnight."

"Was it a loud crash? I mean, were your bedroom doors closed?"

"I don't know how loud the crash was," Nina said. "I only remember waking up because of a noise. And yes, I always sleep with my bedroom doors closed. I don't know how loud the crash was. I only remember waking up because of a noise. I went downstairs, turning lights on as I went. From the top of the stairs, I saw the table in the foyer toppled over, the vase laying in pieces on the floor. Jonathan's den light was on with the door half opened. I thought he had come home and knocked it over. I walked down the stairs toward the den and . . ."

Nina's legs started to bounce under the table. The tapping of her shoes was the only sound in the room.

"And?" Patrick asked.

"And what!" Nina snapped.

"Dr. Grace," I said, getting Nina's attention. "Tell me how you first met Jonathan."

Nina frowned and gave her head a slight shake. "I . . ."

"Was it love at first sight?" I prodded.

The tension in Nina's shoulders visibly relaxed. She pushed her glasses farther up the bridge of her nose. Thick, black, square-framed glasses nicknamed "birth control glasses" in the 70's, retooled as a retro look, that were now popular again.

"No, nothing quite as dramatic as love at first sight." Nina smiled, tucking a strand of hair behind her ear. "It was actually a blind date. Jonathan and I were completely focused on our careers. No time for the clubs and the usual dating scene. We ran in different circles. He had money, in the local commercial real estate business. I was trying to get my private practice off the ground. We had one mutual friend who thought we'd be perfect for each other."

Nina let out a quiet laugh. "I remember Jonnie picked me up that first night, took me to the Columbia Restaurant. The date was horrible. The waiter spilled sauce on my dress, Jonnie's car got towed. I figured I'd never see him again, but the next day he sent me flowers. Pink Asiatic lilies. The card read, 'Now that you've seen me at my worst, how about giving a fellow a second chance to make a better first impression.' Jonnie wooed me. Relentlessly. At the time, I thought it was romantic. I was young, impressionable, had only opened my practice a couple years prior. I was ready to save the world, rebuilding one psyche at a time."

"Jonnie?" I asked, clarifying for the recorded statement.

"My nickname for Jonathan. After the first few dates, I told him the name, Jonathan, sounded too formal and uptight. When he would act too big for his britches, I'd call him Jonnie. It helped deflate the king-sized ego, brought him back down to earth with the rest of us regular folks. You see, Jonathan had created this persona to the outside world. A refined ivy-league-type fellow who looked like he came from money."

"Did Jonathan attend an ivy league school?"

"Hardly. Guess you could say he graduated from the school of hard knocks. Never attended college, but Jonathan was always driven. Almost as if his own inner demons were pushing him to succeed. He never really opened up to me about his childhood, didn't want to be psychoanalyzed. I know he came from nothing and built everything he had from the ground up. Still, he had an inferiority complex around his silver-spooned friends. Most likely brought on by his upbringing. He tried to overcompensate for his feelings of inadequacy. Had to have the best house, best cars, the yacht, and all the other trappings to stay ahead of the Joneses."

Nina nodded her head. "Yes. Appearances were extremely important to Jonathan. I wasn't what you'd call a real catch in the beauty department when we first met. I was more interested in the books I read than the outfits I wore. But Jonnie had a real talent for finding the shining diamond under all the coal soot. I wanted to fit into his world. So much so, I happily traded my own personality for a cookie-cutter look and demeanor. At least when I was on Jonnie's arm. Later, when I got tired of keeping up the public charade, problems started creeping into the marriage."

It was difficult to imagine Nina conforming her personality to the whims of her husband. Sure, I could envision her as a young, inexperienced bookworm, but to think she allowed herself to be paraded around like eye candy was inconceivable. Maybe I didn't know Nina as well as I thought I did.

Patrick jumped in. "We heard Jonathan described as a controlling man. Would you agree?"

"You could say that." Nina answered with a harshness to her tone. She seemed to have a difficult time reigning in her clashing emotions. Like she was warring with herself, trying to soften her expressions, but unable.

Nina sighed. "I'd describe Jonathan as the strong, silent type. He kept his emotions close to the vest. But the times he allowed me close enough to peek underneath his hard exterior, I saw this sweet little boy who only wanted to be loved. It's what most attracted me to him. I don't know, maybe it's the healer in me. I told you I like to fix broken psyches. Jonathan was my own little side project. I had hopes of fixing him, molding him into the man I knew he could be."

Nina wasn't the first wife guilty of being suckered in with the wounded-boy routine. I'd been called out on countless domestic violence calls where the women were stunned when their husbands had beaten them bloody. They would profess their men's tender hearts to anyone who'd listen. Just another reason why I had to get Lucy away from Chuck.

"—marriage is loving the warts and all," Nina was saying. "But after a while, I couldn't stand the warts. Jonathan was motivated by money and status. Two things that meant nothing to me."

"Dr. Grace," I said, getting her attention. "I know this might be difficult, but your housekeeper, Ana Lopez, told me about your problems conceiving—"

"Really, Detective?" Dunbar interrupted, leaning closer into the table. "This woman hasn't been through enough. You have to poke a stick in the wound. What is the point to this line of questioning?"

"Don't worry, Ms. Dunbar. It's okay." Nina patted the table with her hand almost as if she wanted to console her lawyer without actually touching her. "You're right, Detective Springer, Jonathan and I had hoped to start a family once we were married. After a year of trying, my doctor diagnosed me with Polycystic Ovary Syndrome. To make a long story short, we eventually tried a few rounds of in vitro, but it wasn't in the cards."

"You never considered adoption?" I asked.

"No. You have to understand what kind of pressure not being able to conceive a child puts on a marriage. It wasn't a good idea to bring an innocent child into such turmoil. I had fallen into a deep depression, guilty I couldn't give Jonathan the son he'd always wanted. Jonathan retreated emotionally because he couldn't fix me or the situation."

"But Jonathan did have a son," Patrick said. "Bobby Hildabrand."

"Bobby may have been Jonathan's biological child, but the boy wanted nothing to do with his father. Bobby's mother, Tammy, poisoned him against his father. Jonathan wanted a second chance at being a dad. Unfortunately, I couldn't give him that."

I felt guilty. I'd sat in Dr. Grace's uncomfortable chairs for weeks, spilling my guts about my job, family, and hellish childhood when I never gave a second thought to the woman sitting behind the desk. It was amazing the problems plaguing Nina, yet every morning she'd apply her caring doctor mask like it was a coat of makeup. Looks like the shrink needed a shrink of her own.

"How well did you know Tammy and Bobby Hildabrand?" I asked.

"We never actually met. Jonathan wanted to shield me from what he said was, 'the ugliness of his prior bad choices.'"

"Bobby never came over to watch a game or have Sunday dinner?" Patrick asked.

"No. Tammy forbade it. At least that's what Jonathan told me."

Patrick pursed his lips. He couldn't completely hide the disdain he felt for absentee fathers. One of his hot buttons.

"You have to understand, Detective Jessup, what Jonathan wanted, Jonathan got. If he didn't want to discuss something, we didn't."

"Dr. Grace, there's some sensitive material we need to talk about."

"Patrick?" I said, an edge lacing that one word.

My partner shot me a look, shutting me down.

Nina shoulders visibly tensed. Her toes began tapping again.

"And no Ms. Dunbar, I'm not asking these questions merely to add salt to the wound," Patrick said. "This information will help us learn more about Jonathan Grace which could lead us directly to his killer."

Nina took a deep breath. "Understood, Detective. Go ahead and ask."

"Was your husband having an affair?"

"Yes."

Patrick seemed shocked at the matter of fact way she answered. We rarely heard the truth in this room. He recovered quickly. "Can you tell me about it?"

"Which one?"

"Was there more than one affair?"

"I don't know for certain, but I know he'd been banging his secretary, Lauren Tyler. Three months ago, my housekeeper told me she saw Jonathan and Lauren traipsing around my house half-naked. Was it his first affair? His last one? I don't know."

"Did you confront him about it?"

Nina hung her head. "No."

"Why not?"

Nina's head shot up, a fire ignited in her eyes. "What difference would it have made? Jonathan and I were already strangers in our own home. We'd been sleeping in different bedrooms for months. He probably ran to her because she was willing to give him the things I refused to."

"What do you mean?"

Nina smirked. "Jonathan's tastes were always a little on the experimental side. I was game for spicing up our love life. I mean, I'm no cold fish, but once he . . ."

"Yes?"

"He pushed it too far. The bondage. The pain. Love should not hurt. I told Jonathan no more. Maybe Lauren didn't mind."

Patrick leaned in closer, placing his elbows on the table. "You say you didn't tell Jonathan about your knowledge of the affair. Then can you tell me what his reaction was when you asked him for a divorce?"

"What?"

"A divorce. You contacted a divorce attorney, correct?"

Nina chewed her bottom lip for a moment. "All these questions, Detective Jessup? Why are you asking? Do you think I killed my husband?"

"Ma'am, I'm simply trying to find out as much information as possible. If Detective Springer and I are going to solve your husband's murder, we need to know what kind of person he was and who better to give us that information than his wife."

"You have no idea who my husband was. You think I killed him because I gave a shit who he screwed. Hardly. Jonathan was the type of man willing to crush anyone who stood in the way of what he wanted. And what he wanted was power and success. If you'd like a list of his real enemies, Detective, get a bigger pad of paper. This might take a while."

Bethany Dunbar put her hand on Nina's shoulder. "We should call it a day. These questions are obviously taking their toll. I think Dr. Grace should rest now. How about we come back later in the week?"

"Don't be silly." Nina shrugged Bethany's hand away. "I'm here to help them find the person responsible for killing Jonathan. I need to tell them what I know."

"I think—"

"I don't care what you think," Nina snapped.

A loud rapping at the door interrupted. Nina cried out.

Patrick nodded at me, obviously trying to get me to leave and check out the disturbance.

I turned my gaze away from Patrick, looking toward Nina. "I apologize for the interruption, Dr. Grace. Patrick will find out what's going on."

As Patrick stood up to leave, I could feel the heat of his angry stare burning a hole me.

CHAPTER 18

Nina and her lawyer walked out of the interview room just as Patrick returned.

"Where the hell have you been?" I raised my hands in frustration. "You left almost an hour ago. If you're pissed because—"

"That's not it. Listen. You won't believe who showed up."

"My turn for twenty questions?"

"Bobby Hildabrand."

"You're shitting me! What is going on today? Normally you have to pry a suspect's fingernails off the doorframe to get them into this room. Now it's like they've all been sent special delivery wrapped up in one big red bow. What did Jonathan's son have to say?"

"He told me—"

"You bitch! You killed him, didn't you?" The shout came from around the corner. Patrick groaned and ran out the door. I followed.

At the bank of elevators, Bobby Hildabrand tried to push past a detective who stood between him and Bethany Dunbar. Nina cowered behind her lawyer. Bobby pointed at Nina, accusing her again of murder. Spittle ran down his face. He looked like a rabid dog, locking onto frightened prey.

"Who the hell are you?" Bethany Dunbar yelled.

"That gold-digging bitch kept my family apart! If it weren't for her, my parents would still be together."

"Bobby?" Nina said uncertainly. She looked over at me. Her eyes pleaded with me then she seemed to retreat inward, away from the explosive situation.

The elevator dinged and the doors opened. "Let's get you out of here," Bethany Dunbar said. She took Nina by the shoulder, gently guiding her into the empty car.

"What? You're going to let her leave?" Bobby yelled. "You've got to be kidding me."

Patrick moved into Bobby's line of sight. "You need to take it down a notch, son." Patrick put his hand on Bobby's arm trying to lead him back to the interview room. Bobby shrugged off Patrick's touch but still followed him. Inside the room, Bobby refused to sit. Instead he paced, mumbling unintelligibly.

Bobby was in his early twenties. He had his father's mop of dark curls, though Bobby wore it longer. There was also a little more weight around Bobby's middle.

"When you shouted at Dr. Grace," Patrick began, "you said she came between your mother and father. How? They were divorced for seventeen years before Dr. Grace married your father."

Bobby stuck out his lower lip. His faced morphed into one of a petulant child. "Yeah, I know. So."

"Help me understand," Patrick said.

"Did you listen to anything I said earlier?"

"Please, this is my partner, Detective Springer. She really needs to know why you think Dr. Grace killed your dad. Help her see your side of the story. Please, calm down and talk to us."

Bobby exhaled angrily. A stack of curls flopped down across his eyes, and he swiped them back into the fold. "My mom and dad may have been divorced, but they still loved each other. Sure, Dad had other women in his life, off and on, but he always came back to my mom. They were ready to get back together again, permanently, until the bitch took him away."

I pulled out a chair and sat. Bobby ignored my invitation to do the same. I looked over at Patrick who gave me the all clear to take the lead. "Dr. Grace told me when she married Jonathan you weren't in the picture, that you wanted nothing to do with your father."

"What a liar!"

"Her story sounded pretty convincing," I said. "You don't even share his last name."

"Talk to my mother. I was nine when they divorced. She changed my last name from Grace to Hildabrand. She was angry at Dad for leaving. I don't blame her, I was too."

"Yes, you certainly sound angry."

"You're damned right I do. My father tossed us aside for a new piece of ass."

"Come on, Bobby. You're not a little kid anymore. Why are you still hanging onto this pipe dream about your parents getting back together?"

"You sound like my father."

"Did you confront him? Ask why he dropped you from his life?"

"Little good it did. I finally went straight to the bitch and told her she'd better get out of my father's life or she'd regret it. You know what she did? She laughed in my face. Told me she'd finally found her meal ticket and wasn't letting it go for some white trash, reject son who didn't know how to take a hint. You think she's this saint doctor. She's got you snowed."

"What . . . what if Dr. Grace did tell you to kiss off?" I stuttered, thrown off a little. "You think it makes her a killer?"

"No. I think a five million dollar life insurance policy makes her a killer." Bobby looked over at Patrick. "I already told you all this."

It finally hit me that this dog and pony show was for me. Bobby had already told Patrick this story while I'd finished interviewing Nina. I closed my eyes not wanting to let the shock I felt inside show on my face. I bit my lip, trying to control my temper. Patrick let me walk into this blind.

"How do you know Dr. Grace is the beneficiary of a five million dollar life insurance policy?" I asked Bobby, keeping a tight lid on my emotions.

"I don't." Bobby's pouty face remerged. "Not for sure."

"Right, I thought so."

"But, but . . . Dad had a policy with my mother listed as the beneficiary. He probably changed it over into the bitch's name when they got married." Bobby turned toward Patrick looking for an ally. "Why won't you believe me?"

"I do, Bobby. Like I said before, have your mother look through her financial papers and bring in anything having to do with the old life insurance policy. If your dad kept it up and simply changed the beneficiary's name, I can start hunting it down. But until I have the name of the insuring company, my hands are tied."

"Right. Oh, wait, I forgot. Mom's in Buffalo visiting her sister."

"How long has she been there?" Patrick asked.

"All month. Mom always visits Aunt Patty during the summer, but she's cutting the visit short to fly back for Dad's funeral. I'll have Mom check her papers when she gets home."

Patrick stood and the two men shook hands.

I went over to the door and opened it. "By the way, Bobby, where were you Thursday around midnight?"

"Are you kidding me? Now you think I killed my dad? At home. Asleep. Alone. Why don't you try talking to your partner, lady. I'm tired of retelling the same story."

Bobby pushed passed me, leaving the interview room.

I turned my full fury toward Patrick. "You asshole! You set me up."

Patrick extended his hands in front of him, trying to stop the impending explosion. "You're right. I'm sorry. But you know as well as I do, you wouldn't have believed Dr. Grace had a dark side unless you heard it for yourself."

"All I heard was name calling and mudslinging. Bobby has no proof Dr. Grace was involved in her husband's murder. What we have here is a sour, little kid cranky because mommy and daddy got a divorce. Mark my words, Tammy Hildabrand's going to turn out to be a real piece of work. You've seen the type. Mom turns into a vindictive bitch because her husband dumps her. Then Jonathan strings her along, making her think she has a chance to unite the happy family. This makes the woman even more spiteful toward the new lady in Jonathan's life. Who knows what kind of shit she filled Bobby's head with? You saw the level of rage inside that kid. Maybe Bobby finally snapped."

"Now you're saying Bobby killed his father?"

"No. I'm just quoting Detective Patrick Jessup, 'I don't know who killed Jonathan Grace but until I do, I'm going to keep an open mind,'" I mocked.

Patrick nodded. I'd won the round.

"But it sounds like Dr. Grace was the target of Bobby's rage, not Jonathan." Patrick said.

"I'll give you that point, but I'm not taking him off the suspect list. A list, by the way, that is growing longer by the hour. While you were planning your little setup with Bobby Hildabrand, Dr. Grace gave me a list of names over a page long. All people who held grudges against Jonathan. She also said she'd noticed someone watching the house a few days before the murder. Gave a similar description of the vehicle the neighbor girl saw. A white SUV. "

Patrick sighed. "We'll look at it all tomorrow. It's been a long day, and it's shaping up to be an even longer evening." Patrick glanced down at his watch. "Right now all I want to do is drive home and have dinner with my family."

"Good idea. Best to put in some face time before you drop the bomb you'll be hanging out with me at a sex club tonight."

CHAPTER 19

"Sorry to hear about your car, Patrick." I stood on Jessup's front porch bathed in the light shining from his opened door.

"Like I don't have enough to worry about right now. Plunking down a couple grand on a new transmission was not in the budget."

"I have a guy who might be able to give you a good deal. Want me to give him a call?"

"Patrick Jessup, where are your manners?" Alina pushed her husband out of the way, waving me inside. She was a petite brunette with an equally sweet and saucy side. "You'll have to excuse Señor Rude here."

Alina let out a soft whistle. "Look at you," she said, gesturing to my dress.

I glanced down at the black mini hugging my curves in all the right places. "Too much?"

"No way. Good thing I know my husband as well as I do, or I might be a jealous woman."

"Yeah, right." I laughed.

Alina knew Patrick was as loyal as a Labrador. He adored her. Even when beautiful women walked by, Patrick's eyes never wandered.

"Auntie Kate?" Patrick's middle child, Lanie, walked into the living room rubbing the sleep out of her eyes. "I didn't know you were coming."

I bent down on one knee and gave the nine-year-old a big hug. "Aren't you supposed to be in bed, little one? You have to get up early for church."

"But I wanted to tell you the good news."

"What news? Straight A's again?"

"No, even better. Mommy's going to have another baby. Isn't it exciting? Maybe I'll finally get a little brother."

Patrick inhaled sharply. I stole a glance his way and saw hands fisted at his sides. He struggled to keep his composure. His hardened stare was directed toward Alina, but she wouldn't meet his searing gaze. So much for keeping the baby news a secret.

Patrick headed toward Lanie. With the mood he was in, I thought he might scold her for being up late. Instead he swept her off the ground and cradled her like a newborn. All knees and elbows, she overflowed from Patrick's arms. Lanie broke out into a fit of giggles.

"A baby brother, huh?" Patrick teased. "No such luck in this family."

Lanie kissed her father on the cheek.

"Now tell Auntie Kate goodnight. I'm getting you back into bed so I can finish getting dressed."

I told Lanie not to let the bed bugs bite after she blew me a kiss.

Patrick shot Alina one last disappointed look before he left. Once he'd closed the door to their bedroom, she grabbed my arm and led me to the couch.

"Kate, you have to talk to me. I don't know what to do."

"What do you mean?"

"You know Patrick as well as anyone. You're with him more than I am."

"I'm sorry, Alina I—"

"No, that's not what I meant. It's just . . . oh, damn. There goes the waterworks again. Ridiculous hormones!" Like a magician pulling a coin out of thin air, Alina had a tissue. She took a corner and dabbed at her tear-filled eyes. "Ever since I told Patrick about the baby, he's been so angry, always on edge, even snaps at the girls. Little things that never seemed to bother him send him into a tailspin—toys left out, the girls bickering at each other, new shoes on the credit card bill. His reaction wasn't what I'd hoped for. I don't know what to do."

"He loves you, Alina. You and the girls. He'll love this new baby, too."

"It's why I finally told the girls. I wanted to celebrate, to enjoy the excitement of having a baby on the way. Patrick didn't want me to tell them yet, but I couldn't help it. He keeps saying the most hurtful things. Like he wants me to give up the baby or even worse, terminate the pregnancy."

Sly move on her part. Since the kids knew about the pregnancy, Patrick would be forced to stop pressuring her. "He needs time, Alina. Time to adjust to having another mouth to feed, another body to clothe."

"Is that what he told you?"

"You know how men are, Alina. They want to fix things. Patrick can't fix this, and he feels powerless. He wants to provide the best for his family, and he feels like he's already spread too thin financially."

Patrick walked in the room, a chill settling in his wake. "It's getting late, Kate. We need to get this over with." Patrick stormed out the door without saying another word.

I looked over at Alina and saw the hurt in her eyes. "Don't worry, I'll work on him."

***

"Let's park in the garage on 5th Avenue and walk," I suggested to Patrick as we approached downtown Ybor City.

The bumpy drive down the red cobblestone road transported me back to a time when Ybor was known for its industry of hand-rolled cigars. Now the nights belonged to Tampa's disenfranchised youth, inebriated partygoers, and a trannie or two.

"I find it interesting that Bethany Dunbar didn't object to a damn thing until the conversation got around to Jonathan's enemies," I said. "Seemed like Dunbar couldn't care less about keeping Dr. Grace out of jail. Even the worst lawyers object more than she did. If nothing else, to make themselves look good in their clients' eyes."

"Dr. Grace sure hired counsel at lightning speed."

"At first, I thought it was a rich thing. You know, high powered couple has lawyers on speed dial. Then I found out Bethany Dunbar approached Dr. Grace at the hospital. Guess the barracuda had worked for Jonathan in the past."

"I wonder why he needed a criminal lawyer," Patrick said. "He didn't have a record."

"You should have seen Dunbar after you left. Made me think she has a vested interest in covering up for someone. Whether it was for Jonathan's previous dealings or for someone he worked with on a land deal, I don't know, but there's definitely something there."

"Dr. Grace seemed pretty on edge during the interview. And she didn't seem too broken up over her husband's death."

"You heard her shrink," I said. "Acute Distress Disorder manifests itself in a variety of ways. Emotional detachment, irritability. You saw how Dr. Grace reacted to the knock on the door."

"I guess. I know I couldn't read her nonverbal clues very well. I have to say, though, she sure has the wounded wife act down. That is until I got around to asking her about the divorce. A question, by the way, she never answered. Did you see how she deflected the whole thing back on me?"

I rolled my eyes.

"She is a psychologist, Kate. An expert at steering the conversation in the direction she wants it to go. Look how quickly she pointed the finger at Jonathan's enemies."

"All valid if she's not guilty."

"Did you ask Dr. Grace about a life insurance policy or prenup?"

I parked the car in one of the last empty spaces and mumbled no as I turned off the engine. "The woman was spent. It was all I could do to get her to finish talking about the people she thought held grudges against her husband. I'll follow up with her soon. Maybe pop in, check on her when her lawyer's not around."

"Bad idea, Kate."

"Why?"

"You have a past relationship with her. You don't want any hint of impropriety on your part. Without a third party present, she could accuse you of all sorts of things."

"Are you kidding me? Like what? Planting the murder weapon in her purse. Give me a break, Patrick." I opened the car door and got out.

"I'm serious." Patrick slammed his door. "Tell me you won't meet with her unless her lawyer is present or I'm there."

"Sure, fine."

Patrick sighed.

I clapped him on the shoulder as we walked toward the stairwell. "By the way, you didn't let me tell you. I may not have gotten to the prenup or insurance policy, but I did ask Dr. Grace about the ring under the couch. It wasn't Jonathan's. His ring doesn't have an inscription."

Patrick opened the door for me. "Something's been bugging me about the interview though. Dr. Grace said she never met Tammy or Bobby Hildabrand. Yet, when he railed on her in front of the elevators, she knew his name. If they've never met, how did she recognize him?"

"Are you kidding me?"

"What? It's a valid question."

"Bobby is a little mini-me of Jonathan Grace."

"I guess." Patrick shrugged his shoulders. "I just think it's pretty suspicious both our prime suspects happen to be in the precinct at the same time and happen to run into each other on the way out of the building."

"Oh," I said, mocking Patrick. "I think I smell a conspiracy. Dr. Grace is actually having a lurid love affair with Bobby Hildabrand. She convinced him to knock off Jonathan so they could finally be together, five million dollars richer. They're geniuses, throwing us off their trail by making us think Bobby hates her. You figured it out, Sherlock."

"Very funny."

"So . . . are we going to talk about what happened tonight at your house?" This time I opened the door for him.

"It's a lovely evening, don't you think? A little on the warm side but still nice." Patrick looked up in the dark night sky and sucked in a deep breath.

"Don't change the subject."

"There's nothing to change. We're not discussing anything."

We were silent as we reached 7th Avenue. The neon lights covering Centro Ybor lit up the night. I looked down and noticed the sidewalk pavers below our feet. Tiny hexagons engraved with messages from loved ones. Ybor's "Walk of Fame" for the average Joe willing to shell out eighty bucks for a lifelong sentiment.

"Where's the paver you dedicated to Alina?"

Patrick grumbled something under his breath, obviously not wanting to let go of his anger yet. It didn't matter. I knew it was only a block away. I'd brought it up in hopes of reminding Patrick of the love he had for his wife. Memories of when they were first married.

When we reached his paver, I stopped walking. The crowd behind us split apart, moving around us. I read the words decorating the paver aloud. "'Alina Mendoza, will you marry me? Love always, Patrick.' This is where you proposed, isn't it?"

"Why are you doing this?"

"Dammit, Patrick. Why can't you see what a good thing you've got with your family? Yes, it might be difficult, but you cut back. Fewer gymnastics class, not as many Christmas presents, but you make it work. The kids won't suffer. As long as they're loved by both parents, living in a happy home, they'll be fine."

"Kate—"

"No! You don't know how good you've got it, buddy. You're ready to ruin it all just because life's not going the way you planned. Don't you know I'd give my right arm to feel half the love you're surrounded with every day!"

Patrick looked away. We started walking again, both of us quiet, lost in our own thoughts. Love. Only four little letters, but a word layered with so many expectations. I yearned for it, yet was frightened to death of the feeling. For me, love had always come with strings attached. As a young girl, I quickly learned how to play the game—you've got to give a little to get a little.

I still didn't know the rules of a healthy relationship, much less know how to play in one. A relationship where love is given freely without a hidden agenda. Carlos's love felt different from anything I'd ever experienced before. It filled me with uncertainty, made me uncomfortable. I always felt slightly off kilter when I was around him. Like standing inside a kaleidoscope where the view kept changing.

For months, my heart had been pleading with my mind, hoping to persuade it to let me accept what Carlos had to offer. To try out a real relationship and see where it would lead. I don't know what it would take to finally allow myself to let go of control, to free fall into love. I offered up a silent prayer to a god that had never answered me before, hoping this time he'd respond.

"Patrick, how's it hanging?"

I looked back over my shoulder. Patrick had stopped walking to talk to . . . Cher?

Patrick laughed. "Long and to the left. How about you?"

"Tucked in high and tight," Cher said with a signature whip of a curly, black wig.

Patrick clapped the man on the shoulder. "Tell my cousin I said hello when you see him later tonight."

Cher said he would and the two parted ways.

I waited for Patrick to catch up. "How is Keith doing?" I asked. "Is your cousin still impersonating Barbra Streisand at Cheeseburger Sally's?"

"Yep. Belts out *Memories* five nights a week."

CHAPTER 20

We arrived at the Sext Club a little before 11 pm. The only indication of the debauchery housed inside was a golden placard with the name of the club written in an ornate font. The place was located a few streets away from the main drag in a nondescript red brick building.

Patrick fidgeted with the front of his shirt. "You ready?"

"Of course." I grabbed his hand. "Just remember we're a couple. Pretend like you're not mad at all women right now."

The door to the building opened up to an opulent waiting area. Deep reds and dark woods filled the room. Smoky glass doors separated us from the sights and sounds of rest of the club. Patrick and I walked by two couples seated at tables filling out paperwork. One of the couples started arguing. The woman punched the man with a hard right to his shoulder then walked out.

Behind the counter, a raven-haired beauty smiled at us. "Welcome. I'll be with you two in a moment." Her gaze lingered a little longer on Patrick, and then she turned her attention back to the two women holding hands standing in front of her.

While we waited, I leaned into Patrick, acting like I was playfully talking dirty into his ear. "Look up. In the corner over the greeter's head." A camera was expertly camouflaged inside the frame of an ornate mirror. I'd only noticed it because of the slight movement out of the corner of my eye. I'm sure if the patrons knew they were being videotaped, most wouldn't come.

Patrick snuggled into my neck. "What'd you say?"

I swallowed a sigh, instead giggling to mask a whisper repeating what I'd seen.

"How may I help you?" the woman asked us.

"I believe my good friend Lauren Tyler called on our behalf," I answered.

"Yes, Ms. Tyler. Will she be joining you tonight?"

"Hopefully. Lauren said she'd try to make it here a little later. In the meantime, she said you'd take good care of us. Gina, isn't it?"

The young lady flashed a brilliant smile. "Of course. First, I'll need you both to fill out some paperwork. Afterwards, I'll explain our handheld devices."

Patrick and I sat at the recently vacated table. We each had a clipboard with a three-sheet questionnaire. We planned on filling out the forms using an alias created for us on another case. Mr. and Mrs. Reed. If they ran a background check on us while we were at the club, it wouldn't raise any red flags. Kate and Patrick Reed were two married folks from Dunedin, Florida. No kids, but they raked in a combined income of $650,000 a year.

"This is going to be more difficult than I thought, considering the eyes in the sky," Patrick said softly.

"Remember that. You need to lighten up. Every time I look over at you, there's a scowl on your face. We're shooting for old married couple looking to spice up the love life not scorned lovers looking to step out on one another."

"Right. I think that's the answer to question number nine. Have you read these yet?" Patrick blushed. "I'm no Puritan but some of this stuff is . . . not appropriate to discuss outside the confines of the bedroom."

"You mean fantasizing about masturbating in public isn't a topic for discussion in Sunday school?"

Patrick laughed. "No, but if it were, I bet there'd be more converts."

Once we'd completed the questionnaires, Gina handed us two electronic devices similar to high-tech e-readers. She gave us a demonstration using the one in Patrick's hand.

"I don't know how much Ms. Tyler told you, so let me give you the basics. First, choose your avatar," she told Patrick. "This will be the electronic version of you that all of our patrons will see and interact with. Make it look like you or have fun with it. Become the character of your dreams." After a few selections of hair color and clothing choice, a cartoon-like James Bond character popped up on the screen.

"Devilishly handsome." Gina caressed Patrick's hand with her finger. I had to bite my tongue. My first instinct was to tease Patrick about flirting with the help, but it wouldn't do to play the jealous wife. Not here. Though the Sext Club catered to exhibitionists and voyeurs, it was better known for swinging.

Still, I couldn't help myself. I seductively touched her hand with my own. "Any suggestions for me?"

Gina tensed slightly. "Try choosing a completely different look. Half the fun is trying to figure out who is who."

"Honey?" I told Patrick. "You pick. Now's your chance to make me into the woman you've always wanted."

Patrick made his choices on the touch pad and a cartoon representation of his wife appeared. Definitely a loyal Labrador.

"Gina, my husband and I are very guarded with our privacy. How secure are the chats with the other folks in the club?"

"You have nothing to worry about, Mrs. Reed. Everything's internal. The devices won't work outside the club. Once the chat reaches the top of the screen and disappears, you can't scroll back to read it again. The copy's been wiped clean. "

"And video?"

Gina swiped Patrick's new credit card. "We require all our members to leave their cell phones at the desk. Don't worry, you'll get them back once you leave. It's only a precaution. We don't want anyone taking pictures or videotaping what happens inside."

It wasn't the members I worried about. She had deftly sidestepped my question. If the club videotaped its members, I wouldn't be surprised if they also recorded all the chat logs.

"I can tell you're nervous, Mrs. Reed. It's okay. First time jitters, I completely understand. But let me assure you, once you step through those doors, you'll be among like-minded people. People who don't judge, people who like . . . experimenting."

"You're right, I'm being silly. Patrick, dear, are you ready?"

He nodded, linking his arm with mine.

Gina opened the doors to the inner sanctum of the club. "Welcome to Eden. A playground to fulfill your every fantasy."

I closed my eyes, internally shoring up my confidence. Once I felt Patrick lead me through the doors, I opened my eyes expecting to be greeted by naked bodies writhing on top of one another. Instead, I was shocked at the tameness of the room.

This wasn't your average nudie bar found along the blue-collar industrial corridor of Route 60. No fat, middle-aged men creaming their pants as half-naked women showered them with attention. No frat boys in their cut-off shorts and sandals, whooping it up during a bachelor party. This upscale clientele wore designer label and sipped champagne from crystal flutes. Here couples stretched out on oversized couches, most looking down, typing on their handheld devices. Others stood near the bar. A massive structure that looked like it was plucked right out of an old western movie.

"Where are the naked bodies?" Patrick asked.

"Maybe this is a kind of holding area. Foreplay if you will."

"Let's sit over there and strike up a conversation with the others."

Patrick and I found a loveseat for two, and I snuggled in against his chest. Immediately, our devices pinged. We were both asked to join separate private chat rooms.

"The vultures are circling," Patrick said.

"Fresh meat."

"Decline their request. We need to put out some content for the whole club. See if we can hook up with someone who's met Jonathan Grace, get a nonbiased insider's point of view."

Our avatars continued to chat back and forth with other couples. From time to time, I would look over at Patrick's conversation. His sexting was a little too tame to garner much attention, but I took advantage of the situation, exchanging raunchy banter with four strangers probably sitting in this very room.

I laughed, wondering who hid behind the moniker, *sexycowboy21*. "This is like a virtual orgy room, Patrick."

"At least dirty talk is one of *your* fortes."

While sexting, I'd noticed many of the couples heading to the opposite end of the room. From here it looked like a wall blocked their way, but no one had ever come back. They must have disappeared somewhere.

"Come on, Patrick. This isn't getting us anywhere. Let's go check out the rest of the club."

More cameras were expertly hidden around the room camouflaged inside various wall hangings. Unless someone searched for them, they'd go unnoticed.

I squeezed Patrick's hand, nodding my head at the lady who walked by us. "Have you noticed the single ladies initiating contact with the couples?"

"What do you mean?" he whispered.

"Everyone here is gorgeous. I mean hell, money buys a lot of lipo, but look at her." I stared into the corner where a tall blonde with wavy hair, cascading down the middle of her back, laughed at something another woman had said. "She's supermodel gorgeous. Don't you find it odd all these beautiful women are here by themselves?"

Patrick fussed with the collar of his shirt. "This club definitely attracts a rich crowd."

When we reached the end of the room, I saw a hidden exit. To the right, tucked in at an odd angle, were stairs heading up to another level. At the top, Patrick and I had to maneuver around a large, muscular man wearing a tight t-shirt proclaiming his job as security. We'd seen his look-alike down on the first floor. These beefcakes were probably stationed around the club in case encounters got out of hand.

A long hallway shot across in front of us, about sixty feet. Couples stood outside rooms on both sides of the hallway, gazing through windows at the carnal activities happening inside. As the mesmerized couples watched, they grinded their bodies against each other, ignoring the clothing that acted like an unwelcomed barrier.

The doors to the first two rooms were shut and the blinds were closed, ensuring a modicum of privacy. The next room encouraged viewing with a nearly floor-to-ceiling sized glass window. Inside, bodies entwined together like a multi-colored snake. I couldn't tell where one person began and another ended. A sign on the door read, JOIN AT YOUR LEISURE. THE MORE THE MERRIER.

"Here are your naked bodies," I whispered to Patrick.

He wiped the sweat from his brow. "Oh, my."

An early twenty-something couple saddled up beside Patrick. The woman was firmly pushed against the front of her partner's body.

"Would you like to join us inside?" the man asked Patrick, a mischievous smirk on his face.

Patrick coughed. "Thank you for the offer, but I'm the voyeur of the couple."

I don't know if that made me the exhibitionist, but when the man looked over at me, I nixed the idea with one look.

"Vanilla, huh? Well, come back and find us when you're ready for Rocky Road."

The couple laughed, leaving the hallway behind.

"Somehow I don't think he's referring to ice cream," I whispered to Patrick. I hooked my arm through his, leading him past another closed door until we came upon a dungeon-themed room.

"You can't even hear the crack of the whip," Patrick marveled.

When my partner started tapping his toe, obviously in concern for the bound and gagged man inside the room, I tried cutting the tension. "Did you know Komodo dragons have two penises?"

"What?" Patrick stared at me, confusion masking his face.

"And a pig's orgasm lasts thirty minutes."

Patrick let out a belly laugh, his anxiety seeming to ease. The hallway watchers turned facing us. I mouthed a "sorry," and they went back to their viewing pleasures.

"Let me guess. Lucy?"

I nodded. "You don't even want to know how researchers calculated the length of the pig's mating session."

"Let's keep going. We're not accomplishing anything standing around here ogling."

At the end of the hallway, another set of stairs led to the third floor. At the top, multicolored strobe lights chased each other along the wall. Couples looked animalistic on the dance floor, crushing their bodies into each other. Patrick and I stood in the periphery, hands firmly locked together, soaking up the sights around us. A stunning redhead glided over to us. She towered high above me in dangerously tall stiletto heels.

"Mr. and Mrs. Reed, are you enjoying your first visit to our club?"

"Definitely," I said.

"We're just trying to take it all in," Patrick added.

"You're not partaking in any of the festivities?" She balanced a delicate china plate on the palm of her hand. It held a variety of tasty morsels.

"We wanted to take a look at everything first then decide what to partake in. Oh, look Patrick, sushi." I made sure to emphasize the last word.

Patrick gave my hand a quick squeeze of acknowledgment. "Wonderful. We'll be sure and get some."

"The kitchen staff can fix anything your heart desires, Mrs. Reed. For now though, I think you've seen almost everything we have to offer."

"Almost?" I asked.

"If you know the right people, you'll find hidden treasures around every door. Fortunately for you, I'm that special someone." The woman's beauty mark stretched up as a wide smile spread across her face. "Tell me, what's your pleasure?"

"Well," I said, making a show of looking around, "we were waiting for my friend Lauren Tyler, but I'm afraid she's been detained longer than expected. Do you know Lauren? She and Jonathan Grace always gush about this place. They finally wore us down and now, here we are."

The woman's top lip twitched, but her smile never faltered. "Yes, I've had the pleasure of their company before."

"Really? I'm sorry, what was your name?"

"Peyton. Peyton Posey."

"Beautiful name, Peyton. Can I let you in on a little secret? My husband's always been enamored of redheads. He's much too shy to ask, but would you be willing to go somewhere . . . more private?"

Peyton flipped her straight hair away from her shoulders. "I thought you'd never ask." She slipped her well-manicured hand into Patrick's and led us to a hidden room off to the left. It was so expertly concealed by the décor, I hadn't even noticed it. Before I had a chance to latch the door closed, a deep laugh carried across the room. I knew that sound. Intimately.

"Carlos?"

CHAPTER 21

I told Patrick to start without me then stomped over to Carlos Diaz. A curvy blonde sat in his lap, her hands stroking his broad chest, her lips nibbling on his neck. My feisty attitude morphed into fury.

"What the hell are you doing here, Carlos?"

"Kate?"

The logical part of my brain, the part barely able to push through the noise of the cursing in my head reminded me the walls had ears. I couldn't blow my cover no matter how jealous I felt of the skank hanging all over my man.

Carlos stood and whispered something into the woman's ear. She gave me a sad, pathetic smile. Her pity only stoked the white hot embers of my anger. Carlos turned me around, placed his hands on my hips, and pushed me over to a secluded corner of the room. When we reached the long sectional, he made a bold move, picking me up and sitting me in his lap to face him. He moved my head close to his so I could hear his whispers.

"This place is bugged," he said. "The pounding bass will help muffle our conversation, but keep your voice down. And don't bite my ear off."

"What are you doing here?" I said, practically hissing the words.

"I could ask the same of you."

"I'm undercover."

"Me too," Carlos whispered.

"Yeah, right. You saw me with Patrick. You know I'm not here for the scenery. But you . . . you're on the couch, making out with some blonde bimbette."

"If I would have known jealousy was the way to remind you of your feelings for me, I would have tried it earlier. No, seriously Kate, you have nothing to worry about." Carlos ran his hands up my back and gave me a reassuring squeeze. "Rhonda is my editor at the *Tampa Tribune.* We're running an exposé on this place in next week's paper."

"What!" I leaned back, looking him in the face. "You can't."

"And why not?"

"You just can't."

"You're going to have to do better than that." He gently guided my head back down on his shoulder.

"Fine." I exhaled in a rush of air, causing goose-bumps to form on Carlos's neck. "I'm investigating a case with ties to this club. If you start broadcasting all of its dirty little secrets, those involved might get spooked. I won't let you screw up my case, Diaz."

"Hmm. I might be able to push it off for a few weeks. Claim the need for more research. Depends on how important it is to you."

I sat up again, shaking my head. The blackmail infuriated me, but I couldn't help admire his persistence. I felt my resolve soften.

"Name it," I dared.

"No, not here. I'll get back to you. Right now you need to get in there and save your partner." Carlos cocked his head over toward the room Peyton had led Patrick into. "That woman will devour him whole."

"I'll be calling you tomorrow. You can count on it. Plan on telling me everything I want to know about this place." The faint scent of his cologne lingered like a long hug that made me want to nestle in deeper.

I had to force my body to extricate itself from his.

"Yes, ma'am."

I ignored the pinch Carlos gave my ass when I turned to leave but couldn't help contain the smile it brought to my face.

I opened the door to the room my partner had entered earlier and stood at its threshold. Patrick sat on a suede couch, shirt unbuttoned. Peyton had kneeled on the floor in front of him, stroking his thighs. I took a deep breath, gathering the racing thoughts focused on Carlos and shoved them into my mental box. *Focus, Springer.*

Patrick's round eyes pled silently for help.

"You started without me, Patrick."

"Honey, you're back."

"Don't worry, Mrs. Reed," Peyton said in a disappointed tone. "All your husband seems to want to do is talk."

"You should see him in the bedroom. I can't get him to shut up."

Patrick stood, buttoning his shirt on the way over to my side. I put an arm around his shoulders. His body trembled. I knew it was time to wrap up this one-on-one session.

"Bad news, dear. I got a text from Lauren. She asked us to meet her over at Suncatchers. We need to jet."

"Oh, so soon. What a shame."

Patrick about knocked me over on his way out the door. I made our apologies to Peyton, then went and found Patrick standing at the bar across from the dance floor.

I gave him a wink. "Have fun?"

He shot me a cold look. "I haven't had a woman, other than my wife, touch me in fifteen years. I take my marriage vows very seriously, Kate. You know that."

"Then quit your crying about the new baby. Did you find out anything useful while Peyton tried seducing you?"

"Not much." Patrick downed another shot of amber liquid. "I couldn't tip my hand by grilling her. By the way, thanks for leaving me in there all alone with that jackal. You're supposed to be my wingman, remember?"

"Sorry." I motioned for the bartender to set up a round for both of us. "Carlos Diaz was here with some blond bimbo straddling him. Guess I saw red."

"I thought you dumped him."

"I did." I grimaced at the burn trailing down my throat. "Let's get out of here."

Back down on the first floor, we turned in our handheld devices at the reception area. A door from behind the counter opened. Out stepped Mr. GQ complete in his perfectly tailored pinstripe suit. His dark hair was styled in a short pompadour and a dimple on his right cheek appeared when he smiled. "Mr. and Mrs. Reed?"

"Sorry, we were just leaving," I said.

"Didn't you enjoy yourselves at the club?" the man asked.

"Yes, we had a wonderful time," I answered.

"Because if you didn't find what you were looking for, we could always talk about a more . . . private experience. I'm Rob Whitington, owner of the club." He extended his hand only to Patrick.

At first glance, this man looked like he worked in the stock market, not the sex trade. He was all pressed shirts, lots of starch, trying to carve out an image classier than his profession normally allowed.

I looked at Patrick. "Darling, I know we need to meet up with Lauren, but Mr. Whitington has me intrigued. Can't we stay a minute longer?"

"Anything for you." Patrick gave me a smooch on the cheek. It probably looked more like what a brother would give his sister, but as rattled as Patrick was at this moment, I had to give him props. Maybe the drinks he'd consumed had given him a bit of liquid courage.

"Hey, babe," Whitington said getting Gina's attention. "Go get us some champagne."

Gina gave a slight eye roll then noticed me watching her. She seemed worried at getting caught disrespecting her boss. She smiled hesitantly and briskly walked away.

"Follow me." Whitington led us into his inner sanctum, a small but elegant office. It had plush deep-green carpeting, a dark mahogany desk, and matching antique wingbacked chairs. On the opposite side of the room, another door remained closed. It was probably where the bank of television sets played a continuous loop of the members' escapades. A real pervert's dream come true.

"A private experience?" I asked after we were all seated.

"Yes. I believe holding in our fantasies, not allowing ourselves to live them out, stunts us emotionally. Mr. Reed, there has to be one or two fantasies you've held close to the vest. Afraid you'll be judged. Well, I'm here to tell you, at the Sext Club you have no need to worry. This is a judgment free zone."

While Whitington gave us the hard sell, he spoke directly to Patrick. The man directed all his comments to my partner, even though Patrick had never engaged him in conversation. It showed a lack of respect for women. Whitington may have appeared charming at first, but slowly his true colors began leaking out. Turns out he was just a sleazy car salesman selling fantasies instead of broken down Chevettes.

"Mr. Reed, is there something you've always wanted to try sexually? Something you've either never had the opportunity to indulge in or were too afraid to ask for?"

When Patrick remained silent, I decided to speak up and show how I was the eager wife willing to serve her husband in any way he wanted. I knew a submissive wife would loosen Whitington's tongue more than a dominant one.

"Yes, dear. Tell us. You know how I love to indulge your fantasies. Is there anything we haven't done you've been hesitant to share with me?"

"Don't worry, Mr. Reed, most of the time the fantasies men have . . . well they think they're pretty hard core, when in truth, they're very tame. No matter what's on your mind, I'm sure I've heard it before."

"There is one thing." Patrick hesitated. "Kate, I discussed it with Jonathan once. I'm talking about Jonathan Grace, Mr. Whitington. We're close friends. Anyway, I discovered we share a fantasy. I like to watch women in pain. I don't want to be the one inflicting it, just watching from the sidelines."

Nice move, Patrick. He'd also picked up on Whitington's disdain for women and created a fantasy that would hopefully endear him to the club owner.

"Jonathan's the reason we're here tonight," Patrick continued. "He told me you were the man who could make my fantasy happen. My wife and I got back from a working vacation in Belgium a few days ago, and this is the first we've been able to check out the place for ourselves."

Whitington's expression made me uneasy. Since the moment Patrick had mentioned Jonathan Grace, Whitington's demeanor had changed. His posture became more rigid, his jaw tightened. Maybe he already knew about Jonathan's death. If so, hopefully he bought Patrick's excuse for our ignorance of the murder.

"Mr. Grace is correct," Whitington said. "I can make that happen. But this scenario will take a little bit of time to put together. I want to make sure all the details are just right. Will Mrs. Reed be participating?"

I looked at Patrick.

"No," he said, "but can you get someone who looks like her?"

"Of course. Now let's talk about payment."

I leaned in closer to Whitington's desk. "If it's only a matter of money, that's the easy part. What my husband wants, he gets."

Rob Whitington flashed a wide smile. "Wonderful. I'll be in touch."

On our way out of the club, Gina finally showed up with the champagne. I looked back over my shoulder and saw Whitington jerk her arm, causing her body to stumble closer to him. She barely kept her fragile items balanced on the tray. Anger rolled off Whitington liked waves as he cursed at her. Even from across the room, I could see the defeat in Gina's eyes.

SUNDAY

CHAPTER 22

I slammed the snooze button on the blaring alarm clock. Another ten minutes is all I needed.

Buzz. Buzz.

Dammit!

I picked up my phone and read the incoming text: CHARLES DUMPED ME.

Shit! With the late night, I'd completely forgotten about my threat against Lucy's boyfriend. I texted her back the message, COME OVER.

Patrick and I had agreed that after all our hard work at the Sext Club last night, we deserved a little extra sleep this morning. But I'd forgotten to turn off my alarm. Now it was 7 am and five measly hours of sleep wasn't enough. My head ached and my body yearned for a nice hot shower. Maybe I could sneak one in before Lucy arrived.

A knock on the door announced another interruption. *Guess not.* I opened the door and found Lucy standing on the porch, puffy red eyes under smeared glasses. A clump of tangled hair stuck up on the crown of her head.

"Lucy, if you were already here, why did you bother texting?" I moved out of the way allowing her to come inside. She put her coffee cup on the table.

"I knew you had a late night. I didn't want to wake you but . . ." Lucy couldn't continue. She broke down into body wrenching sobs. Her shoulders jerked with every breath. I pulled her into my arms, holding her until the tsunami wave of emotion carried itself back out to sea.

"Come sit down." I pulled her over to the couch. "Tell me what happened."

"I don't want to . . . I don't want to . . ." Hiccups interrupted her sentences. Lucy took a few deep breaths then continued. "I don't want to keep you. I'm sure you're itching to get back to your case."

"Don't be silly. I always have time for my best friend. What happened?"

"Last night, I met Charles for dinner at Bern's. I thought the evening had some serious potential for romance. Boy was I wrong. From the moment I saw him, I knew something was wrong. Charles always lights up when I enter the room, but when I got there, he was sitting at the table with his shoulders slumped and the twinkle in his eye extinguished."

Frank jumped into Lucy's lap, instinctively knowing she needed soothing. She absently stroked her fur. "I thought maybe one of Charles's patients had died, a dog involved in a hit and run, but work wasn't the reason for his dour mood. I was. He broke into the, 'it's not you, it's me' speech. What did I do, Kate? Why did he dump me?"

This time silent tears rolled down Lucy's face. I wondered if I'd made the right move. The way she'd described Chuck made him seem like he genuinely cared about Lucy. Guilt strummed its sad song, plucking at my conscience-stricken heart.

No! I couldn't second guess myself. Wife beaters were master manipulators, sucking women in until they were completely brainwashed and unwilling to leave their abusive relationships. I couldn't let my best friend fall into that trap. Sure Chuck was charming now. It was part of the lure. But Lucy had lived through enough heartache in her life. She and I were kindred spirits in that way, each living through our own horrific childhood.

When Lucy was ten, her little sister had been abducted from their parent's farmhouse. Less than twenty-four hours later, Lucy's dad found the body discarded in a ditch near the property. A jury handed down a fifty-year sentence to a farmhand who'd drifted into town looking for seasonal work. Forensic evidence convicted the killer. The investigation, the trial, they were the seeds setting Lucy on her future career path.

So I refused to let Lucy be played. I would see her through the pain of this breakup. In a few weeks, her heart would heal.

***

After a couple of hours soothing Lucy, I watched her cry herself to sleep on my couch. Poor girl said she'd been up all night bawling. I took a quick shower then jotted down a note telling her we'd pick up where we left off later that evening. A couple of tear jerkers on TV, some popcorn, and lots of ice cream. In the meantime, Frank would keep an eye on her.

Patrick had called earlier asking about a ride. I explained the situation with Lucy, and he begrudgingly agreed to ask his wife for a ride downtown before all the girls headed to church. I brought in a couple of jumbo-sized muffins with me to the squad room to say thanks.

"I'll take the blueberry one," Patrick said.

Only one other detective was in the room besides us. He gave me a quick nod then went back to his phone conversation. I sat down, unpacked breakfast, and handed Patrick's favorite to him. "Did you assuage your guilt by telling Alina what happened last night?"

"No. The only thing greeting me when I got home was a pillow and blanket sitting on the couch."

"Ouch."

"You said it. I don't know what she's pissed about. She's the one who went behind my back and told the girls she's pregnant. We still haven't had a chance to talk about it. Looks like I have a fun conversation ahead of me tonight." Patrick grumbled, yanking off a crumbly piece of his muffin.

I thought pregnant women were the hormonal, bitchy ones. I hoped I didn't have to put up with this attitude for six more months.

"I know things are tough at home, Patrick, but I want to thank you for coming in today. You didn't have to."

Patrick shrugged. "No problem. I know you want to get this case solved as quickly as possible."

I nodded at the understatement. "What have you been working on?"

"I gave Dr. Grace's receptionist, Donna Milhouse, a call this morning. She wasn't too happy to hear from me on a Sunday morning, but I confirmed Dr. Grace went home early the day of her husband's murder. Dr. Grace asked Donna to cancel her afternoon appointments due to a migraine. Her two o'clock was already sitting in the waiting room and had to be rescheduled. When I pushed Donna about Dr. Grace's attitude during the weeks leading up to her husband's death, Donna tried to sidestep the question. She finally conceded Dr. Grace had been on edge with the worst of it on the morning of the murder. Donna said her boss had come in wired and very jumpy."

"Hmm." I balled up the muffin wrapper, lost in thought.

"Is that all you have to say?"

I crossed my arms. "What do you want me to say? How about, 'Wow you cracked the case wide open. Good job, you proved Dr. Grace is the killer.'"

Patrick smiled. "Sounds pretty good to me."

"Smartass. What have you got there?" I pointed at the file in front of him.

"The ME's final report."

"On a Sunday?"

"Ellis wants to get caught up on the backlog before he goes on vacation."

"Right, the Galapagos Islands."

Patrick handed me the report. I took a few minutes to read the findings while he cleaned up his breakfast and grabbed another cup of coffee from the pot across the room.

"Nothing much new here," I said when he got back. "Although, Ellis surmised the large contusion to the back of Grace's head was administered with the smaller end of a mag light. The bruising shows the killer hit Jonathan in a downward arc. The light impacted his head almost dead center in the top part of his head." Possible scenarios rushed through my mind. "What if the initial blow came from the mag light?"

Patrick thought about it for a moment. "Killer's waiting for Grace in his den. Grace arrives and gets smacked on the back of the head when he walks through the door, rendering him unconscious while the killer binds Grace to the chair."

I looked down at the report. "It says here, Jonathan was 6'1"."

Patrick held his coffee cup in one hand while making lazy circles with a red stirrer in the other. "What about it?"

"Bear with me. How tall do you think Dr. Grace is?" I raised my hand to my brow line to estimate her height.

"Slightly shorter than you, probably 5'7"," Patrick estimated.

"That means the killer had to be as tall as or taller than Jonathan. Dr. Grace is too short."

"Wait up, Kate. That proves nothing. The blow to the head could have come after the killer bound Jonathan to the chair. And even if the mag light provided the initial blow, it only proves Dr. Grace didn't kill her husband with her own two hands. She still could have hired the person who did."

"But look at our suspect pool," I said, refusing to let it go. "Lauren Tyler's pushing six feet, and you can't count out Bobby Hildabrand.

We'll have to ask Wozniack about Owen Mitchell, the hater from Defenders of the Earth."

"Okay, okay." Patrick put down his #1 Dad mug on his desk. "Let's table this for now but—"

When I tried to interrupt, Patrick continued speaking over me. "—but we'll continue to keep *all* suspects front and center."

"Fine," I conceded. "Speaking of Wozniack, have you heard back from him? Let me guess, he decided to stay an extra night in Orlando so he could ride Space Mountain."

"He hasn't called me."

"Well you know he won't call me." I laughed. "The big baby's still holding a grudge. After ratting me out to the newspaper last year, the payback wasn't nearly what he deserved."

"Not in your eyes, but when Mr. Wee Willie Winkie is exposed in public, it can scar a man."

"Do you call yours Mr. Winkie for short?"

"Ha, ha."

"Can I see the photographs of the body?"

Patrick handed me the prints. "I wonder if Jonathan will test positive for narcotics."

"Won't know for a couple of weeks, not until we get FDLE's findings back."

"Besides the tox screen, we're also waiting on analysis of a bunch of items—all the clothing, hair and fiber samples found on the body, and the spit collected from Jonathan's cheek. What else?"

"The ring," I answered absently, still leafing through the photos.

"Right, the ring belonging to Snookums. Maybe the lab will find skin cells on it and match it to the spit, proving the same person who killed Jonathan owned the ring."

"That's a long list of what we still don't know."

"Yeah, it would make our job a hell of a lot easier if we didn't have to wait three weeks for the results. If one of the hairs discovered on the body had a root intact, we could at least narrow down race and sex of the killer."

"When do you think we'll have the report from our own forensics team?" Patrick took another drink of his coffee.

"Definitely won't be today. Lucy's sleeping off a long night on my couch. I'll sweet talk her tonight, but it still might be a while. Her team had to do a lot of reconstruction since the EMTs destroyed the crime scene."

"Then what's the game plan?"

"I want to interview Jonathan Grace's business rivals today. Catch them off guard in their home enjoying a leisurely Sunday afternoon. They might be more forthcoming if they're not sitting on their office thrones."

"Sounds good," Patrick said. "Since I'm stuck with no car, I'll hang out here. I'm going to finish tracking down the phone numbers on Jonathan Grace's cell. I also need to check in with Wozniack."

"Any luck getting the transcripts of the Graces' text messages?"

Patrick sighed. "Not yet, but the cell phone company promised I'd get them tomorrow. We did get the reports back from Intelligence Bureau on the contents of Jonathan Grace's two computers. The one at the house and the other from his office."

"Sounds like a fun day."

"Speaking of fun, are you going to call Carlos Diaz?"

I groaned.

"You may not like it, Kate, but if he's been undercover at the club, Carlos could provide details we wouldn't get any other way. Just knowing more about the players involved would be beneficial. It looks like the club was a major part of Jonathan's life. At least according to his financial records and what Lauren Tyler told us."

I tapped my pen on the desk, thinking out loud. "There's a chunk of time the night of the murder still unaccounted for. The time from when Jonathan left Jamar Washington in Orlando to when he arrived home.

Approximately an hour if you subtract driving time."

"We know Jonathan ate sushi for his last meal, a food they served at the Sext Club. My money says he was there during the missing time. At least some of it."

I nodded.

"I know that look, Kate. What's on your mind?"

"Maybe we've got it all wrong. What if Jonathan brought his killer home with him from the club? Could be the reason there's no forced entry. What if—"

My cell phone rang. I raised my hand, pausing the conversation.

"Springer."

"Kate, this is Carlos."

"Speak of the devil."

"Meet me outside. We're having lunch."

"It's not even 11 am."

"Fine then, brunch," Carlos corrected.

"Why?"

"You said you wanted information on the Sext Club. If I'm going to tell you what I know, it's going to be on my terms. Outside in ten minutes."

Carlos hung up.

"Where are you going?" Patrick asked me as I stood up and pushed my chair under my desk.

"Out on a wire with no net."

CHAPTER 23

"You do know it's the middle of July, right?"

Carlos sat on a blanket under a shady oak tree in the middle of the plaza. He held out a plate of food like a peace offering, flashing a boyish grin.

"It's why we're having lunch early."

Each plate was layered with all the fixings for a mid-morning picnic. I told my traitorous stomach to shut up.

"Are you purposefully trying to embarrass me in front of my colleagues?" I stood looking down at him, hands on my hips. "Anyone working at One Police Plaza could look out the window and see me sitting here."

A hurt look crept into Carlos's eyes. He extinguished it quickly, playing it off well. "Tell them you were meeting with a confidential informant."

"Fine." I yanked the plate away and sat down beside him. He handed me a cup of lemonade. "But after this, we're even. You're not publishing the exposé article on the Sext Club until I give the go ahead."

"Oh, you are so mistaken." Carlos wagged his chicken drumstick back and forth like a finger telling me what for. "You wanted information on the club. This is you getting information on the club. I simply chose the forum in which I dispensed the details. I still have yet to decide what will be the payment for holding off on my story."

"You are wicked Carlos Diaz. To the core."

Carlos laughed. A sound like a soft pounding rain. A sound that threatened to melt my heart like butter.

"What tipped you off to the club?" I asked gruffly.

"Three weeks ago, I received a letter postmarked Dade City, Florida. It was written in the tone of guilty churchgoer seduced by the sins of the big city. This man had talked his wife into going to the Sext Club. They went once, participated in its offerings, and afterward felt guilty about it. As an act of repentance, the man felt it important to expose the club publically so others wouldn't fall prey to its lure. That's where I came in."

"Did he give his name, an address?"

"No, the letter was anonymous, and the envelope didn't have a return address."

"Chicken," I said, finishing off my macaroni salad. "Guess he wasn't too repentant. Didn't want his pew buddies seeing his name in print."

Carlos smiled. "The writer explained how the club owner hired gorgeous women to have sex with the patrons. These decoys would walk around, posing as fellow members, and entice people into having relations. The mythical unicorn."

"Unicorn?"

"It's the term swingers use for a single female, usually bisexual. She's quite the sought after being. Anyway, strategically placing women in this way is all an ingenious ploy to hook patrons into paying high monthly memberships."

"I see. Set the hook by letting the guy get a little taste of what could be, then reel in his pocketbook when he agrees to pay thousands of dollars in monthly fees. But why would one of these ladies let this slip? I saw how Rob Whitington treated his women. I can't imagine they'd want to cross him."

"The unicorn was trying to set up a list of clientele on the side, offering a cheaper rate." Carlos rubbed his greasy hands on a napkin.

"That's a dangerous game. Did the anonymous writer name the woman who made the offer?"

"He described her as having hair the color of the flames that would engulf his immortal soul into the fiery pit of damnation for all eternity."

"Ah, Peyton Posey."

"Yes. She approached Rhonda and me asking about a private get together."

"Did you take her up on her offer?" I asked, looking into my lap.

"Of course not." Carlos lifted my chin. Looking into his eyes, I could see the sincerity of his words. "It was our first night at the club. We feigned a vanilla attitude."

"Vanilla? I heard the term at the club last night."

"It's a word used for people who go to swinger clubs but don't swing."

"Well aren't you well-versed in all the terminology."

Carlos laughed. "Always be prepared," he said, adding in the Boy Scout salute.

I smirked thinking of Carlos as an enthusiastic, little nine-year-old racing cars in the Pinewood Derby. "Did you have the pleasure of meeting Rob Whitington?"

"You mean Mr. Male Chauvinist in the two thousand dollar suit?"

"That's him." When I spoke, a bit of food flew out of my mouth.

Carlos handed me his extra napkin, smiling. I hurriedly cleaned up my face, a blush spread across my cheeks. That's one of the things I liked about Carlos. Even at my worst, he didn't tease or hold my failings against me. The delight in his eyes never waned.

"Did you get the whole 'we're here to indulge in your every fantasy speech'?" Carlos asked.

"The exact one. Patrick and I could tell Whitington was a sexist pig, so Patrick played that angle, ingratiating himself to the club owner. We're waiting to hear back on our request."

"I'm sure the higher your bank account, the quicker you'll get a call." Carlos brought his cup up to his lips.

"I hope *your* fantasy didn't involve a donkey."

Carlos snorted. I think a little lemonade shot out his nose. I gave his back a few hard pats.

"No," he said. "No animals were involved. But I did take a rather unsavory angle. You know how bad sex trafficking has gotten in Tampa."

"Unfortunately. Florida is the number three hub in the United States just behind New York and California, with Tampa showing the most activity. You combine the seaman from the port and the truckers travelling along the long corridor of I-4 running from Tampa to Orlando, and you've got plenty of men willing to fork over money for young girls."

"I've written a few stories in the *Tribune* about the trafficking problem, but I hoped to tie Whitington and his club to some illegal operations. I told him my fantasies included young girls. The younger the better. I don't know if I spooked him or what, but he claimed the illegality of the request. Whitington told me he could get a girl who looked young, but she would definitely be of age. I kicked myself for pushing too hard too fast. I should have waited after we'd visited the club a few more times."

"How did you know they bugged the club?" I asked.

"When Rhonda and I sat talking to Whitington in his office, a man came out of a room. I think he expected to find an empty office. The door opened a little too far, and I saw a bank of television sets. I recognized the dance club area on one of the screens. Afterwards, I started searching for the hidden cameras."

"When Patrick and I were leaving the club, it looked like you and Rhonda were pretty chummy with another couple."

"We met those two the first night. They're swingers who live in a small town near Ocala. They've been driving over here twice a month for the last year. "

"Did they share any juicy gossip about the people who work at the club?"

"Not really. They were more interested in trying to talk us into checking out the rainbow room with them. I'm assuming all of these questions have to do with your new case. Jonathan Grace's murder."

I pursed my lips, felt the heat rise on my neck.

"Don't, Kate. I've freely given you every detail I've uncovered about the club without any expectation of a reciprocal agreement. You can't expect to keep me completely in the dark."

I remained quiet.

Carlos gently took my hands into his. "Listen. We need to set some ground rules if we ever expect to make a relationship work between a reporter and a detective."

I cocked an eyebrow in question. If *we* expect to have a relationship?

When I offered no verbal resistance at his proposal, Carlos kept talking. "I'm giving you my word. I will never use anything you say in one of my stories without your prior approval. I love my job, Kate, but I love you more. I want to make us work, and I will figure out a way our careers won't interfere with our relationship. Will you step out on a limb and trust me?"

Before I could allow myself to rest my entire weight on that branch, I decided to take a baby step to see how the tree held up. "Yes, all these questions are in relation to the Jonathan Grace murder. According to his financial records and a very reliable source, Grace frequented the club quite often."

Carlos gave my hands a squeeze. We both sat quietly, enjoying the moment of being together, of touching again.

Carlos furrowed his brow.

"What's wrong?" I asked.

"Do you have a picture of Jonathan Grace?"

"A picture?"

"Yes. Over the last couple of weeks, Rhonda and I have spent quite a few nights at the club. I may have seen him there."

I fumbled with my cell phone, trying to get my fingers to cooperate. "Here's a picture." I brought up the same photo from the article in *The Maddux Business Report*, the one I'd shown Patrick yesterday.

"I *have* seen him before."

"What?"

"Yes. He was pretty inebriated that night. Grace made a scene, yelling gibberish really. Something about fantasies turning into nightmares. Rob Whitington showed up with a couple of his security guys and escorted Grace out of the room. It only sticks out in my mind because Rhonda and I had arrived only moments before. When we got inside, Grace was already making a spectacle. I don't know what set him off."

"When was this?"

"Sometime Thursday night. I'd say between 10:30 and 11 pm. I remember Rhonda was running late because of an issue with a babysitter."

"You're kidding me?"

"No, why?"

"I haven't been able to definitively nail down Jonathan Grace's movements the night of his murder. What I know for sure is he travelled to Orlando for business then stopped for gas when he got back in town. After that, a credit card payment showed Jonathan went to the Blue Martini for drinks, but there's still over an hour of unaccounted time before his death. We didn't know if Jonathan went home after he left the bar or stopped somewhere else. We thought he might have stopped at the club but had no proof. Are you sure you saw Grace there Thursday night?"

"Positive."

"This is great news, Carlos."

"How do you mean?"

"Now I have a witness placing Grace at the Sext Club right before he was murdered. Grace made a scene and the last person to potentially see him alive was Rob Whitington."

"Slow down, Kate." Carlos squeezed my hands again, but I was too excited to keep them still. I sat up on my knees absently drumming my fingers against my legs. I ran through the possible scenarios in my head.

"Whitington just made my official suspect list. I wonder if Nina has ever met him. I'm going to have to talk to her—"

"Wait a minute." Carlos guided me back down onto the blanket. "Do you really think Nina is innocent?"

"Of course." I was confused Carlos would ask such a question.

"Why are you putting everything on the line for her?"

I sighed. "I don't have time for this, Carlos."

"Indulge me, please. I know how much your job means to you. The last thing I want is for your blind loyalty to bite you in the ass."

"You know the nightmarish childhood I endured. I never could shake the tight grip the past had on me. Not completely. It wasn't just a matter of mentally willing away the ugliness that had set up shop in my heart. Believe me, I tried. Nothing worked. Until Dr. Grace. For some unknown reason, I connected with her. She stopped the hellish internal soundtrack in my head. Before her, I was locked into a perpetual state of always waiting for the other shoe to drop. I could never enjoy the present moment. Do you know what that feels like?"

I shook my head, clearing the memories that had seized me. "I don't know how she did it, can't explain the transformation, I only know she changed me. I'm not saying I turned into a raving optimist, but there is a difference in me. Something like that, you don't forget it. The marines never leave a man behind. Neither do I."

I stood up, dusted my pants off. "I don't expect you to understand, but I do want to thank you for your help today."

"What—"

"I promise we'll talk soon. Right now, I need to give this case my complete attention, but after I've found the killer . . . who knows, maybe we can talk about giving our relationship another try."

CHAPTER 24

"Patrick, you're not going to believe what Carlos told me."

"He knows who shot JFK."

"Better." I sat down at my desk and looked around the eerily quiet squad room. Except for us, it was deserted.

"He knows the recipe to McDonald's Big Mac secret sauce."

"Really?"

"What?"

"Have you heard of Google?" I said. "Ten seconds on the computer, and I could find every ingredient in that recipe. Now are you done?"

"You started it."

I sighed. "Anyway . . . Carlos told me he saw Jonathan Grace at the Sext Club around 10:30 pm the night Grace died."

"You're shitting me."

"No." I relayed everything Carlos had told me about the club.

"It's all great information," Patrick said, "but it doesn't get us any closer to solving the case."

"At least we have another suspect to add to the list." I picked up a file folder off the desk and waved it in front of my face, trying to circulate the air to cool me off. A picnic in the middle of July. What was Carlos thinking?

"It won't help us get a warrant for Whitington's place," Patrick countered.

"No, but we could at least send Wozniack in to question the slime ball. Maybe rattle Whitington's cage a little. It'd also ensure our cover stayed intact."

"Speaking of Wozniack, he called while you were out. He met with Owen Mitchell over in Orlando yesterday."

"How'd that go?"

"Mitchell had a real hard-on for Jonathan Grace. Didn't even try to hide his anger at what he called the 'destruction of mother earth by corporate greed'."

"Did Mitchell change his tune after he found out about Grace's murder?"

"Nope." Patrick leaned back in his chair, cradling his head in the palms of his hands. "Woz said the guy almost creamed his pants when he found out. Mitchell's only response was, 'Karma's a real bitch.'"

"What a peach."

"Wozniack or Mitchell?"

"Both."

"Wozniack said Mitchell's been picked up in Orlando on a few misdemeanor charges for protesting, as well as breaking and entering. Each time he only got a slap on the wrist."

"Did Wozniack call the guy out on the hate mail?" I asked.

"Mitchell gave the excuse of just trying to get Grace's attention. Wozniack told me he got a weird vibe off Mitchell. He's staying close by today, poking around to see if anything shakes loose."

"Wozniack taking the initiative? Must be some serious kind of bad vibe."

Patrick laughed. "That's exactly what I thought."

I nodded over to the stack of papers sitting on the desk in front of Patrick. "Making any headway?"

"A little. While you were out having lunch," Patrick practically grumbled the last word, "I continued calling Jonathan Grace's cell contacts from the phone dump."

"Don't blame me if you haven't eaten. Go get some food."

"It's Sunday afternoon. All the good downtown restaurants are closed. It's not like I can jump in the car and grab something."

"You big baby." I picked up the phone and ordered delivery. "Happy now?"

Patrick smiled brightly, enough that both dimples appeared.

"Good," I said.

"While you were out, I called people who'd had phone conversations with Jonathan in the last month before his murder. I wanted to see if any of them were close friends. See if they could provide us with some insight into his last few weeks of life. So far, nothing's panned out, but I'll keep at it."

"Sounds good. Next up on my list is tracking down the men Dr. Grace thought might have held grudges against her husband." I dropped the file folder and started fanning my shirt up and down. "You sure you don't want to come along?"

"No, I'm not really in the mood. Think I'll stick around here for a few more hours."

I was thankful I'd be riding solo this afternoon. I wanted to talk to Nina privately and purposefully didn't tell Patrick. He'd already made his feelings known about my suggestion of having a secret meeting without her lawyer present. Hopefully, Nina's loyalty would ensure our conversation remained private. With Patrick's volatile mood, if he found out, it could cause irrevocable damage to our relationship.

"Do you need a ride home later?" I asked him.

"No. Alina said she and the girls would pick me up. Might as well face the music."

"Good luck with that."

***

"Hi, Dr. Grace. This is Detective Springer. I called to find out how you're holding up." I'd dialed Ana Lopez's number from the car, hoping to reach Nina to set up a meeting with her before I attacked the grudge list.

Nina cleared her throat. "I'm okay, I guess."

"I know this whole thing is . . . awkward. Yesterday with my partner in the interview room and your lawyer . . . well, I wanted you to know I'm sorry for your loss, and I think we should talk."

"Thank you, Kate. I know I seemed a mess yesterday. You and Detective Jessup must think the worst of me. I just can't help it. I can't seem to pull myself together."

"What you've been through, it's understandable. Give yourself a break, Dr. Grace. It's only been three days since you lost your husband."

"I know. I'll try."

"Are you staying at Ana Lopez's house?" I rubbed the gearshift's leather with my fingers.

"Yes. My family wants me to come back to Miami, but I'm not ready to deal with them yet. They mean well, but they're a bit too . . . smothering."

"You should have family around. Someone to lean on."

"Don't worry, I've got Ana, and no matter how hard I tried, I couldn't talk my brother out of coming up. After he takes care of a few loose ends with his business, he'll be here. Most likely midweek. The rest of the family will be here for the funeral."

"Would you mind if I come over to talk?"

"I don't think that would be a very good idea."

"Dr. Grace, you called me that night. Remember. You told me 'I think I killed my husband.' A fact I haven't disclosed to anyone. But if I'm going to stick my neck out for you, the least you could do is be candid with me."

"You want candid?" Nina's voice took on a hysterical edge. "I can't eat, I can't sleep. All I see when I close my eyes is blood. Red dripping blood everywhere. I'm supposed to be the strong one, the one everybody else comes to for answers. Don't you get it, Kate? I have no answers for you. I can't help you. I can't even help myself. I'm just . . . so . . . tired." Nina let out a sob. I thought more tears would follow, but she reigned in her emotions. "Do you know how embarrassing it is for people to see me as this pitifully weak woman? You don't need to stick your neck out for me. I don't care what happens anymore."

"That's not true, Dr. Grace. It's the depression talking. You've been through a horrifying event, and you need to talk to someone."

"Ha," Nina cackled. "How poetic. The shrink needs a shrink."

"I'm serious. Is there somebody you'd feel comfortable talking to? If not, I can put you in touch with a—"

"Give me a break. What are you going to do? Go through the rolodex of shrinks you've visited in the last ten years? They did a real bang up job with you, didn't they?"

I inhaled sharply, the stinging comment striking a nerve. My first instinct was to hang up on Nina, but the detective in me knew she was only striking out blindly. Anyone in her path would suffer her sharp tongue. Nina wanted everyone to feel as badly as she did.

"I know you didn't mean that, Dr. Grace. You may have given up on yourself, but I haven't. I won't. Do you hear me?" This time I heard unrestrained sobbing over the line. "Call me when you're ready to let me help you."

Immediately after I disconnected the call, my phone rang.

"Detective Springer," I answered.

"This is Jude Campion over at the Falkenburg jail. A couple of hours ago one of my officers picked up a woman for possession with intent to sell. We were going to process her, but she said she had critical information regarding a high profile case. Wanted to trade for it. Are you the detective working the Jonathan Grace murder?"

"Yes. Yes I am. What's the woman's name?"

I could hear the rustling of papers in the background. "Posey. A Peyton Posey."

CHAPTER 25

"Are you sure we should meet with her?" Patrick asked me again. "We'll blow our cover at the club."

After the call from the sheriff, I headed back inside the precinct and told Patrick about the call. He snapped out of his mood and accompanied me to the jail. We were sitting in an interview room, waiting for an officer to escort Peyton Posey to us.

"You saw how Whitington treats the women who work for him. Peyton's ready to turn on him, I can feel it. This is our best option. Unless of course, you're willing to go through with your little bondage fantasy."

Patrick shivered.

I got out my notebook and pen and set them on the table. "This might be our only chance to infiltrate the club. Anyway, Carlos is still posing as a member. He can work that angle if need be."

A loud buzzer sounded outside the room. I turned around in time to see Peyton being led toward the glass door in handcuffs. Outside the glitz and glam of the club, Peyton's luster had waned. Her red hair hung limp over her shoulders, dark circles aged her once flawless skin.

The closer she got, the more her confusion grew. "Mr. & Mrs. Reed?"

"No, Peyton. I'm Detective Kate Springer and this is Detective Patrick Jessup with the Tampa Police Department."

The officer uncuffed Peyton and moved to the side, allowing her to walk around the table to the empty chair.

"Now last night makes sense," she said. "I thought I'd lost my touch." Peyton flashed a sly smile and a wink toward Patrick that only came off as desperate.

"I heard you wanted to make a deal," I said, taking the lead.

Peyton chewed on her bottom lip and fidgeted in her chair.

"Come on, Peyton. You know it's only a matter of time before your boss gets busted. The TPD has been collecting information on his club for months. We've got almost everything we need to take him down. You have to get ahead of this thing. Count yourself lucky. Another week and there'd be nothing to trade for."

Peyton rapidly blinked her eyes. Her restlessness increased until she sprang up from her chair, nervously pacing behind it. She trailed her red, chipped fingernails across the white cement blocks. "I'm no snitch, you hear me? But these bastards have me in a corner." She glared at the officer standing bored in the corner of the room. "This is my third offense. I'm looking at real jail time. That means I lose my daughter. And that means foster care."

Peyton rushed back to the table, slamming her palms against the metal. The sound reverberated off the cold walls. "If I tell you what I know, you have to promise to expunge this trumped up charge. I mean it. I want no record of this arrest."

"Peyton, before I take this to the Assistant State Attorney, I have to know you're not blowing smoke up my ass. I don't want to jump through hoops only to find what's really behind all this is a lovers' quarrel. You need to tell me something, anything to prove you've got the real goods."

"Fine. I know for a fact Rob Whitington was blackmailing Jonathan Grace."

That got my attention. With a poker face, I told Peyton I'd contact ASA Randolph and set up a deal in exchange for her testimony. Since she hadn't been processed yet, it would be easier to extricate her from this situation.

Once all the parties had signed off on the deal, we were ready to video Peyton's get out of jail free card. The three of us were seated around the table in the same interrogation room.

"For the record," I began, "this interview is being videotaped on Sunday, July 18, 2011, at 2:36 pm. Those participating in this interview are Peyton Posey, Detective Kate Springer, and Detective Patrick Jessup. Ms. Posey approached the Tampa Police Department with information about Rob Whitington's possible involvement in the Jonathan Grace murder investigation. In exchange for this information, ASA Jack Randolph has brokered a deal expunging Ms. Posey's recent charge of possession with intent to sell. All parties understand this deal is null and void if Ms. Posey attempts to warn Rob Whitington of this exchange. Ms. Posey has declined representation during this interview. Do you agree with everything I've said, Ms. Posey?"

"Yes." Peyton made a half-hearted attempt to fix her hair for the camera then went back to picking at her cuticle.

"Ms. Posey, can you tell us what you know about Rob Whitington and Jonathan Grace's relationship?"

"You mean now?"

"Yes. Go ahead and start. If we need clarification, we'll ask."

Peyton let out a soft sigh and closed her eyes, seeming to get her thoughts in order. When she opened them, the green color seemed to shine brighter with a new resolve. "When couples come to the club, they're told all their activity is completely confidential. It's a lie. There are hidden cameras and microphones camouflaged throughout the place. All three floors, in every room. Rob tells the people who work for him that it's for our own protection. He doesn't want one of the members taking a fantasy too far. It's bullshit. I know better."

"How's that, Peyton?"

She cast her stare toward the wall, refusing to look at me.

"Peyton?"

"I used to date Rob."

"This is a lovers' quarrel." I pounded my fists on the table. "Dammit!"

"No, no. Give me a second, would ya."

I stood up from the table, playing the infuriated detective. I wanted to make sure Peyton knew I wasn't screwing around. I didn't want her holding back key details from her story.

"Would you wait! I'm not talking to you because I want to jam Rob up. You wanted to know how I got all this information. I was in his inner circle. I came to the Sext Club in November 2010. Rob quickly singled me out. We started dating within the month. It definitely had its perks. I rose up the ladder overnight. Went from working on my back to signing up new members as the greeter in the front of the club."

Satisfied with the explanation, I sat down. "The job Gina has now?"

"Yes." Peyton practically hissed the word. "She's the soup de jour, and I'm back to spreading my legs for the whims of the members."

"Why didn't you leave?"

Peyton let out a hard laugh, one that said it all. "You don't leave. Not unless you're on a gurney." Peyton stilled for a moment, obviously stuck in a memory. "Rob's a real sadist, but I know how to handle him. Playing the submissive role kept me in the front of the house, raking in the dough. It was better than the titty bar I used to work at over on Adamo Drive."

"Let's get back to the surveillance Rob Whitington kept on the patrons of his club."

"Right. One night, not long after Rob and I started dating, this couple took the dungeon room too far with my best friend, Angie. I went off on Rob, asking why he didn't have someone stop them. I mean, if that's what the surveillance room was for. He laughed. Said the monitors weren't for the ladies, they were his retirement plan."

"What did he mean, retirement plan?"

"I found out a few weeks later. Rob told me it was time to start earning my higher paycheck. That I was crazy if I thought an extra $500 a week was for sitting behind a desk smiling."

When Peyton saw the confusion on my face she explained. "Whenever a big fish came into the club for the first time, I'd flagged their file. Rob would research the couple, finding out how much dough they had. If their net worth was high enough, Rob would introduce himself as they were leaving and bait them into coming back to fulfill some dark fantasy. I was the star of those fantasies. Rob would videotape the encounter and use it as blackmail."

"Peyton, I'm confused." Patrick rubbed the corner of his eyebrow. "You sound happy about changing jobs, moving up to the front of the house. But when you think about it, weren't you still working on your back? The promotion doesn't seem like much of an improvement."

Peyton gave Patrick what I call a "duh look." She probably couldn't fathom the idea that even though her new position in the club was better, it still sucked.

"Are you kidding me?" she said. "More pay, more perks. What was there to complain about? And anyway, the sex only happened once in a while in that job, not every night."

I gave Patrick's arm a slight bump with my elbow. "How many of these encounters did you participate in?" I asked Peyton.

"Who knows? Ten, maybe more. Rob and I only dated for about six months. Jonathan Grace is the reason we broke up."

I threw a quick look toward Patrick.

"Start at the beginning," I said. "When did you first meet Jonathan Grace?"

Peyton chewed on the cuticle skin around her pinkie, searching her memory. "Early April sometime. I remember it was before tax time. He came in with a member. Lauren something."

"Lauren Tyler?"

"Is she the 40s pinup chick?"

I nodded. "Yeah, that's her."

"I flagged Jonathan's file. He had a look that screamed money. Lauren didn't last long at his side though. Seemed like once he got his invitation into the club, he didn't need her anymore. He acted like a kid in a candy store, trying all the flavors at once. But I was surprised he showed up with his wife once."

I dropped my pen. Patrick placed a light hand on my leg bouncing underneath the table.

Peyton smiled. "Yeah, usually if the guy doesn't start out with his wife on his arm, she never makes an appearance."

"Do you remember anything about the night Jonathan and his wife were at the club?" Patrick asked.

"It was a hoot. Jonathan walks in as handsome as ever. His wife," Peyton stops and laughs. "She's clinging to his arm. Looks like a gazelle walking into the lion's den. Probably afraid someone would pin her to the wall and do her right there."

Peyton laughed again.

"Why is that funny?" Patrick asked.

"That kind of thing doesn't happen at the club. I mean unless you ask for it. Everything is always consensual. Rob never forced anyone to be a part of something they weren't totally comfortable with."

I shook my head. "Didn't you say earlier no one ever left the club? That once you started working for Rob Whitington, there was no way out?"

Peyton only shrugged. "All I'm saying is Rob never physically forced us to go through with a fantasy. Even with the real weirdo's who came in. The girls always had to agree."

"Intimidation is a form of force," I said. "Whitington might not have strong armed you, but I'm sure every girl at the club knew the consequences of saying no."

Peyton shrugged indifference again. I wanted to shake the woman, tell her to wake up. But I wasn't surprised at her attitude. Many women just like her had been beaten down their entire lives. So much so, that when a man showed interest in them and didn't use his fists, they thought life was wonderful. The women didn't realize verbal abuse was still abuse. They were so used to hearing themselves belittled regularly, that to not incur the daily verbal assaults would've made them more uncomfortable.

"Do you remember anything else about the Graces' visit to the club?" Patrick asked.

"Rob thought it odd the two of them showing up together. He asked me to keep an eye on them. It was pretty vanilla though. Jonathan showed his wife around, introduced her to a few couples. You would've thought the members had cooties the way she shook their hands. After Jonathan and her spent a little time watching the groups in the observation hallway, they retreated to a private room. I would've loved to be in the control room listening to that conversation. And trust me, as short a time as they were in there, I'm sure talking was all they did."

Peyton snickered. "The wife stormed out of the room. Jonathan didn't even follow her. He came out naked, wearing only a smirk on his face. He winked at me, then joined the group across the hall in the orgy room."

CHAPTER 26

"You got a root beer in this joint?" Peyton said after a long bout of coughing. "My blood sugar's getting low."

Patrick stopped the video recorder and left to retrieve a drink for Peyton. After he handed it to her, I motioned for him to step outside the room.

"What's going on?" Patrick asked, handing me a can of Coke.

"Thanks. I'm just trying to wrap my head around the fact that Dr. Grace went to the club with Jonathan."

"Once she walked in, she must have known what he'd been up to. His extracurricular activities."

"If Peyton's being honest with us, that is."

"What would she gain by lying?"

I rubbed my eyes, holding the exhaustion at bay. "You're right. It doesn't look good for Dr. Grace."

"Better get back in there." Patrick nodded toward the glass door. "Peyton's looking a little antsy."

"We need to get her back on topic. Find out more about the blackmail."

Once we were seated inside the room, I cracked open my pop can. I mumbled an apology when the noise made everyone jump.

"Peyton, this is all great information you're giving us," Patrick began, "but I think you got a little sidetracked. Earlier, you mentioned flagging Jonathan Grace's file as a potential blackmail mark. You also said Jonathan was the reason your relationship with Rob Whitington ended. Can you tell us more about those two things?"

"I don't know. Haven't I told you enough? I mean if you bust Rob, where am I going to work?"

"The better question is when we bust you, where's your kid going to end up?" Patrick countered.

Peyton began looking around the room like she was searching for a way out.

"Peyton," I said, getting her attention. "I'll help you find a new gig. I have a friend over at First Steps who will get you connected with a reeducation counselor. Trust me. The writing's on the wall. You don't want to be anywhere near the club when we take it down. You'll just end up in here again."

Peyton pinched the bridge of her nose, a look of defeat settled over her. "This really sucks. Why does this kind of shit always happen to me?"

"You've got it backwards," I said. "I think your luck's finally changing. You have a chance to break free from this kind of life."

Peyton exhaled. She seemed to make a decision, one that got her talking again. "Rob hadn't been able to get Jonathan to open up about his fantasies, so Rob told me to get close to Jonathan. I worked my magic, catching Jonathan's eye. Over the next few weeks, we met in the private rooms and sometimes we'd join other couples. It was going pretty good, Jonathan started trusting me, but for some reason he still refused to confide in me. I don't know, maybe he thought I'd be turned off by his secret desires. He was real into public perception, that one. Finally though, I got him to at least agree to another discussion with Rob. It must have gone well because Rob surprised me with a bonus.

But whatever happened didn't happen with me. Rob must have set up Jonathan's fantasy with someone else. And it didn't take place at the club, which was odd." Peyton tilted her head to the side, frowning.

"You mean all the taped fantasies you participated in happened at the Sext Club?" Patrick asked.

"Always. Find that tape and you'll find out what Jonathan was into."

"Do you know where Rob Whitington hides the blackmail tapes?" I asked.

"No."

I let the subject drop for now, but I was suspicious at how quickly she answered the question.

"What role did Jonathan Grace have in breaking up you and Rob Whitington?" I asked.

Peyton blushed, looking away from me. "Number one rule—don't fall for the mark."

I shook my head. "I'm not buying this helpful, Girl Scout routine, Peyton. A woman like you always plays the angles. You're not telling me everything you know. This vague bullshit has to go if you want us to honor our agreement. You want to come out of this smelling like roses, but I'm thinking you must have stepped in some shit somewhere along the way for Rob to move you to the back of the house."

Peyton's face morphed right in front of me. Her eyes narrowed, her lips pursed. She looked more like a ferret than the innocent little lamb she'd pretended to be three seconds ago.

"Screw you."

"Peyton, I'm sure you're worried about your culpability," Patrick began.

"My what?"

"What I'm trying to say is that I understand if you're worried. Worried you might be held responsible if your actions caused harm to come to Jonathan Grace."

Peyton raised her hands in frustration. "What are you talking about?"

I jumped in. "You say you fell for Jonathan. Whatever happened, I'm sure it came from a position of caring for him, trying to help. If you did or said something that led Rob to murder Jonathan Grace, that's on Rob. I can't see the ASA holding you responsible for someone else's actions."

"That's right. I'm not responsible. It's not my fault." Peyton went back to chewing on her cuticle. This time blood trickled down her thumb and she sucked on the skin, making the red droplets disappear.

"Can you tell me more about the blackmail tape Rob Whitington had on Jonathan Grace?" Patrick flashed his dimpled smile.

Peyton returned the smile, smoothing her hair down again.

I inwardly groaned, wondering how women could fall for that. But then throw even the smallest amount of kindness toward a woman like Peyton, and she'd lap it up. A smile, a compliment, any compassion would be soaked up like a sponge, wetting her hard crusty edges.

Peyton started talking directly to Patrick. "As I said before, Jonathan shared his fantasy with Rob. I couldn't get Rob to tell me what it was, but he said he'd make a fortune off Grace. Jonathan stayed away from the club for a couple weeks. Then one night he showed up hammered. He pulled me into one of the private rooms, started yelling at me, accusing me of being in on it. At first, I didn't know what he meant, but I quickly gathered Jonathan had gone through with his fantasy, and Rob had started blackmailing him. I knew Rob was watching us through the monitors, so I played dumb. One of the security guys escorted Jonathan out of the club."

When Peyton got quiet again, Patrick prodded. "What happened next?"

"I called Jonathan at work. Asked him to meet me. We got together at a hotel near his office and made love. He was so tender." Peyton sighed. The tightened muscles in her face loosened with the memory. "Jonathan told me he loved me that day. He said he was going to divorce his bitch of a wife. We could finally be together, but first we had to figure out a way to destroy the blackmail tape Rob had made. If it went public, Jonathan's reputation would be ruined. He'd lose all his money in an ugly divorce. He might even go to jail."

"What was Jonathan Grace's fantasy?"

Peyton looked down at her lap. "I don't know. He never would tell me." When she finally looked up, her eyes glistened. "But I didn't care. I loved him, and he loved me. We were going to be together."

"Did you help Jonathan Grace find the blackmail tape?" Patrick asked.

Peyton nodded. "I'd seen Rob hide the tapes in a hidey hole in the wall of the monitoring room. I came up with the plan that Jonathan would keep paying Rob the blackmail money and continue going to the club like usual. Then one night, I paid one of the girls to create a diversion with her client. Everyone cleared out of Rob's office. I showed the fake wall panel to Jonathan and waited outside to keep a look out. Only . . ."

Peyton stopped talking.

"Only what?" Patrick asked.

"Only Jonathan took way too long looking through the tapes. Idiot spent too much time searching for his own. He should have listened to me—grabbed all of them and split. Rob came back to the office quicker than I thought. I knew he would've suspected something if I'd tried to stall. I had to do it."

"Do what?" Patrick asked.

"I told Rob I'd seen Jonathan go into his office." Peyton narrowed her eyes when she saw my expression. "Don't you dare judge me. Why should we both get busted?"

"You sold him out to save your own ass," I said.

Under the table, Patrick placed a hand on my leg again.

"I understand why you did it, Peyton," he said. "You have a child at home. We know what Rob would have done to you if he'd learned you were in on it."

Peyton kept nodding, agreeing with Patrick.

"You made the right decision," he said. "Can you tell me what happened when Rob Whitington discovered Jonathan Grace in his office?"

"Don't know. I'd tried calling Jonathan to explain, but he never would pick up. All I know is that he didn't find his tape. I heard one of the security guys say it wasn't worth the beat down they gave him. The night it happened, Rob made me get ice for his split knuckles. Asshole wanted to intimidate me. It worked. Scared the shit out of me. Rob questioned me over and over, but I held firm. He couldn't get the truth out of me, but he still didn't believe me. Rob fired me from the front of the house because I'd seen Jonathan go into his office and didn't come find him immediately. Rob said he couldn't trust me anymore. I asked if it would be better if I left. He laughed, told me he wanted me at the club where he could keep an eye on me."

"When did all this go down?" Patrick asked.

"Jonathan got caught looking for the blackmail tape last month, end of June sometime."

At the autopsy, the ME reported old rib fractures. It could have been the result of an ass kicking by Whitington's men that night.

"Was that the last time you saw Jonathan Grace?" Patrick asked.

"No. He came to the club the night he was murdered. He hadn't been there since Gina took over the front desk. Rob must have forgotten to warn her about him. Frankly, I'm surprised Jonathan's account hadn't been closed. Anyway, Thursday night I finished up with a private session around 10:30 pm. I went to grab a bite and found Jonathan standing around with a plate full of food, three sheets to the wind. I asked him what the hell he was doing at the club, told him he'd get another beat down if he didn't stay away. I pulled on his arm, trying to get him to leave. The only thing I got for my troubles was spilled champagne all over my dress."

"Do you know why Jonathan came to the club Thursday night?" I asked.

"He said something about having a plan, wanting to talk to Rob. I don't know, I could barely understand his slurring words, but it sounded like Jonathan had been stupid enough to stop paying the blackmail and now he needed to . . . what did he say? Oh right, 'renegotiate the terms of their agreement.' I didn't have time to get much more out of him. The security guys showed up, and Jonathan made a real spectacle. They had to drag him out. It was the last time I ever saw him."

CHAPTER 27

"Do you think Peyton will warn the girls working for Whitington?" Patrick asked. We were back at the precinct, coordinating our efforts with Wozniack, Jung, and a couple crime scene techs.

"If she does, you can bet it will get back to Whitington," Jung said. "He might destroy the tapes before we can serve him with a warrant."

I shook my head. "Nah. Women like Peyton, their number one concern is for themselves. Now that she finally has a chance to get out from under Rob's control, she's not going to do anything to screw it up."

"Still, she has an abused woman's mentality," Patrick said. "Always making excuses why her man treats her badly. Always going back either because she thinks she deserves the abuse or believes she can't make it on her own."

"Doesn't matter," I answered. "Those blackmail tapes are Rob's winning lottery ticket. He's not going to destroy them. Hide them better, maybe, but not destroy them."

"I hope you're right," Patrick said. "You know it's one thing for Whitington to blackmail Jonathan Grace, another to kill him. I mean what's the motive? Can't collect money from a corpse."

"According to Peyton, Jonathan stopped paying," I said. "It must have seriously pissed Whitington off. If Jonathan really did show up at the club to renegotiate, you can imagine how that conversation went. It's not a stretch to think Whitington sent one of his guys home with Jonathan to rough him up. The ME said he thought the slit to the throat was accidental. Whitington's guy could have taken it too far."

Patrick mulled over the possibility as Jung walked off to answer his ringing cell phone. Wozniack and the crime scene techs also stepped away.

"Sorry you didn't get a chance to go home this afternoon," I told Patrick.

"Are you kidding me? Home's the last place I want to be right now, but it looks like you'll have to cancel chick flick night with Lucy."

"Dammit." I looked down at my watch. Half past four. "I completely forgot about her."

I pulled out my phone and punched in Lucy's cell number. No answer. When I tried calling my house, the phone rang until voice mail picked up. "Hmm, she's not there."

Wozniack ambled back over, adjusting the belt under his massive gut. "Are you girls going to jaw all day, or are we going to serve these damn warrants?"

"Which location do you want?" Patrick asked Wozniack.

"Jung and I've got dibs on the club. From what you said, I can't wait to get a look inside."

I shook my head. "Don't worry, Wozniack. It's still early. The boobs aren't going anywhere."

Wozniack handed Patrick the search warrant granting us access to search Rob Whitington's home.

"Once you get a look inside the hidden compartment at the club, don't forget to give me a call Wozniack," Patrick said.

I nodded. "If you don't find a tape labeled Jonathan Grace at the club, we need to know right away. We'll tear Whitington's house apart brick by brick if we have to."

***

A shocked Rob Whitington opened the door to his Clearwater beachfront property. I was happy we'd caught him at home, wanting to see the surprised look on his face.

"Well, look who's home," I said.

"Mr. and Mrs. Reed, what are you doing here?"

Patrick slapped Rob's chest with a warrant, walking past him inside the house.

"You can't barge into my home," Rob said. "What the hell are you doing? "

"Read that little paper. It gives me all the right I need to be here. And it's Jessup, not Reed. Detective Patrick Jessup."

Rob looked over at me.

"Nope, not the Mrs., but I am his partner, Detective Kate Springer. We're here to serve you with a warrant to search your home, car, boat, and any outlying buildings. We're looking for videotape and blackmail pictures of your club members. If you'd like to save us the hassle of ransacking your place, feel free to tell us your hiding spots."

Rob grabbed the cell phone clipped to his belt.

"Don't bother," I said. "Five minutes ago, detectives served a warrant on your club. The secret compartment where you keep all your blackmail tapes, they're ours now."

Rob's gaze darted back and forth between Patrick and me. Finally his eyes rested on the front door. Before Rob could act on his instinct to flee, two officers stepped inside, blocking his escape route. A crime scene technician followed them in.

"Please escort Mr. Whitington to the couch," Patrick told one of the officers. "Search him and make sure he doesn't leave." The other officer stood sentry at the door.

Rob's phone rang. He held onto it like a life line. "I know," he said. "They're here too. Keep your mouth shut until I can get Bethany Dunbar to send someone over there."

"Bethany Dunbar's your lawyer?" I asked Rob after he'd disconnected his call.

He crossed his arms over his broad chest, ignoring my question. Rob's hair looked wet. He had on a pair of crisp jeans and a pressed, button-down shirt. Even though Rob had the fresh out of the shower look, I don't think a few minutes under a spray of hot water could remove the slime oozing off this guy.

"Forget it," Patrick said. "He's not going to talk."

For some reason, I couldn't drop it. I wanted to wipe the smug little look off Rob's face. "You know we're going to tear your place apart, right? We're going to find every single thing you've tried so hard to hide. Sure you don't want to save yourself the trouble of cleaning up and tell us where the tapes are?"

Rob let out an arrogant laugh. "That's what I got my bitches for."

Patrick grabbed my shoulder and twisted me around. "Come on, Kate. He's not worth it."

I shrugged his hands off.

"Hey, Jessup," Rob said getting Patrick's attention. "It's a shame your partner carries your balls in her pocket. I knew you two weren't on the up and up last night. Pretending you want to dominate some woman. Yeah, right. I could tell you were pussy whipped from the moment she led you into the office."

"What!" Spittle flew out of Patrick's mouth.

"Not worth it, remember," I whispered.

I pulled Patrick down the hallway out of earshot.

"I am not whipped. Am I?" But Patrick didn't wait for an answer; he kept ranting. "Just because I don't treat women like ho's doesn't mean I let them walk all over me."

Usually a perp's verbal jabs didn't get under Patrick's skin. Maybe Rob's comment struck a chord because of Patrick and Alina's recent arguments. "Come on, Patrick. The best revenge is finding something incriminating on Whitington. Have him stewing on a cold, metal bunk this time tomorrow. Let's—"

Patrick's phone rang. "Jessup . . . What'd you find, Wozniack? . . . Damn. Okay, call me if anything else comes up."

"What?" I asked.

"The good news is Wozniack found twenty-seven mini video cassettes in the false wall Peyton told us about. Guess Rob's ego was too inflated to think they'd ever be discovered. Bad news—none of the tapes had Jonathan Grace's name on it."

I looked down both ends of the long hallway, wondering where a scumbag like Whitington would hide a blackmail tape. Peyton had told us the cassettes measured the length of her index finger and about half as wide. "You ready to rip this place apart?"

Patrick tugged at the buttons holding his shirt sleeves closed and rolled up the fabric past his elbows. He bent his neck to the side. A popping noise indicated he was all in.

***

"This is ridiculous. We've been here for three hours." Patrick wiped the sweat from his brow with the back of his hand. "You know, Kate, the tape might not even be here."

"Oh, it's here. There's no way Whitington would trust it out of his sight. Let's stop, take a breather, and talk it out. Where would a guy like this hide a tape? It's small."

"Compact," Patrick added. "Can fit into a tight spot."

Shelby, the crime scene tech had already finished searching Whitington's computer. There were no sexual pictures on the hard drive. She'd come in the room, standing nearby, trying to keep up with our back and forth.

"Get in Whitington's head, Patrick. What does he like to do at his club? Think about the cameras. They're cleverly hidden in plain sight."

Patrick snapped his fingers. "Right. A man like Whitington would figure if cops ever searched his home, they'd look for hiding spots. Look for false walls, loose tiles."

"Instead, what if he arranged the tape case in a way that blended into its surroundings? It could be right in front of us, staring us straight in the face."

Patrick looked around at all the destruction we'd caused. "Okay, but where do we start?"

"In a room Whitington is more apt to spend most of his time in. Think about a serial killer wanting to keep his trophies close. I bet he looks at his hiding spot daily, patting himself on the back for how clever he is."

"I'll take the bedroom, Kate. You take the living area, and you," Patrick pointed at Shelby, "can start in the kitchen. We've already gone through everything thoroughly. This time stand in the room and think about where a tape could be hidden in plain sight."

We left the workout room and went to our respective areas.

Whitington sneered when I walked in the room. "Having fun, Detective?"

Bethany Dunbar, who'd showed up a couple hours earlier, shushed her client.

"I'm not having nearly as much fun as you'll have cleaning up this mess," I said. "Oh, right. You don't clean up your own messes, you have your bitches do it. Shame they'll be busy at the station all night answering questions."

Whitington's sneer grew wider, showing off teeth that looked like they wanted to rip out my throat. I couldn't help but add another dig. "You like being one of Whitington's bitches, Ms. Dunbar? Cleaning up his legal messes?"

I turned my back on the two of them as they whispered back and forth. Whitington's home had an open floor plan. One enormous room housed an overstuffed sectional that had been torn apart, the stuffing scattered on the floor around it. A smoky glass bar stood at one end of the room near a door leading to an outdoor patio area. Patrick had already checked the hot tub to make sure the tape hadn't been stuffed into a waterproof container and submerged under the water.

Walking towards the abstract wall paintings on the opposite side of the room, I noticed Rob glancing my way with a slight grin on his face. He and his lawyer were sitting in a bay window, one of the few places where a seat was still available. I looked away, continuing over to the piano sitting in the corner of the room. I ran my gloved hands underneath the piano's belly. I knew Patrick had already checked here, this was purely for Rob's benefit.

A quick glance over my shoulder confirmed my suspicion. Rob's grin had turned into a full-fledged smile. I got off my knees and walked back toward the bar. As I got closer, Rob's smile faltered.

I moved around to the back, looking at the liquor bottles sitting on the bar top. Nothing looked out of the ordinary. Glasses were arranged upside down in the corner, tongs hung over an empty ice bucket. Again, I slowly stepped around to the front of the bar, sneaking a peek at Rob's still concerned body language. I heard him tell his lawyer to shut up. His voice as sharp as the knife he probably used to slit Jonathan Grace's throat.

Something about the bar nagged at me. My subconscious begged me to open myself up to the image it had already discovered. I closed my eyes, trying to clear my head. I pushed the voices out—mine telling me not to screw this up, Nina's telling me she might have killed her husband, Patrick's reminding me to remain objective.

I opened my eyes. The waning sunlight seeping through the window reflected on a portion of the glass directly under the leather bar top.

I knelt down. Rob sprang up. The officer standing near him bolted, blocking his way.

Earlier when I'd been standing across the room, it'd looked like a decorative band of smoky gray crystals had been mounted into the bar's dark glass base. Upon closer inspection, I realized they weren't rectangular crystals at all but plastic pieces expertly disguised to blend into the bar's stand. I used my knuckles to knock on each piece until a sound, a more hollow sound, rang out from the fourth rectangle on the left.

I shouted for Patrick and the crime scene tech to join me. Shelby took pictures of the bar and fingerprinted the decorative pieces. She removed a miniature crow bar from her case, and with one quick flick of her wrist, she popped out the rectangular piece. The jarring action caused the case to pop apart and a mini video cassette tape fell out onto the tile floor. J. GRACE was scrawled across the top of the cassette in all caps.

CHAPTER 28

"I'm wired, want to get a drink?" I looked at Patrick expectantly over the hood of my car.

The officers had taken Rob Whitington into custody, charging him with twenty-nine counts of blackmail. The charges would be appended depending on what else Wozniack discovered at the club. For now, Whitington wouldn't talk, so he'd spend the night in lock up.

"No thanks." Patrick opened the car door and got in. "Better take me home. Time to face my wife. Anyway, shouldn't you get back to Lucy?"

"I've called a couple of times. No answer. She probably got tired of waiting around and went home. I'll catch up with her tomorrow. With all this excess energy, I wish I could stay up to see what's on those tapes."

"I can't believe we found a second one. I wonder which bigwig got caught with his pants down." After a misfire, the car's engine roared to life.

"Whitington stashed the tape at his house instead of keeping it with the others at his club. There's got to be a story behind it."

"Shelby said she'd put a rush on the tapes. Hopefully, we can watch them tomorrow."

The crime scene tech had taken all the seized evidence, including the two mini video cartridges, back to the crime lab. The second tape was sealed tightly in its plastic case. It had to be opened back at the lab to ensure the evidence wasn't damaged.

"Wozniack and Jung can watch all the tapes they confiscated," I said. "Make sure nothing was mislabeled."

"Woz will love that assignment."

"I bet a lot of people will be shitting their pants tomorrow when they turn on the morning news to find out the club was raided."

***

"Lucy, you're still here?" I'd walked into my house to find my best friend sitting on the couch stroking Frank's fur. "It's almost 10 pm. Wait a minute. Why didn't you answer any of my calls?"

"How could you?"

"How could I what?" I kicked the front door closed and headed toward the kitchen to store my gun and charge my phone. When I saw Lucy's face, I stopped at the archway and grabbed onto the molding. "What?"

"I didn't trust myself to talk on the phone, so I waited until you got home. Do you have something to tell me?"

My heart beat faster. I didn't know what I'd done, but it felt like I was sixteen again and my mother had caught me coming home after curfew. I chuckled, hoping to make light of Lucy's serious demeanor. "Please don't ground me, Mom. Sorry I'm home late."

"Charles called."

Uh-oh.

"Remember now?"

I averted my eyes from her piercing stare. "What do you mean?"

"Don't you dare, Kate. Don't you lie to me."

Maybe I could have kept up the façade if Lucy had lashed out in anger. Instead, she seemed to recoil inside herself. Resignation and disappointment lay like a thick blanket wrapped around her. Seems my name had just been added to the long list of people who'd failed her.

I sat down beside her on the couch. "Your friendship means everything to me, Lucy."

"Then why would you tell Charles to dump me? Don't I deserve to be happy?"

"Of course you do. Why do you think I wanted the relationship between you two to end? I care about you, and I don't want to see you hurt. After the stories you told me about this guy . . . well, there was something off about him. I could feel it. At first, I thought he was married because he refused to show you where he lived. After a little digging, I discovered he'd been arrested for spousal abuse. He's the bad guy here, not me."

"You had no right to invade his privacy. You promised me you'd never do that again."

"You're right, I'm sorry, but when I saw you were falling for him . . . oh, I don't know, Lucy. With your track record, I only wanted to check him out, make sure there was nothing in his past that could harm you."

"Don't you dare pretend you did this for anyone but yourself, Kate Springer. You are a selfish woman. I've tried telling myself you're a good friend, only looking out for my well-being but ever since we became close, you've somehow sabotaged every one of my romantic relationships."

"Fine! If you want to date thieves and wife beaters, go right ahead. I won't stop you."

"Don't you dare try to change the subject, putting this off on me. Admit it. You can't stand to see me with any man. Why? Because you're selfish. You want me all to yourself. You need meek little Lucy around to bolster your ego, hanging on your every word. Can't you see, Kate,

I'm not that timid girl anymore."

"Isn't it better to find out Chuck is a wife beater now instead of down the line when you two are engaged."

"Damn you, Kate!" At the outburst, Frank jumped off Lucy's lap. The look of condemnation the cat gave me said what I already knew. I had to fix this fast or my best friend would leave. Leave forever.

Lucy's short lived flame of anger fizzled out quickly. She hung her head. Her hair fanned forward around her glasses.

"Lucy? Lucy?"

Slowly she raised her head. A look I'd never seen before blazed in her eyes.

"Lucy, I—"

"Don't. When Charles called me tonight, he explained the situation surrounding the arrest. The police misconstrued the scene. His ex-wife recanted her story."

"And you believe him?"

"He also told me what you said at the clinic. That he had better leave me or you'd ruin his life. Charles apologized for calling off the relationship, begged me to come back. He doesn't care about the repercussions, he loves me."

I could hear the cracks shooting through my heart. One tore open at the thought Chuck really did love Lucy. To incur my wrath, he must. Another crack spread out when I realized there would be no easy repair to the damage I'd done to my friendship with Lucy.

I went for the Hail Mary. "Do you know how many times I've picked up the pieces to your failed relationships? Sat on this couch while you cried on my shoulder. What are you going to do when you and Chuck break up? Huh?"

"Do you mean all the relationships you blew out of the water so you could sit back and be the hero who came to my rescue? Tell your shoulder not to worry. If Charles and I don't make it, you won't be around to pick up the pieces."

MONDAY

CHAPTER 29

"Thanks for catching a ride in with Cunningham," I told Patrick after arriving at the precinct. The squad room was abuzz with detectives busy working at their desks.

"No problem. By the way, you look like shit."

I gently patted my swollen, red eyes. "Damn pollen."

After Lucy had stormed out of my house last night, I sobbed into my pillow for hours. In a moment of weakness, I broke down and called Carlos Diaz. I didn't even let him get through the front door before I fell apart again. The waves of sadness that had threatened to pull me under outweighed any embarrassment I might have felt at the pitiful display of vulnerability I showed. Carlos's embrace was like a lifeline I used to pull myself out of the black pit attempting to swallow me.

Last night, I finally allowed myself to let go. To sit surrounded by Carlos's strong arms, soaking in his love, feeling his devotion. His intent seemed so pure to me, and for the briefest moment, I allowed myself to dream. To let the emotions soar instead of stamping them down, destroying them with the usual what-if scenarios. I eventually cried myself to sleep, lying across his lap snuggled into his chest.

Patrick looked at me like he was waiting for an answer to a question

I hadn't heard him ask. I coughed, embarrassed by the memories that had gripped me. I turned toward my desk, busying myself with straightening it. "Have you had time to look into the white SUV sighting?"

"Sure go ahead and ignore me. Well to answer *your* question, I actually checked into it this morning before I dived back into Jonathan Grace's phone calls. The neighbors with cameras pointed at the street don't have recording capabilities, so I checked with the city. They'll send us footage of the traffic cam nearest to the Graces' house. I should get it tomorrow. It's a long shot though."

"Still, tell me when it arrives. I'll go through it." I pointed at the pictures spread across Patrick's desk. "What are you looking at?"

"Copies of the photos Wozniack found at the Sext Club. Whitington, that egotistical bastard, had them sitting in a filing cabinet."

I took off my navy blue blazer, hanging it on the back of my chair. "Have we gotten the video found at Whitington's house back from the lab yet?"

"No, but they know we're chomping at the bit to get anything we can."

"Have you found any pictures in there of Jonathan Grace?"

"No, but I only started looking fifteen minutes ago. Want half?"

"Sure." I took a large stack.

"Need a magnifying glass?"

"What?"

Patrick cocked his head and pointed at his eyes. "How are you going to see anything? Your eyes look almost swollen shut."

We both knew he wasn't buying my allergy excuse.

"Keep it up and we'll have some quality sharing time about your evening at home with the wife."

Patrick quickly buried his head in his pile of photographs. We took our time looking through each picture, studying the faces when they were exposed, searching the backgrounds when they weren't. Some of the scenes were extremely graphic in their depiction of pain. We couldn't help but remark on them. It helped to alleviate the tension we felt.

"How can wearing leather from head to toe be comfortable?" I turned the picture around to show Patrick.

"I would think it'd chaff."

Patrick went back to looking through his photos.

"Wait a minute, Kate. Look at this one. It's dated 5/20/11." He handed it to me. "It only shows the guy's back, but notice the hair and build. It could be Jonathan Grace."

"I think you're right. Look at the watch. It's hard to tell for sure, but I think it could be the one I saw in pieces collected off Grace's body. Do you have any other pictures with this same background?"

The camera angle implied it was mounted above the two people in the room. A man's back faced the camera, and over his shoulder I could see the face of a frightened young girl lying on a dirty bare mattress. She had dark blond hair with the bottom couple inches of the straight strands dyed a bright pink. Tall floodlights bathed the room in bright light, revealing wallpaper peeling away from the ceiling down. Water stains marked the bare areas of the wall.

"There aren't any more photos matching these surroundings or having the same date stamp," Patrick said. "Look through yours, too. See if they got out of order."

I looked through my entire stack twice. "Nothing here."

"I searched all of mine again, too. This girl doesn't show up in any of them." Patrick tapped his finger on the picture sitting between us. "This has to be Jonathan Grace. Remember what Peyton told us about his fantasy. He acted it out somewhere other than the club."

"You're right. All the pictures in my pile show elaborately decorated rooms. I even found some taken in the jungle-themed room. The same one Lauren Tyler was photographed in. Even the dungeon room, which you wouldn't necessarily consider beautiful, still has an embellished feel. This picture showing the man and the girl has a rawness to it."

"How old do you think the girl is?" Patrick asked.

"Definitely underage, maybe fifteen."

"Rob Whitington told us he never used underage girls."

"Bullshit. He's just too smart to admit to a crime."

"If this *is* a picture of Jonathan Grace, I wonder why Whitington left it at the club."

"Do you think Whitington got spooked after he caught Jonathan looking through the files?"

"Makes sense," Patrick said. "If Whitington did move the pictures, he could have missed this one."

"Hell, we almost did."

"We never discovered any photos at Whitington's house."

"Just because we didn't find any, doesn't mean they weren't there," I said.

"We were damn lucky to find the videotapes. Let's hope they show something blackmail worthy."

I checked my notebook. "Jonathan Grace made six $5,000 cash withdrawals during the time Peyton said Whitington blackmailed him. That's one payment every Saturday until July 2 rolled around. Then nothing. Who knows what went down those twelve days before Grace was murdered, but if we had the actual blackmail tape used against Grace, it would be seriously damning for Rob Whitington."

"While we're waiting to watch the tapes, we need to keep wading through our suspect pool. By the way—"

"Wait a minute, Patrick. The first cash advance was taken off Grace's credit card on May 21. That's one day after this photo was taken."

"It can't be a coincidence."

I shook my head. "It has to be Jonathan Grace in this photo. Let me roll this around in my head for a while, figure out what implications it has on the case."

"First let me get back to what I tried to tell you earlier. You know when you came in and completely ignored me. I asked if you wanted to interview Sean O'Brien."

"What?"

Patrick sighed. "You know, Jonathan Grace's ex-business partner. Jonathan gave Sean O'Brien a call two days before the murder. I called O'Brien. He said he'd be happy to talk, but it had to be in person. Sounded very cloak and dagger."

"Do you mind taking the interview? If I went out looking like this," I said patting my swollen eyes, "I might scare him away."

"Do I get to borrow your car?"

Right, Patrick's vehicle was still in the shop. I raised an eyebrow until the stretching of the skin around my eye area caused me pain. I drive a Porsche 911. An older model with some patches of faded black paint, some rusting in a few other spots, but the engine purred like a panther on the prowl. "And how careful are you going to be?"

"I'm packing gloves." With a magician's sleight of hand, Patrick produced a pair of latex gloves out of thin air.

I smiled and threw him the keys.

***

I wound my way around the detectives' desks, my arms holding the last two boxes from the Graces' house. Laziness prohibited me from making another trip to evidence lockup, so now I could barely see.

I set the boxes on the corner of my desk. They wobbled precariously on the edge until I used my body to push them farther onto the flat surface. Out of the corner of my eye, I saw my phone scoot forward until it teetered on the end of the desk. When I made a grab for it, my elbow knocked the top box onto the ground.

"Augh!" I yelled in frustration. A hush came over the room as the other detectives looked my way. Five seconds later, their attention turned back to their own tasks. Outbursts in this squad were pretty common.

It's going to be one of those days. Problem was I still couldn't get the look on Lucy's face out of my head. It's one thing to screw up, pissing somebody off. It's a whole other ballgame when I disappointed someone. I'd worried so much Lucy would end our friendship once she became romantically involved, that in the end, my own actions caused it to happen. It turned out to be a self-fulfilling prophecy.

I absently picked up the spilled contents of the box, unable to get my mind off Lucy. My soul ached over the hole her leaving created. The things she'd told me last night stung. Selfish. Sure I knew I was selfish, always had been, but sabotaging her relationships to be the hero? No way. She always picked the wrong type of guy. That's why things never worked out. Sure, Lucy was upset with me now, but it wouldn't last. It couldn't. Some crisis would arise, she'd realize she needed me, and all would be forgiven.

My phone rang. "Detective Springer."

"Kate? Kate?"

"Dr. Grace?"

"Kate, he was here."

"Who?"

"Bobby. Bobby Hildabrand."

"Where are you?"

"Ana's house. He was here outside, banging on the front door. Yelling at me, accusing me of killing his father."

"I'll be right over. Wait. Dammit! Patrick has my car."

"I'm leaving anyway. I don't want to be here if Bobby comes back. All of this is so overwhelming—the cards, the flowers, all this damn food from fake friends offering empty platitudes."

"Are you alright to drive?" Her skittish tone concerned me.

"Of course," Nina answered harshly. "Why is everyone handling me with kid gloves?"

"I'm sorry. I'm only worried about your welfare."

Nina made a noise, a mixture between a growl and an exhale. "No, I'm sorry. I know you're only trying to help. I appreciate it. Really I do."

"Look, I'll find a way over to Ana's house and pick you up. It sounds like you could use time away to clear your head. I'll take you wherever you want to go."

"Are you sure?"

"Of course."

"Thank you, Kate."

After I disconnected the call, a plan began to formulate in my head. I looked over at Detective Jung's desk. He was oblivious to the noise surrounding him, typing on his keyboard. I hesitated a moment then turned around, grabbing the photograph of what might have been Jonathan Grace off my desk. It was time to get some real answers.

CHAPTER 30

"Thanks for getting me settled into a hotel," Nina told me. She dropped a large duffle bag at the foot of one of the double-sized beds. "With all the planning for Jonathan's funeral and the constant barrage of calls from family and friends, I feel like I'm going to crack."

"No problem. I'll stop by Bobby Hildabrand's house later today. Have a talk with him. He won't be harassing you anymore."

"No!"

I stared at her, confused by her demeanor. Maybe her disorder still had a firm grip. It looked like Nina hadn't showered in a couple of days. Her hair was tangled in clumps, and I could see mismatched socks peeking out beneath a pair of well-worn sweatpants.

"I mean . . ." Nina sank down onto the edge of the bed. She motioned to the other bed, and I sat facing her. "What I meant to say is that it's not necessary. Bobby's obviously in a lot of pain, and he's striking out at the one person closest to his dad. Me."

"But on the way over here, you told me about the threats he made. Bobby could be dangerous."

"Please don't confront him, Kate. I've counseled enough men like him to know he's only blowing off a little steam, but challenge him and his behavior might escalate. Don't worry. I'll call you if he shows up again."

I wasn't happy about her assessment of the situation, but I had to trust her. I didn't want to make things worse. "I know I should leave, that we shouldn't be speaking without your counsel present but—"

"No. I think we should talk. I wanted to thank you. Please know I appreciate all you're doing to find Jonathan's killer. Do you have any leads?" Nina moved her glasses up off the bridge of her nose, rubbing her eyes.

"Nothing concrete, but we're working the suspects we have."

"Your partner thinks I killed my husband, doesn't he?"

I hesitated.

"Don't worry," Nina said. "I knew from his tone during the interview he considers me the prime suspect."

"That's why I'm on the case, Dr. Grace. To make sure the department doesn't get tunnel vision."

"Thank you. I know you're putting your career at risk for me. Can you do me a favor though?"

"Anything."

"Stop calling me Dr. Grace. I think we've both been through too much together to stand on such formalities. Anyway, you're no longer my patient."

"I'll try."

"How have you been holding up since the kidnapping?" Nina asked.

"Worrying about me is the last thing you need to do."

"I only want to make sure you have a support system in place."

That was one of the things that made Nina special. Even in the midst of her own personal tragedy, she reached out to others, demonstrating how much she cared about them. "Yes, I took your advice. Patrick knows about my past, and I even opened up to . . . to Lucy."

A pang of emptiness punched me in the gut like a hard-hitting fist. I didn't know how I'd handle not being able to pick up the phone and call my best friend. To just talk about my day or complain about the men in my life. Lucy had always been my shoulder to lean on, to cry on.

I shook my head, trying to clear my thoughts. "I'm sorry, what?"

"Oh, it's nothing important. I was rambling on about my brother."

"You said earlier you were worried about my job. Don't. It's not in jeopardy. I know you're not responsible for your husband's murder. I'll clear your name. It just might take a little longer than we'd like. I need to ask you . . ." I hesitated, wondering if I really wanted to hear the answer to the question I'd already asked Nina yesterday but had gotten no response to.

"What, Kate? Please ask."

"The night of the murder you called me. I know I was half asleep, and we had a poor connection, but I swear you said, 'I think I killed my husband.' I don't mean to sound heartless, but from the look of Jonathan strapped to that chair, I don't understand how there could be any question. You'd know if you had killed him or not."

Nina cleared her throat and looked down at her lap. "Is that why Detective Jessup thinks I'm guilty?"

"Are you kidding me? I didn't tell anyone. A declaration like that would immediately put a red target on your back."

Nina looked up, tears swelled in the corners of her eyes. "I didn't hold the knife to Jonathan's throat but that doesn't make me any less responsible."

"What? How do you mean?"

"I told Jonathan about the man in the white SUV, sitting across the street watching our house. Jonathan said I should call the company that monitors our alarm system, increase the security of the house." The unshed tears now streamed down Nina's face. "I waited. I don't know why, but I did. By the time I called Janz Security, they couldn't get me an appointment until Friday. It's my fault, Kate. It's my fault Jonathan's dead."

"We have no idea if the guy in the SUV is the killer. Don't beat yourself up like this." It was clear she felt guilty for her procrastination, but her attitude seemed a little over the top. I couldn't help but wonder if she was telling me the whole story. "Can you give me a description of the man?"

"No. I told you the other day; I never really got a good look at him. I was outside picking up the mail. He was parked down the road a little ways. It was a scorcher of a day, and the man had his window down. When I looked his way, he immediately started his vehicle, rolled up the windows, and drove away. The only thing I had time to register was a man behind the wheel. I didn't think anything of it until I saw the same white SUV a second time when I looked out the window."

"Do you think the driver could have been Jonathan's son, Bobby?" Patrick had already told me none of our suspects had a white SUV registered in their name, but that didn't mean one of them couldn't have rented or borrowed one.

"I don't know, maybe."

I pulled out my cell phone, punching a few buttons to bring up a picture of Owen Mitchell. "What about him?"

Nina shrugged.

"How about this guy?" The picture was of Rob Whitington, one I'd snapped after serving him with the search warrant at his house.

"He looks familiar, but I told you, I didn't get a good look."

Deciding to move on, I closed my phone and opened my notebook. I jotted down the dates and approximate times Nina saw the white SUV. "Thanks. This will help when I'm searching the traffic camera recordings. You know I'm glad we had this time to talk . . . away from your counsel. Are you sure Bethany Dunbar has your best interest at heart?"

"What do you mean?" Nina grabbed her purse, rummaging around inside until she found a crumpled up tissue.

"How did Ms. Dunbar come to represent you?"

"She showed up the hospital. Told me she'd heard about Jonathan's murder and that they had worked together in the past."

"In what capacity?"

Nina tilted her head, seemingly searching for the memory. "You know, I don't recall if she told me. I was pretty out of it, just happy she showed up. She got me released, brought me some clothes and toiletry items. On the way over to Ana's house, Ms. Dunbar explained how the police would put my life under a microscope. She suggested we go on the offense. Talk to the police first to see if they had any evidence against me."

I'm sure Bethany Dunbar was interested in discovering what evidence we had, but for a completely different reason. The real party she represented probably wanted to find out if the investigation would lead the police to their doorstep. Nina was simply the tool to get the information.

"I think you should find new representation. Detective Jessup and I served Rob Whitington with a search warrant. Bethany Dunbar is his attorney. There's a real conflict of interest."

"What do you mean? Who is Rob Whitington?"

"Nina, have you ever been to the Sext Club?"

An explosion of red spread across Nina's face. "Once."

"Did you meet the club owner?"

"No."

"Rob Whitington is the owner of the Sext Club." I showed Nina his picture again. "This is him."

"I don't understand." Nina bowed her head, rubbing her temples. She grabbed her purse again, this time taking out a prescription bottle.

"Migraine?"

"Yes, still in the early stages, but I can feel it coming." She stood and walked to the bathroom.

I heard the water run, the clink of a glass against the faucet spout. If a migraine was about to hit Nina, I knew I wouldn't have much more time with her. She'd need a dark, quiet space to stave off the pain. There were a hundred more questions I wanted to ask, but I decided to jump ahead to the ones mattering most.

I leaned over laying the photograph on the bed Nina had been sitting on. When she returned to the room, she stopped short as her eyes locked onto the picture.

"Where did you get that?"

In my heart, I knew Nina couldn't be responsible for her husband's death, but I still had to play this like I had all the cards. "Who's the girl with Jonathan?"

"I don't know what you're talking about." Nina's gaze darted around the room. She went to sit on the bed then remembered the photograph and jumped back up. Almost as if she'd received a shock from the close proximity. Nina walked over to the small table in the corner of the room and stood by it. She picked up the pen lying on a pad of hotel stationery and started clicking the top repeatedly.

"Nina, I can tell you've seen the photograph before. Please talk to me. I'm in your corner. How can I help you if I don't know all the information?"

Click, click click. She kept punching the top of the pen with her thumb, seemingly calculating her options. I couldn't help but wonder how much of the truth I'd get or what version. The thought threw me. If I truly believed in Nina's innocence, why would I question her trustworthiness?

"A copy of that photograph," she said with clear disdain, "was in a stack of others delivered to my office. It's the least offensive one out of the bunch."

"Tell me about them."

Nina dropped the pen and began rubbing the taunt tendons at the base of her neck. "It was the end of the day, Friday, July 8. My receptionist handed me an envelope with my name inscribed on the front. No address or return information. She said a courier had dropped it off. Luckily, I had the sense not to open it in front of her." Nina got quiet, lost in her own thoughts.

I walked over to the table and sat in one of the chairs. "And?" I pointed to the empty seat across from me. Nina almost melted into it.

"I knew my husband was controlling, demanding, domineering but I never knew . . ."

"What Nina?"

"I never knew his deviant behavior included raping little girls."

I pursed my lips and jerked my neck to the side causing a rush of popping sounds. Pointing at the photograph on the bed I said, "Is this same girl in all of the pictures you received?"

Nina bobbed her head slowly. "It looked as if the girl had been held in a condemned room. The photos showed the evolution of Jonathan binding her to metal rings screwed into the floor and savagely raping her. I can't get those images out of my mind, Kate. He did horrible things to her."

"Are you sure it wasn't staged?"

"Staged?" Nina's forehead wrinkled in confusion. "How could it have been staged?"

"We know Rob Whitington set up fantasies for his rich clientele. He may have set up a mock rape scenario for Jonathan. The girl could have been in on the whole thing. I know it sounds repulsive that a woman would put herself in that kind of situation, but it's been known to happen. The internet is full of videos of women subjecting themselves to the humiliation of bondage, gang rape—all for a dollar."

Nina shook her head emphatically. "No. No way, Kate. Her face. In the first few shots, she wasn't scared, more confused. When Jonathan got rough, her expression changed to one of complete terror. And there's no faking the blood I saw." Nina kept shaking her head. "Now to hear Jonathan may have paid money to have this girl . . . spread out for him like some sexual buffet. It's unimaginable."

"Do you think the girl was eighteen and only looked younger? I ask because when Patrick and I went undercover at the Sext Club, we talked privately with Rob Whitington. Patrick asked about the possibility of acting out a fantasy with a minor. Whitington said he didn't cater to that kind of thing, though he admitted he could find girls who looked younger than they were."

Nina shuddered. "No. Her body . . . her body development clearly indicated she was younger than eighteen. But what does her age have to do with anything? Jonathan raped that girl."

"I'm simply trying to gather as much information as I can. Was a note included in the envelope of photographs?"

"Yes. It read, 'Tell your husband if he doesn't keep paying, the media gets the next set of pictures.' I don't know who sent it, but a man didn't write the letter. It looked like a girl's flowery handwriting."

"Did you confront your husband with the pictures?"

Nina looked away for a moment then back at me. "Jonathan was out of town the weekend they were delivered. I spent three days rehearsing what to say. I planned on confronting him Monday morning before work. I knew if I didn't, there'd be no concentrating on my clients later in the day."

"What happened?"

"He was acting erratically. He screamed at Ana when she didn't have his shirts back from the dry cleaners. His anger scared me. I'd planned on asking for a divorce after confronting him with the pictures. I envisioned myself telling him I would keep his secret if he'd only let me go, not contest the divorce. I knew it was my only shot at getting out of the marriage."

"If you didn't confront him with the pictures, what was the argument your neighbor saw you two having outside the house Monday morning?"

Nina let out a dry, emotionless laugh. "Jonathan was itching for a fight with anyone unlucky enough to be in his line of sight. I'd followed him outside and stopped him before he drove off, asking if he'd be home after work. I told him I wanted to talk to him about something. He went off on me. Saying I was trying to control him. Ha! What a joke. It set me off. All the emotion stirred up from seeing those pictures had me a ball of nervous energy waiting to confront him. My anger got away from me."

"Are you telling me you had those photographs in your possession for over a week before Jonathan died and did nothing with them?"

Nina avoided my gaze.

"Nina? Did you ever show them to your husband?"

She shook her head. "I couldn't find the nerve. The morning of Jonathan's death I met with my divorce attorney. Rutledge is a real shark, and I wanted to see if he'd confront Jonathan about the pictures for me. Drop the d-word on him. I know, I know, I'm a chicken."

"No, I understand. Really I do. If Jonathan was as volatile as you described, there's no telling what he would have done. You have no idea how many crime scenes I've been called out to where a domestic altercation turned deadly. So what happened between your husband and your lawyer?"

Nina rubbed circular motions across her brow. "Jonathan was murdered before Rutledge ever got a chance to sit down with him."

"Why didn't you tell me about the blackmail pictures earlier?"

Nina stopped rubbing. She looked at me shocked. "Are you kidding me? I was too embarrassed. I'm married to a rapist, Kate. What does that say about me? A psychologist who doesn't even know her husband's predilection for . . . I can't even say it."

"Don't you understand? Those pictures represent one more nail in Rob Whitington's coffin. Your financial records show Jonathan took out six weekly cash advances of five grand each. Hush money to Rob Whitington for the pictures. I've uncovered a scam Whitington ran from his club. He enlisted the help of his female workers to set up wealthy members. Create embarrassing situations to later blackmail them with."

"You said one more nail. What other evidence do you have against this guy?"

I hesitated a moment, reviewing the details in my head to make sure divulging the information wouldn't hurt the case. "We know from a worker at the Sext Club that Whitington allegedly set up a fantasy for Jonathan. We don't know what kind, but based on the pictures you received, let's assume for now it was a rape fantasy with an underage girl. As I mentioned earlier, transactions from Jonathan's credit card show regular withdrawals we're assuming paid a blackmail threat. Your husband got caught searching Whitington's office for the incriminating tape. Jonathan received a beating that night, a fact the ME can confirm from partially healed rib fractures on the body. An eyewitness also placed Jonathan in the club an hour and a half before he died Thursday night. Whitington and his goons escorted Jonathan out of the club, potentially the last ones to see him alive. One of them could have followed Jonathan home, tortured and murdered him."

Nina's hand nervously rubbed her neck. "I'm lucky I didn't wake up any earlier. I could have met the same horrible fate."

"Your husband wasn't the only man to fall victim to Whitington's schemes. During the raid on Whitington's house and club, we found a great deal of incriminating evidence." I leaned in closer. "Nina, please tell me you still have those blackmail pictures."

Nina's eyes were closed as she nodded slowly, her head in obvious pain. "They're with my divorce attorney. Do you want me to have him send them over to your precinct?"

"No. I'll have an officer stop by and pick up the evidence. I don't want to take the chance of them disappearing."

I pulled out my cell phone and handed it to Nina, asking her to call Emmitt Rutledge to okay the transfer of photographs from his possession to the TPD. Nina made the necessary arrangements, then handed back my phone. Excited we'd soon have more proof against Rob Whitington, I smacked my hand on the table. Still though, I was frustrated. "Now if we could only find out who the girl is in the pictures."

Nina stilled. She slowly opened her eyes and locked them onto mine.

"I might be able to help with that."

CHAPTER 31

"What do you mean, Nina? Do you know the girl's identity?"

"You have to understand, Kate. I was devastated after seeing those pictures. I couldn't get the vision of that young girl out of my head. I thought if I could only find her, make sure she's okay. I don't know . . . make some kind of restitution." Nina let out a sound, a cross between a sigh and a growl. "I don't know what I thought."

"How'd you figure it out? Did Whitington put the girl's name on the back of one of the pictures?"

Nina shook her head. "No, I had a lot of time on my hands that weekend. I studied those photos for hours looking for a clue. I was at a loss until I woke up in the middle of the night thinking about the blazer."

I walked over to the picture and looked at it. "There's no blazer in this photograph."

"It was only in the first one of my bunch. A burgundy school jacket thrown on the floor, half out of the picture. I got a magnifying glass and saw a crest on the pocket. Tampa Conservatory. It took me a while to figure out what to do with the information. School was out for the summer. I scoured the school's website searching for . . . I don't know, the answer to fall into my lap I guess. In a way it did. The site had a link to a yearbook website. You know the kind where you can reorder a past yearbook from a list of participating schools. Tampa Conservatory was on the list, so I ordered last year's copy, requesting overnight delivery. The school teaches kids in sixth grade up through their senior year in high school. I was hopeful I'd find her picture, even if she were younger than I'd initially guessed."

"Look at you, Nancy Drew." I returned to my chair, still clutching the picture under the table.

"Must run in the family. Uncle Manny's been a sheriff for more than twenty years."

"I'm assuming you found the girl."

Nina nodded. "Julia Eaton. Sophomore. That put her age at fifteen or sixteen depending on when her birthday fell. I paid for one of those online searches and got her address and phone number. I also scoured the internet looking for anything I could find. Besides her social networking sites, which I wasn't privy to, I found one article about her in the *Tampa Tribune*. One of those articles spotlighting teens who make a difference in our community. Julia Eaton raised $10,000 in a fundraiser benefiting the American Cancer Society. She was only fourteen at the time. The story explained how her grass roots campaign enlisted the help of fellow classmates as well as teenagers across the country."

"Nina, what did you do?"

"The guilt was eating me alive." Nina took off her glasses, laying them on the table. "Logically, I knew I wasn't responsible for Jonathan's actions but remaining silent about it felt like it made me . . . an accomplice somehow. I called Julia's house."

"You did what?"

"I know it was dumb. But I've counseled enough girls to understand how keeping that kind of secret stuffed away leads to tremendous self-abuse. Men take their pain out on the world. Women internalize their feelings. If she never sought counseling, refused to verbalize her feelings about the rape, she'd suffer a lifetime of pain. It could manifest as an eating disorder, self-mutilation, promiscuity, or an inability to maintain healthy relationships."

Check, check, check. Sounded like a laundry list of my twenties. And thirties.

"When I called Julia's house, her dad, Greg Eaton, answered. I didn't want to let on about the real reason for my call. I didn't know if Julia had told him about the rape yet. When I asked to speak to Julia, Greg got suspicious. He started grilling me about how I knew his daughter."

Nina nervously fiddled with her glasses, pushing the frames up and down like a teeter totter. "On the fly, I concocted a story about being a doctor, a liaison for the American Cancer Society. I told him we were resurrecting some of the old stories of outstanding individuals who'd helped the organization. Stories to try to revitalize our current campaign. I asked again to speak to Julia and he said . . . he said . . ."

"What did he say, Nina?"

She let out a choke-filled sob. "I couldn't speak to Julia. She was dead."

"What?"

"Yes. Suicide. I was stunned, at a loss for words. Maybe it was unethical of me, but I had to find out the details of Julia's death. I told her dad how sorry I was for his loss and suggested we write another article memorializing her. I hated to play on the man's pain, but at this point, I was in too deep to walk away. I knew he'd never openly speak about his daughter without a good reason. But he—"

Nina grabbed her head, trying to stifle the pain.

"Migraine taking over?"

She tried to nod but stopped in obvious misery.

"Come over to the bed and lie down," I said.

After I settled Nina under the covers, I turned out all the lights except for the one in the bathroom. I cracked the door enough to light my way back across the room. I sat down on the bed opposite Nina. "You know, I'm going to have to talk to Julia's dad, right? I won't be able to keep your husband's actions a secret."

Nina spoke quietly, every word laced with pain. "I understand. I wouldn't ask you to."

"Only a couple more questions then I'll leave. Did Greg Eaton ever open up to you about Julia's suicide?"

"No, the wounds were still too fresh. He broke down crying. Asked me to call back later."

"Did you use your real name? Give any indication as to your real identity?"

"No, I was extremely careful. Kate, can we finish this—."

"Later? Yes, we'll talk more tomorrow."

I walked to the door, grabbing the do-not-disturb hanger before leaving the room. I placed it on the outside door handle, hoping Nina would be able to get some uninterrupted sleep.

What did all this mean to the case? My head was dizzy from the possibilities. I knew I needed to talk to Greg Eaton about his daughter. Find out what Julia had told him about the rape. Or if she had even confided in him. Either way it would be a difficult conversation, probably the last one Greg would want to have.

On the flip side, he'd finally get the name of his daughter's rapist. As I saw it, we already had visual proof the rape occurred, or at least we would when Nina's lawyer handed over the pictures. Most likely, the video footage at our crime lab showed the same attack. Because Rob Whitington commissioned the crime, he was just as responsible for the rape as Jonathan Grace. Now all I had to do was prove Whitington, or one of his men, followed Jonathan home the night of his murder and killed him.

Time to get Patrick in the loop. He'd be angry I'd met with Nina alone, but after I shared everything I'd learned, he'd forgive me. It was always easier to obtain forgiveness than permission.

I pulled out my cell phone, dialing as I walked through the front lobby of the hotel. My partner picked up on the second ring. "Patrick, you're never going to believe this."

CHAPTER 32

Back at the squad room, I dropped Detective Jung's keys on his desk. "Thanks for letting me borrow your car. I owe you one."

Jung looked up from his computer screen, eyes bloodshot. "No problem." It looked like he hadn't moved in the three hours I'd been gone.

"Have you seen Patrick around?" I asked.

"Nope."

"Good talking with you, Jung."

"Yep."

Under my shirt, I undid the top button on my pants. My stomach begged for relief after quickly gorging on lunch in the car.

Patrick walked into the squad room and threw me my keys. They slipped out of my fingers. "Looks like we're playing musical cars today," I said, bending over to grab the keys off the floor. My belly groaned at the movement.

"Not much longer," Patrick said. "The shop called and said I could pick mine up tomorrow morning. Finally something's going right." Patrick sat down at his desk and opened a brown paper bag. He pulled out a carton of Chinese food. "Damn. How do they always forget the chopsticks? It's not rocket science, people. Doesn't anyone take pride in their work anymore?"

"Chill out, partner." I dug around in my desk drawer until I found a pair of chopsticks. "Here."

"These aren't used . . . are they?"

I bent over and slammed my drawer shut. "Really?"

"Hey, you never know what's in that desk of yours."

I shrugged. "Are you still pissed I went to see Dr. Grace alone?"

When I'd talked to Patrick on the phone earlier, he was furious I'd met with Nina by myself. He gave me a five-minute lecture on the inadmissibility of interviews without lawyers present before he'd even let me speak. Eventually, he simmered down. Yet, even after I told him everything I'd discovered, he wouldn't admit I'd done the right thing.

Patrick stopped eating and sighed. "You know, I'm really sick of the women in my life hiding things from me. First, I find out Alina met with her obstetrics doctor without me. She also forgot to mention the riskiness of the pregnancy due to her having placenta previa when she carried our last daughter. Now you drop *your* bombshell on me. No more, Kate. I'm serious. From now on, you keep me in the loop. Don't hide anything from me and don't inadvertently forget to tell me something because you think it will piss me off."

I kicked at a gum wrapper on the floor. "You're right. I went off half-cocked again."

"Stop yourself next time." Patrick stabbed at his orange chicken.

Agreeing with a salute, I sat down at my desk. "Go ahead, finish eating. I'll start a computer search on the Eaton's. See what I can dig up. When you're done, you can update me on the meeting with Jonathan's old partner, Sean O'Brien. I know you were too mad to talk about it on the phone.

"No, the conversation won't take long. I can take bites in between."

"The abridged version then."

"Jonathan called Sean O'Brien two days before his murder, asking if they could meet. Said he wanted to talk about something important. O'Brien suggested they get together for lunch, but Jonathan wanted to talk somewhere more private. Guess Jonathan showed up at this guy's office looking like hell, unshaven, had a stain on his shirt. You get the idea. Nothing really noticeable to anyone else, but O'Brien knowing Jonathan like he did, realized something serious was going on. His appearance seemed completely out of character."

Patrick paused a moment, taking a bite of chicken. "Jonathan said he'd gotten himself into a jam. Didn't give any details but admitted he was being blackmailed by a guy and wanted an opinion on how to fix the mess. O'Brien said, and I quote, 'Only three ways to get out from under it. Keep paying, stop paying and let the shit hit the fan, or go after the fucker holding the goods on you.'"

"He actually said that?"

"Yep. You should have seen this guy. Short, thick, tree trunk kind of a guy. I'm guessing if the roles were reversed, O'Brien would have chosen option number three."

"So what happened?"

"Jonathan told O'Brien what we already knew. That Jonathan had stopped paying and tried to find the blackmail tape himself. Got an ass beating for his troubles. O'Brien told Jonathan he'd have a talk with the blackmailer, persuade him to make a different choice."

"That's ballsy to admit."

"Only because he never ended up talking to Whitington. Jonathan thanked his friend for the offer, but it seemed like an idea had struck Jonathan while the two of them were talking. Guess Jonathan wanted to try out something before he took O'Brien up on his proposition. He didn't say what."

Patrick took another bite of food, quickly chewed it, and continued. "At the end of the conversation, O'Brien seemed to get upset over Jonathan's murder. As much as a thug Irishman can let on anyway. The guy said he'd been straight up with me in hopes that it would help catch the killer."

"Interesting a guy like Jonathan Grace was in business with a guy like Sean O'Brien. I'd love to have seen their company's mission statement. 'Let us build where we want, or we'll break your kneecaps.'"

Patrick laughed, barely able to keep the food in his mouth.

"Though my money's still on Whitington," I said, "tomorrow we need to start looking into the grudge list Dr. Grace provided. Who knows what kind of shady dealings Jonathan was involved in and how many people he pissed off along the way?"

I turned my attention to my computer, searching for information about the Eaton family. When I came across an important detail, I read it aloud. "Although there's not much information in Julia Eaton's obituary, the death certificate reports she overdosed on Cytoxan. Do you know what kind of drug that is, Patrick?"

I confirmed the spelling of the drug's name, and Patrick typed in a search on his computer.

"It's an oral chemotherapy drug used to fight leukemia and lymphoma," he said. "Also lung, ovarian, and breast cancers. How does a kid get ahold of a powerful drug like that?"

"Don't know. Let me keep looking for more information on the Eatons." After a few minutes of reading, I snapped my fingers.

"What?"

"Hey, Jung," I yelled across the squad room. "I know you're knee deep into the Masterson case, but can you spare a minute?"

Detective Jung looked up from his computer and rubbed his eyes. Through a yawn he said, "Sure. I need a break anyway." He stood, popped his neck, and stretched his arms over his head.

"You caught a case a little over four weeks ago," I said as he walked over to my desk. "A Caucasian girl, sixteen, found overdosed on oral chemotherapy pills. Do you remember the case?"

"Sure. Over on Van Dyke Rd. Dispatch got a 911 call from the father—"

"Greg Eaton?" I asked.

"Yeah. Greg Eaton. Said he was heading out for work, checked on his daughter, and found her not breathing. When Wozniack and I got on the scene, the father was distraught. Poor guy had lost his wife to cancer only a couple months earlier. Come to find out, the daughter had finished off her mom's chemo pills. ME ruled it a suicide. Why? Does this have something to do with the Jonathan Grace case?"

"Sure does."

Jung nodded at the case file I'd brought up on my computer screen. "Did you see the footnote?"

"Which one?"

Jung pointed at the one on the bottom of the last page. "It's the case number for Julia Eaton's missing person report. Greg Eaton filed one on her May 3 of this year. We classified her as a runaway. Eaton cancelled it when his daughter showed up three weeks later."

"Wait a minute. I can't keep up with all these dates." I walked over to the whiteboard and grabbed the black dry erase marker. Detective Jung took over my chair, reading off the dates I asked for.

"Look at this Patrick. April 8 mom dies. May 3 Julia runs away. May 22 Julia returns home. Remember what happened two days before on May 20?"

Patrick thought for a moment. He snapped his fingers. "The date stamp on the one blackmail picture found in Rob Whitington's office."

"Right." I wrote May 20 on the board. The day Jonathan Grace raped Julia Eaton.

Detective Jung looked confused. I took a few moments to get him up to speed.

"How about this for a possible scenario? Julia's mom—what's her name?" I looked down at the computer. "Maggie, right. Maggie Eaton dies of cancer. Julia can't handle the grief, runs away. Somehow she gets hooked up with Rob Whitington who sets up a rape fantasy for Jonathan Grace, with her as the star. Maybe Julia needed money out on the streets, she could have . . . hell, I don't know, point is, Whitington is responsible for setting up the rape. We have pictures and hopefully video of the crime coming soon."

"After the attack, Julia goes back home," Patrick said, picking up the conversation's thread. "The rape causes her to spiral further down into a depression until she takes her own life."

"Whitington may or may not have known Julia Eaton committed suicide," I said, "but it doesn't matter. He had what he wanted— blackmail on Jonathan Grace. Julia was a means to an end, one Whitington discarded when he was through with her."

"Does this bring you any closer to finding out who killed Jonathan Grace?" Jung asked.

"Nothing concrete," I said, "but it definitely helps fill in some of the holes.

"Assuming Julia Eaton was actually the girl in the blackmail pictures," Patrick said. "We don't know for sure yet."

"We'll know soon enough. As we speak, an officer is on his way back from Rutledge's office with the photographs Nina received." I jammed the cap back onto the marker. "I still like Whitington for the murder. Even if he didn't hold the knife to Jonathan's throat, he sent one of his guys in his place."

Patrick shook his head. "I know I'm repeating myself, but I'll say it again. Dead men don't pay blackmail. Whitington wouldn't kill his cash cow."

"Remember what Peyton said? Grace refused to pay Whitington any more blackmail money. Maybe the goon was only supposed to rough Grace up, enough to hammer home Whitington's point about paying. The guy could have gone overboard. I told you what Harry Ellis said during the autopsy. The killer may have pressed too hard on the trachea. Jonathan Grace suffocated on his own blood. Maybe the killer didn't mean to finish him off."

"That's one scenario," Patrick said.

By this time, Jung had rolled his chair out of the crossfire, deciding to watch the show rather than participate in it.

"I suppose you have a better one?" I asked.

"Not better but an alternative."

"By all means."

"Dr. Nina Grace receives pictures depicting the rape of a girl by her husband. She confronts Jonathan, hoping this is her ticket to freedom. She demands a divorce. He refuses. She realizes if this doesn't get him away from her, nothing ever will. Dr. Grace hires a killer. Says to make it painful, payback for the girl."

"That's ridiculous, Patrick. If Dr. Grace had photographic proof of her husband raping a girl, why not turn him into the police? Seems like a much easier way to get rid of him."

"The pictures might not prove rape. A good criminal attorney could have Jonathan out of jail in twenty-four hours. Then what do you think would happen? Put yourself in Dr. Grace's shoes. Jonathan comes home in a rage, ready to take out his anger on the person who turned him in."

Patrick and I stared at each other, neither of us willing to back down.

Jung stood up once again stretching his arms over his head. "No matter what scenario you like, you guys should talk to Greg Eaton. Find out if his daughter told him about the rape. He might have more dirt on Whitington. Or at least confirm Dr. Grace's version of the conversation they had."

CHAPTER 33

"I can't believe Wozniack uncovered Owen Mitchell's plot to blow up a power plant," I said.

"According to Wozniack, Mitchell will be arraigned later today." Patrick clipped his phone back onto his belt. "Looks like we might need to make a trip over to Orlando after all. We should interrogate him ourselves. Mitchell's obviously unstable."

"You know what this means, right? Wozniack's going to be an even bigger pain in the ass than he already is."

"Give him a little credit, Kate. He saved hundreds of lives."

"A regular hero." I sighed. "Before we take a deeper look into Mitchell, let's get this done first."

Patrick and I stood at Greg Eaton's front door. When I pressed the doorbell, a melodic chime rang out.

"Why don't you take the lead on questioning Eaton?" I said. "This is going to be one hell of a difficult conversation. He might feel more comfortable with you at the helm."

"You sure?"

"Definitely. I'll be your second set of eyes. Watch his demeanor. Get a good look around the place."

We knew from Detective Jung, even though it was a Monday afternoon, Greg Eaton would be home. He worked as a freelance computer programmer out of his house.

The door opened and a lean man towered over us. He was so tall his head nearly touched the top of the door frame. His uncombed, short brown hair stood up in spiked patches. Even though it was the middle of July, he wore sweatpants with threadbare knees and a holey, long-sleeved shirt. Eaton must not do a lot of videoconferencing for his job.

"Mr. Eaton?" Patrick asked.

"Yes?"

"Hello, my name is Detective Patrick Jessup and this is my partner, Detective Kate Springer."

I nodded to Greg. He wiped sweat from his flushed cheeks.

"Sorry, wasn't expecting company," Greg said. "Not feeling too well today. Can I help you with something?"

Patrick nodded, a friendly smile on his face. "May we come in?"

"Sure." Greg closed the door behind us. "What's this about?" He stood with his back against the door, his hand on the doorknob, twisting it back and forth.

"I know you worked with a Detective Jung on your daughter's case. First, I want to tell you how sorry we both are for your loss. I know you still must be grieving Julia's death. I promise we won't take long, but we'd appreciate your help."

"I don't understand. Julia died a month ago. What more could you need from me?"

"We have some questions. Questions that might be tough to hear, but please understand, we wouldn't ask if it wasn't necessary. Your daughter's name came up in a recent investigation."

Greg looked unsure, his eyes scanning the room behind us. "Do you want to sit down?" He extended his arm toward the living room to the right of us. As we followed behind him, I looked farther into the house and saw a filthy kitchen, counters full of dirty dishes and takeout boxes.

Greg sat on the couch, Patrick beside him. I sat in the rose-colored chair facing the couch. The room had a feminine touch to it, soft pinks and floral prints. A layer of dust covered the room, speaking to its lack of use. A large portrait of Julia hung on the wall between a smattering of frames, containing prints of family members, some together, some separate. Though she looked older than her age, I could tell Julia was the girl in the pictures we'd gotten from Rutledge's office. No pink stained the ends of her hair in the portrait on the wall.

"You said Julia was involved in a crime." Greg sat slightly hunched over, his elbows on his legs, hands clasped together tightly between his knees. He looked uncomfortable, his tall frame trying to find space on the small couch next to Patrick.

"No, sir. Julia didn't commit a crime. Her name recently surfaced in a case we're investigating. You might have heard about it on the news. The murder of real estate mogul Jonathan Grace."

"Sure, I heard about it. Hey, before we get started, I need to use the bathroom. Sorry. Told you I wasn't feeling real hot."

Patrick stood when Greg Eaton did.

"Don't worry about it," Patrick said. "Would you like us to come back at a better time?"

I shot Patrick a stern look.

"No," Greg said. "As long as you don't mind waiting a few minutes. I'll be right back." He walked down the hallway and quietly shut the door.

"What's your take on this guy?" Patrick asked.

"He's got the sweats. He's flushed, but still bundled up. Looks like he has a bad summer cold."

"That's not what I meant."

"Then what? We just got here. By the way, what was all the 'do you want us to come back later' crap? We don't have time for that bullshit. This conversation is going to suck whether he's sick or not. Best to get it over with as quickly as possible."

"Wow, when did you turn into such a heartless person?"

"What do mean by that?"

"You've changed, Kate. Ever since we caught this case, you've been more concerned with proving Dr. Grace's innocence than finding Jonathan's killer."

"The guy's a rapist."

"What if he is? Doesn't mean he deserves to die for it. We're not the judge, jury, and executioner. I've never seen you show such indifference toward a victim before."

I was shocked at the mirror Patrick had forced in front of my face. Had I been that callous, only thinking of Nina and how to help her? I cringed at Patrick's words, realizing I'd always been the one championing for the victim. Fighting for those who'd had their voices extinguished far too early. A battle raged inside me—loyalty versus my moral compass.

Patrick continued holding up the mirror. "And then your selfish response toward Greg Eaton? The guy looks like hell. He's still reeling over the loss of his family. Have some freaking compassion."

"You're right, I can't believe—"

I stopped talking when I heard a door close. Footsteps announced Eaton's return. I sat shell-shocked. Twice in two days, those closest to me had told me how selfish I was. If I didn't change, I'd end up pushing away the people I loved most in this world. Hell, I'd already accomplished it with Lucy.

Greg walked into the room wearing a fresh set of clothes. He'd exchanged his sweats for a pair of jeans and one long-sleeved shirt for a new one.

"Sorry," Greg apologized. "I didn't mean to keep you waiting so long." He sat in the same place he'd vacated earlier.

"Are you sure about this?" Patrick asked him. "We can come back later in the week, talk when you're feeling better."

"No, let's get on with it. Not knowing has a way of eating you up inside, you know?"

Patrick nodded. "Detective Jung told us Julia ran away. It must have been an agonizing time for you. I have three daughters myself. I can't imagine the hell you went through not knowing where she was."

"You're lucky to have such a big family, Detective. You should thank God every day He allows you the chance to come home to them."

Patrick looked down into his lap. I knew thoughts of the new baby weighed heavy on his mind.

"Julia couldn't cope with her mom's death," Greg continued, sadness and regret punctuating each word. "You always hear about daddy's girl. Not Julia, she was definitely a mama's girl. Those two were inseparable. Getting their nails done on the weekend, watching sappy love stories on television. Julia was a teenager, a time when hormones usually tore mothers and daughters apart, but not my girls. When Maggie got diagnosed with ovarian cancer, Julia was devastated."

Greg's voice changed, becoming almost robotic sounding. "Maggie had malignant epithelial ovarian tumors. The surgeons removed her ovaries, fallopian tubes, uterus, and nearby lymph nodes. She followed it up with chemotherapy, but Maggie couldn't handle the depressing mood of the treatment center. Said everyone else's sadness made her feel heavy for days afterwards. My wife had been an elementary school teacher. You'd never find a more caring woman. She could always handle her own pain, but the cancer had weakened her too much to deal with the emotional pain of others. Maggie quickly switched to an oral chemotherapy treatment in order to stay home. We thought it was working, until Maggie took a turn for the worse. The cancer spread. She was dead seven months after receiving her initial diagnosis."

Patrick remained quiet for a moment longer, waiting to see if Greg would continue talking. Many times family members who'd lost a loved one found it easier to talk to strangers. During an interview, they would finally unload their pent up feelings for the first time since their loved one's death. If that's what it was like with Greg Eaton, he wouldn't need much prompting to talk.

"Julia was so quiet after her mother's death. I couldn't get her to open up, to talk about her feelings of loss. I naively thought it was her way of grieving."

Greg let out a heart wrenching sob. He put a fist up to his mouth, biting his knuckles to get his emotions under control. "Julia probably thought I left her alone to grieve, but I swear it wasn't my intention. I only thought she needed a little space. One morning, I went into her room to wake her for school. It had been a constant battle getting her to go. Julia's room was empty. The only thing I found was a note that had fallen on the floor."

When Greg remained silent, Patrick asked what had been written in the note.

"Julia said she couldn't handle the silence in the house. Said if she didn't leave, it would drive her crazy. She told me she'd only to be gone for a little while, only until she could get her head wrapped around a few things. Julia promised me she'd call. She never did."

"Do you know what finally prompted your daughter to come home?"

Greg was startled by Patrick's question. Greg's already flushed face dripped sweat from his brow. He anxiously started muttering to himself, shaking his head back and forth.

"Mr. Eaton, are you okay?"

Greg stood abruptly. He walked behind the couch and began pacing. Though Patrick sat calmly with his back facing Greg's agitated movements, my partner's raised eyebrows confirmed his agreement that things were getting a little weird.

Caught up in his ramblings, Greg vigorously rubbed his index finger back and forth over the spot where his wedding ring should have been. Surprising he took it off so soon after his wife's death. Maybe he put it in her casket the day she was buried.

Greg continued pacing. The volume of his fractured speech varied between barely a whisper and just loud enough to hear. "My wife, my wife . . . she said . . . 'Take care of our daughter, Snookums,' she said . . . said to me before she died . . . 'Promise me. You're all she's got now.' . . . I let my wife down. . . Didn't protect Julia."

Snookums? My heart jumped in my chest.

Greg stopped moving. He watched my expression, reading me, somehow knowing my thoughts. I chanced a glance at Patrick, but he hadn't caught Greg's slip-up. My hand darted to my holster, unclipping it, pulling out my gun. Greg's hand also moved, brandishing a knife he'd taken out from underneath the back of his shirt. He jerked Patrick up off the couch. The crook of Greg's arm hooked around Patrick's neck, pulling it up at a sideways angle. Greg positioned the long, straight edge blade over the blanched skin of Patrick's Adam's apple. Greg wrapped his other arm around Patrick's ribs using Patrick's body as a shield against my weapon.

"Put down the knife!" I yelled, aiming my Smith & Wesson at the men. Years of training ensured my nerves didn't impact the steadiness of my hands.

Patrick struggled. Greg's knife nicked the skin, a line of blood dripped down Patrick's neck, staining his white collar.

"Stop!" I yelled.

Patrick listened, Greg did not. The hand gripping the knife continued to shake, causing blood to drip faster. I looked into Patrick's eyes. They were awash with a mixture of fear and concern. Probably thinking about what would happen to his loved ones if the situation went south. My heart groaned at the thought he may never see his newest child enter the world.

Patrick blinked once very slowly. Purposeful in its intent. An innocent action in and of itself, yet to me filled with underlying meaning. He wanted me to know he trusted me. Trusted me to talk Greg out of this situation, or if need be, to take the man down.

"You don't have to do this," Patrick finally managed in a shaky voice.

"Shut up! Both of you." Greg squinted as the sweat from his brow dripped into his eyes. "Do you know what that monster did to my little girl? DO YOU?"

"Are you talking about Jonathan Grace?" I asked in a soothing, calm voice.

"Yes, the late Mr. Grace." The words oozed venomous disdain. "The man who thought money could buy him anything he wanted. The man who thought he was entitled to having his every fantasy fulfilled. He ripped the innocence away from my daughter."

Anger flared behind Greg's bright eyes. "When Julia came back home, she was a shell of the girl I used to know. I'd hold her for hours while she cried, but she never would tell me what happened."

While Greg ranted, I'd hoped he would move the knife away from Patrick's throat, enough for me to take a shot. His grip never wavered.

"Greg, I know you don't want to hurt Patrick. Please lower your knife."

"NO! No one would listen to me before. I begged and begged for someone to listen to me. For someone to help me find my daughter. You damn cops sat on your asses while that bastard raped my daughter! Well, you'll listen to me now. You'll hear every word."

"I want to listen to you, Greg. I want to hear Julia's story. It's why we're here. Please. Move the knife away from Patrick's neck. You're hurting him. Look at all the blood."

"Then drop your gun."

"You know I can't do that."

"Neither can I."

Standing with my gun drawn, I may have looked the pillar of strength but on the inside, self-doubt nagged at me. Greg and Patrick stood behind the very edge of the couch about eight feet away. If it came down to it, could I pull the trigger knowing a miss might cause my partner's death?

"If Julia didn't open up to you, how did you find out Jonathan Grace raped your daughter?" I asked.

Greg exhaled sharply like the wind had been knocked out of him. He moved the knife, creating another blood trail along the side of Patrick's neck.

I winced, watching Patrick grit his teeth as he endured the pain silently.

"I found a diary lying on the bed next to her dead body. I kept it from the police."

"What did it say?"

"Julia wrote about the horrific attack. Everything she was too ashamed to say out loud, she wrote in her diary. That bastard!" Greg flexed his arm, causing Patrick's chin to stretch higher. The tendons on the side of Patrick's neck bulged from the pressure.

"Greg, I want to help you put the monster responsible for your daughter's rape behind bars, but you have to help me."

"What are you talking about? I killed Jonathan Grace. I made him recount every detail. Every painstakingly vivid detail." Greg smiled. "It was easy. I just had to provide the right motivation."

"No, not Jonathan Grace. The man responsible for putting Julia inside that room in the first place. Can you get me Julia's diary, Greg? Can we look to see if she wrote about that man?"

"Nice try." Greg's smile grew wide as he used his fist holding the knife to squeeze down blocking Patrick's airway.

"Wait! I'm sorry. I didn't mean . . . I thought maybe you were confused, forgot what Julia wrote."

Greg loosened his hold just enough to let Patrick breathe again. Patrick gasped, trying to pull enough oxygen into his lungs without causing more damage from the knife. I couldn't tear my eyes away from the blood-soaked collar of Patrick's shirt now a vibrant red. In my mind's eye, I pictured the bloody scene at the Graces' house and how the ME said the fatal cut to Jonathan's neck had been accidental. Greg Eaton looked unstable, at times shaking with anger. I had no doubt he was capable of slitting Patrick's throat either purposefully or by accident.

"Do you really think I could forget any of the words Julia wrote?" Greg's voice softened as he quoted his daughter. "I miss you so much, Mommy. Why can't you be here, now when I need you the most? Since God won't bring you back, I'm coming to find you. I feel horrible about leaving Daddy behind. I love him, but he can't heal my pain. Nothing will take away this pain. Look for me, Mommy. I'm coming."

Tears made slow tracks down Greg's face, wetting Patrick's hair. "Julia wrote about how she ran out of money a week after she left home. Naive girl thought she could live on her own with only a couple hundred dollars in her pocket. She tried getting a job but no respectable place would take her. When she described the strip clubs she'd visited, I wanted to be sick. The thought of men staring at my daughter while she gyrated on a stage for dollar bills disgusted me."

An anguished noise erupted from deep inside Greg. His hand, the one holding the knife to Patrick's throat, was wet with the blood from my partner's cuts.

"I don't understand why she just didn't come home," Greg said. "Julia wrote about how she was ready to give up, to come back, but then she ran into some guy named Rob. He offered her a job."

"Rob? Are you sure Julia said his name was Rob? Did she describe him or say where he worked?"

"No, only Rob. I pieced together what happened by reading her later journal entries. Julia wrote about a man with the initials J.G. raping her. She'd never met him before, but she saw his initials on a handkerchief. Now you're saying this Rob guy is responsible for setting up Julia's rape? How?"

"We know who he is. We have Rob Whitington in custody. Put down your weapon, and we'll talk. I'll tell you everything."

Greg looked like he was considering the option, but he continued his strong hold.

"Greg, do you remember when you told me how agonizing it was, not knowing? Give me the knife, and I'll tell you about this guy. Explain how all the evidence we have on Rob will put him away for life."

Greg shook his head, trying to block out my voice. Patrick's hair moved with each swing of Greg's chin.

"It's okay, Greg. You did your fatherly duty. You took out the man who hurt your little girl. No one can blame you. Hell, I'd do the same thing in your position. Let us take over. You've got to be tired, Greg. Let us get vengeance for Julia. There's no need to hurt anyone else. Patrick's one of the good guys. He has a wife at home, three little girls, a new baby on the way. You don't want those kids to grow up without a father, do you? You know how devastating the loss of a parent can be to a child. Please, put the knife down."

Greg's features morphed. I could see the physical manifestation of the rage welling up inside him, begging to be released. He growled at me, the animalistic growl of a wounded predator. Greg pointed the knife at me shouting, "Why should he get to go home to his family when mine's been taken away!"

When Greg moved the knife away from Patrick's throat, Patrick took the split second of freedom to elbow Greg in the ribs. Patrick dropped to the ground and rolled out of the way. Greg looked pained and bewildered for a moment then turned his focus toward me. Greg charged. I shot twice. The impact of the bullets spun him around, leaving him face down over the side of the couch.

I rushed to Greg, rolling him onto his back. Blood poured down his chest. He'd been hit near the right shoulder. Patrick appeared beside me, as I yanked off my blazer. He took it from me, balled it up, and pressed it over Greg's wounds. Greg laid still, the mewing sounds of pain the only indicator he was still conscious. I ran to find a towel then tied it around Patrick's neck. After I radioed dispatch requesting an ambulance, I took over holding the impromptu field dressing against Greg's chest.

Patrick slumped back against the couch, a tear trail still wetting his cheek. "I owe you one, partner."

"Looks like you handled yourself just fine without my help."

"No. You kept it together. Kept him talking long enough for me to find my moment."

"How's your neck feel?"

Patrick shrugged his shoulders. "Do you know what kept running through my mind while Greg held the knife to my throat? That I can't believe how selfish I've been. Complaining about money instead of feeling gratitude that God's going to bless my family with a new little life."

"Selfishness seems to be going around lately. I've got a lot of work to do on that one myself."

"I can't believe I'm walking out of here alive. That I get a second chance."

"Today was a close call. Too close. Maybe it can be my second chance, too. I need to use this as a wakeup call to pay attention to all the things I've been taking for granted. It's time I make some serious changes in my own life."

TUESDAY

CHAPTER 34

Though I was sure to be cleared in the shooting, I'd been put on paid leave until internal affairs finished their investigation. Normally after an event like yesterdays, I'd spend the evening ruminating with friends, but understandably Patrick wanted to spend time with his family. Nothing like a crazed killer holding a knife to your throat to make you reevaluate your priorities. That only left Lucy and well, she wasn't interested in hearing about my day. So I'd spent the night by myself, soul searching.

I'd realized my sensitivity toward domestic violence had caused me to overstep my boundaries with Lucy. A lifetime of watching a string of stepfathers knock around my mother had made me overly sensitive. I couldn't stand the thought of seeing my best friend live through the same hell. Unfortunately, I didn't recognize the feelings quickly enough.

This morning, I left a three-page note in Lucy's mailbox. I only hoped curiosity would compel her to read it instead of throwing it in the trash. In the apology letter, I took ownership for my selfishness. What I'd done to Charles Kent was unforgiveable. I told her I didn't expect absolution, only wanted her to find all the happiness she deserved. I couldn't bring myself to write about the personal impact domestic violence had on my life. It would just look like one more excuse in a long line of them.

Patrick's accusations of selfishness had also caused me to spend time examining my heart. I realized I'd pushed those closest to me away because of my selfish actions. I'd gotten lucky with Patrick, but I knew it was time to change.

I stood at the doorstep to Ana Lopez's house, waiting for someone to answer my knock. Nina opened the door. Her hair was styled up in a loose bun. She wore a green, floral dress. Her appearance seemed markedly improved from yesterday. I don't know if the lightness of the dress made her seem more carefree, but she definitely seemed calmer.

"Kate?" Nina seemed surprised but pleased to see me. "Would you like to come in? Ana's out with my brother shopping."

"Sure. You're looking better."

"Feeling better, too. I'm less jittery, not as anxious. Maybe it's because Jonathan's killer is off the streets. By the way, thank you for calling me last night at the hotel to give me the details of what happened."

We walked into Ana's kitchen. I sat in the same chair I'd interviewed the housekeeper less than a week ago. It seemed like so much had happened in such a short amount of time. I laid my keys and phone on the table.

"Sorry I wasn't able to give you the news about Greg Eaton in person," I said. "Most of my afternoon was spent giving statements and filling out paperwork. But I figured you'd want to hear it from me before you saw it on TV."

"I appreciate it. What will happen to Greg Eaton and Rob Whitington?"

"They'll each have their own trial. Whitington's been charged with multiple counts of blackmail. The ASA also tacked on an accessory to rape charge, but I don't know if a jury will go for it. Greg Eaton's been charged with your husband's murder and the attempted murder of a police officer."

I wondered how Greg Eaton's trial would shake out. The man had been under an inordinate amount of stress dealing with the death of his wife. Then to find the body of his dead daughter, it must have pushed him over the edge.

"How is Patrick doing?" Nina asked.

"A little shaken, but he'll be fine."

"I want to thank you, Kate. Thank you for everything. You believed in me when no one else did. You hunted down Jonathan's killer. You're amazing."

"We need to talk."

"So serious," Nina said smiling. "Tell me, what's going on?"

"Something about Greg Eaton's story bothered me. He said Julia didn't know who raped her. In her journal, she'd written the initials, J. G., when she discovered the embroidery on Jonathan's handkerchief. Yet, she had no other identifying information. It made me wonder how Greg found your husband."

"Jonathan and Julia are dead. Greg Eaton and Rob Whitington are in jail. Do we really need to revisit all of this?"

"Yes, we do. You lied to me."

Nina looked out the window, avoiding my gaze.

"When we spoke in your hotel room, Nina, you said you didn't tell Greg Eaton your name. You lied, didn't you?"

Nina remained silent.

"That's why the night you found Jonathan dead you told me over the phone, 'I think I killed my husband.' You felt responsible for his death. You felt guilty that you somehow must have accidentally let Greg know your identity."

"Accidentally?" Acidic hate oozed from that one word. "You're absolutely right. I *accidentally* told Greg Eaton my name was Dr. Nina Grace. Oops." Nina covered her mouth in mock shock. "You look surprised, Kate."

"I trusted you. I believed in you."

"And I appreciate that blind loyalty. I really do. After our counseling sessions, I knew you'd be the one I could count on."

"How could you, Nina? How could you set up your husband?"

"My husband? You mean the monster I married. When I received those pictures of Jonathan raping that little girl, I confronted him, demanded a divorce. You know what he said? After he smacked me across the face, he told me he'd never let me go. I threatened to go to the police, turn him in. He laughed. Said I couldn't squeal if I didn't have a tongue. He listed in excruciating detail the vile things he would do to me if I didn't shape up, go back to performing my wifely duties. I was terrified, Kate."

"You could have come to me. I would have moved heaven and earth to protect you."

"It wasn't your mess to clean up." Nina leaned forward, her eyes bright, begging me to understand. "Do you know how many abused women I've listened to over the years, the number of lives shattered by the devastation of rape? Women just like you, Kate. I couldn't get those women's voices out of my head. They cried out for justice. So when I discovered Julia Eaton had committed suicide after her mom died, I knew Greg Eaton would be ripe for revenge."

I shook my head, saddened by the choices Nina had made.

"Don't look at me like that," she said, jutting out her chin. "It's not like I spoon fed him. He had to work for it, or he would have been suspicious. I made sure I only left enough clues that if he were so inclined, it would leave a bread trail straight back to Jonathan. I just can't believe the idiot killed Jonathan in our own house. And while I was upstairs."

"What did you say to Greg Eaton that led him to your husband?"

Nina wagged her finger at me.

"Fine, I don't need to hear the details to know that you're still responsible for your husband's death. An accessory."

"I'm not responsible for Greg Eaton murdering my husband." Nina's facial expression morphed, now taking on the look of an innocent choir girl. "I mean, I was in the bedroom when it all happened. I could have been killed. Why would I knowingly put myself in harm's way?" Nina grinned. "There's no proof I aided Eaton in the commission of a felony."

"Until now." I pushed a button on my phone, turning off the recording app I'd downloaded that morning. "Sorry, Nina. Guess you didn't know me as well as you thought you did."

Nina's eyes narrowed, her nostrils flared.

"You were right about the loyalty part," I said. "Most of the time I'm loyal to a fault. Unless it bumps head with my moral compass. You see, I'm a bit of a stickler when it comes to right and wrong. You know the pesky little thing about finding justice for the victim. It's kind of a big deal to me. Patrick reminded me I'd been neglectful in this because of my loyalty to you. After a lot of thought, I made myself a vow I would find justice for Jonathan Grace, no matter how big of a scumbag he was. Because no matter what kind of sentence he deserved, it sure as hell wasn't a death sentence. And even if you were the helpless martyr you claim to be in your story, which I seriously doubt, you had no right to pass judgment on him."

I removed the handcuffs from my utility belt. "Dr. Nina Grace, you have the right to remain silent."

CHAPTER 35

"Nina set up her husband?" Carlos was shocked.

I'd called him after Nina had been booked, asking if he could stop by my house after work. We were seated on the couch facing each other. His fingers lazily stroked my hand resting on the back of the couch.

"Looks that way. I can't believe I ever blindly trusted her."

"Don't feel duped. Nina helped you through a really tough time. I understand. You felt you owed her. Looking for the good in people is never a bad thing. Neither is trying to help a friend."

"Unfortunately, I think duped is exactly what happened. Nina's a shrink. She knew exactly what she was doing. She looked for someone like me, someone who doesn't make friends easily. A person who when they make a bond, they hold on for dear life. Nina knew I'd come to her rescue. I played my part perfectly, with Nina directing every scene."

"Don't be too hard on yourself, Kate. You caught her in the end."

I took Carlos's hand in mine, squeezing it. "I did, didn't I?"

When Greg Eaton had been questioned in his hospital room, he filled in the last few puzzle pieces, giving us a clearer picture of what had happened the night of Jonathan Grace's murder. Eaton had been camped out in front of the Graces' house and saw Jonathan pull up, parking his car in the garage. Jonathan forgot to lower the door, probably due to all the alcohol he'd consumed that evening. By Greg's own admission, he snapped. He saw his opportunity and took it.

Greg was surprised to hear Jonathan's wife had been home during the murder, sleeping through the whole thing. He refused to speak about the conversation he'd had with Nina, insisting all the blame laid solely on him. Who knew if the accessory to murder charge against Nina would hold up in court, but at least I'd done my job. I'd gotten justice for both victims—Jonathan and Julia.

My mind drifted to thoughts of my partner, and I couldn't help but laugh.

"What's so funny?" Carlos asked.

"Life with Patrick's going to be unbearable. 'I told you so' doesn't even begin to scratch the surface of how bad it'll be."

"Don't worry, a little crow never hurt anyone. But Patrick doesn't strike me as the kind of person to lord mistakes over his friends."

"Right, his friends," I mumbled to myself. The word conjured up so many conflicting emotions lately. I was just thankful I still had Patrick's friendship.

Carlos looked at our intertwined hands. "What is . . . this?"

I took both of his hands in mine, pulling them up, kissing each knuckle. "I don't want to be that person, Carlos."

"What person?"

"The kind of person who can't connect with others. The one who always pushes those she loves away until she's bitter and alone. More than once, I've teetered on the edge of destroying the most important relationships in my life. Hell, I actually succeeded in sabotaging my friendship with Lucy."

"And what about us?"

"I tried my hardest to push you away, too. Didn't I? But you're too damn stubborn to listen."

"You're right, I am stubborn. I won't give up on you, Kate. I love you, and I'm in it for the long haul. I know you have baggage. We all do. I don't expect to hear the words 'I love you.' You've explained why they're so painful to say. It's not the words I'm after; it's the sentiment behind them that matters." Carlos brought my hands up to his lips and tenderly kissed them. "How about we try this again? Take it a little slower this time. We can make it work if we do it together."

I moved forward, kissing him lightly on the lips. I had to catch my breath before I could speak again. "Patrick almost lost his life yesterday. It made me realize we're not promised one more day on this earth. Last night when I was thinking about the future, trying to figure out what I wanted out of life, one question kept running through my head. If I knew I only had one day left, how would I spend it? You know what I realized?"

"What?"

"I would want to spend it with you."

Carlos pulled me to his chest, enfolding me in his warm embrace.

I sighed. "Why have I been so pig headed about us?"

"I'm not the only one around here who's stubborn."

I laughed. "The only thing keeping us apart is me, my hang-ups, my fear."

I looked up into Carlos's eyes. They were so full of promise—the promise to treat me kindly, the promise to love me without strings.

"I'm done with the excuses, Carlos. Living my life, waiting on the chance I might get hurt if I open myself up. I'm done. I'm jumping in head first. Even though I have no idea what's waiting for me below, I'm all in. Do you know why?"

Carlos shook his head.

"Because . . . because I love you."

DEAD LIKE ME

Find out how the Detective Springer Series started with the first book, *Dead Like Me,* which is available in ebook and paperback on Amazon.

On edge after a two-week mandatory leave, Detective Kate Springer is blindsided when she discovers she shares a link with Tampa's newest murder victim—a troubled teen found strangled and dumped in a remote part of town.

The bond between them threatens to expose Detective Springer's past—one she's been hell-bent on keeping secret.

When the killer finally emerges from the shadows, Kate's secrets aren't the only thing on the line. So is her life.

SPLINTERED

In Kelly Miller's third novel, *Splintered,* she introduces her readers to a whole new cast of characters. Now available on Amazon in ebook and paperback.

Life turns from barely tolerable to complete hell when Maddy Eastin's impulsive plan to win back the attention of her absentee father backfires. Word of her scheme spreads through her high school, but when mockery escalates to cyberbullying, Maddy and her failed stunt become headline news. But the worst is yet to come ...

A disturbed man is fighting the overwhelming urge to surrender to his true nature—a moral code molded by a sadistic father who taught him that a girl needs proper training to become the perfect subservient woman. As he watches Maddy on the evening news, his already fractured psyche completely splinters. She's the girl he's been waiting for.

When Maddy disappears, she's labeled a runaway even though her mother believes it was foul play. Will the two detectives investigating Maddy's disappearance find her before it's too late? Or has she already fallen prey to the vicious stranger hunting her?

This psychological thriller unfolds through the viewpoints of five deeply flawed characters. Each is on their own emotionally charged journey that ultimately intersects in a collision course of devastating consequences.

MY BLUE NIGHTMARE

Get Kelly Miller's latest novelette, *My Blue Nightmare,* for free on her website at www.kellymillerauthor.com.

Maggie Hamilton's brother and sister died shortly after turning sixteen. Cops say their deaths were tragic accidents but Maggie knows better. Two days from now she celebrates her sixteenth birthday, and she believes she's next on death's list. Frantic for help, Maggie shows up at the police station. But will anyone believe the twisted story of her family's tragedy?

Detectives are shocked when Maggie names her siblings' killer—their own father. Is the girl telling the truth or is she suffering from delusions brought on by the stress of grief? One detective who empathizes with this troubled girl vows to investigate the accusations and keep her safe. No matter what the cost.

Photo Credit: Ruth Kegel

KELLY MILLER grew up shivering in Illinois but now enjoys the year-round sunshine in Tampa, FL. The first book in this series, *Dead Like Me,* won second place in the best mystery category of the 2011 FWA Royal Palm Literary Awards competition. It was also named a semi-finalist in the mystery category of The Kindle Book Review's 2013 Best Indie Books Awards competition. The Detective Kate Springer series continues with the second book, *Deadly Fantasies.* In Kelly's psychological thriller, *Splintered,* she introduces her readers to a whole new cast of characters. *Splintered* was named a 2015 Kindle Scout winner and the e-book is published by Amazon's Kindle Press. Her latest work, *My Blue Nightmare,* is the first novelette in the *My Nightmare Series.* She's offering it free as a thank you to all her supporters.

Visit **www.kellymillerauthor.com** to get a glimpse into the inner workings of her writing life, to download a free ebook, or sign up for her author newsletter.